T

THE DESPOILERS

Other Five Star Titles
by Johnny D. Boggs:

The Lonesome Chisholm Trail (2000)
Once They Wore the Gray (2001)
Lonely Trumpet (2002)

THE DESPOILERS

A FRONTIER STORY

JOHNNY D. BOGGS

Five Star • Waterville, Maine

Five Star First Edition Western Series.

Published in 2002 in conjunction with
Golden West Literary Agency.

Set in 11 pt. Plantin by Elena Picard.

Printed in the United States on permanent paper.

Library of Congress Cataloging-in-Publication Data

Boggs, Johnny D.
    The despoilers : a frontier story / by Johnny D. Boggs.
        p. cm.
    ISBN 0-7862-3535-7 (hc : alk. paper)
    1. United States—History—Revolution, 1775–1783—
Fiction.   2. Marion, Francis, 1732–1795—Fiction.
3. Frontier and pioneer life—Fiction.   I. Title.
PS3552.O4375 D47 2002
813'.54—dc21   2002026642

For Chris and Leigh

"In no part of the South was the war conducted with such asperity as in this quarter. It often sank into barbarity."

Light Horse Harry Lee
MEMOIRS

PROLOGUE

The sign at the stoplight on U.S. 76 told me to take a left to get to Darlington, so I hit the signal in the Nissan Pulsar I had rented back at Columbia Regional Airport, and yielded to the oncoming John Deere tractor before turning. I passed old houses, Victorian- to 1950s-style, crossed the railroad tracks, saw a crumbling livery stable on my left, with the date **1901** on the façade, and drove on, out of town and into the country—decrepit barns, piney woods, and well-picked rows of tobacco my only scenery.

Labor Day weekend, 1985, and the roads leading to Darlington were all but abandoned, which I knew wouldn't be the case Sunday. The *Dallas Times Herald* had sent me to South Carolina to cover a stock-car race. Some driver could earn a bonus of a million bucks by winning this race—not a big amount by today's standards, but certainly an event worth covering back then—so the sports editor had given me the assignment. I had once worked at a paper we journalists jokingly dubbed the *Charleston Newsless Courier*, therefore he figured I knew all about stock-car racing. Never mind the fact that I had never, ever, covered one of those events and didn't even know where to find Darlington.

I flew from Dallas to Columbia, rented a car, and spent Thursday night with a friend, a former *Courier* colleague

7

now working at the *Daily Item* in Sumter. After breakfast, I said good bye and headed for Darlington. Now I realized I probably should have studied the map a little better.

Well, at least I was on the right road. How hard could it be to find this burg? I had plenty of time.

That's why I pulled onto the shoulder after spotting the Darlington County sign. Bruce Springsteen's *Born in the U.S.A.* was the boss on rock radio, and a friend of mine in Dallas idolized the New Jersey singer-songwriter. One of the cuts on the album was called "Darlington County", so I figured to take a picture of my rental car parked by the sign. She'd get a kick out of that. OK, maybe she wouldn't, but it seemed funny at the time. I snapped the photo, started back for the car, and noticed a church, cemetery, and historical marker just up the road.

I drove up to the marker, and stepped outside. The brick chapel's sign across the road read **Cameron Branch Baptist Church**. An ancient, pale blue Impala was parked out front while the cemetery looked like one of a thousand boneyards I had passed since landing in Columbia. The historical marker caught my interest. It had been erected by the Daughters of the American Revolution in the 1930s and had been the target for several shotguns and at least one .30-30 or similar caliber. I could, however, still make out the words.

AUGUSTIN DRUMMOND

About 50 yards due east, a cannon barrel marks the final resting place of Augustin Drummond. Born in North Carolina in 1753, Drummond settled near here during the Revolutionary War. He later served with the legendary Francis Marion, the "Swamp Fox", against the British, and also

fought a gang of renegades called "The Despoilers". In 1783, he married a second time—
legend has it that his first wife was Cherokee—
and farmed. He died on December 29, 1829.

Wanting to finish off a roll of film, I fetched my Pentax
K1000 from the passenger seat and walked among the
tombstones, searching for the cannon and Drummond's
grave. Andersons. Atkinsons. Murrays. McGees. Fletchers.
No Drummonds. Certainly no cannon barrel. The earliest
date of death that I found was 1892. I still had time to kill—
the sign down the road said Darlington was twenty-two
miles, and I had already traveled six or seven—so I continued my quest.

"Lookin' for the cannon, I take it."

The voice, sugary as hominy, startled me. I looked up to
discover a large man, probably in his late fifties or early six-
ties, with a tobacco-stained smile. He wore a polyester suit
the color of the Impala, wing-tips, and a Ronald Reagan-like
tie hanging loosely from an unbuttoned collar. Sweat damp-
ened his face as it did mine—South Carolina on Labor Day
can be a furnace—and he grunted as he approached me.

"I think it was over yonder," he said, pointing a fat
finger to the far corner of the boneyard. "Only thing is that
the cannon barrel sank, just disappeared, I guess twenty
years ago or more."

"Really?" It was the only thing I could think to say.

"Yeah. Before I got here, mind you. I spent a while
lookin' for that thing myself. So now, when I see tourists
huntin' for it, I come over to tell them they ain't gonna find
it. I'm Stan McIntyre, preacher here."

We shook hands. I gave him my name, told him I was a
sportswriter.

"Come here for the race?"

"Yes, sir. I'm covering it for the *Dallas Times Herald.*"

"Dallas? You don't say. Well, I reckon that million dollars will draw a lot of you reporters."

"I guess so."

"Think he'll win it?"

"Don't know."

"Well, folks say that's one tough track. Never been to a race myself. Kind of a conflict. They race on Sundays. I work on Sundays." I grinned in reply, and he blurted out: "Want some iced tea, young man? I'm sorry. I've forgotten your name."

"Ray Price," I told him. I always found it a hard name to forget.

"Like the singer!"

"Yes, sir."

"Bet you've heard that before."

"Plenty," I answered, and we both laughed.

I really don't know why I took him up on the offer. Maybe I was thirsty. Maybe I figured he could tell me how to get to the speedway. Perhaps it was just another way of killing time, but I'm glad I went.

His office was ice cold. *I'd hate to pay for the air conditioning,* I thought, as he went to pour the tea. I looked at his bookcase: Bibles and concordances, religious topics, a first edition of *To Kill a Mockingbird,* and several books on South Carolina history, most of them dealing with the Revolution. One book that caught my eye. It didn't seem to fit in. *Abandon Ship!* by Richard F. Newcomb. I read the subtitle: *The Saga of the U.S.S. Indianapolis, The Navy's Greatest Sea Disaster.*

"Good book," the Reverend McIntyre told me. I returned the book to the shelves and took a tumbler of tea. It was heavy on the sugar, but I didn't complain. I should have told him that I took mine unsweetened.

"Good tea," I lied.

McIntyre gestured at the book. "Are you familiar with the *Indianapolis*, Ray?"

"Not really. I remember Robert Shaw mentions it in *Jaws*." He stared at me blankly. "The movie?" I added.

"Never saw it. Let's see, last movie I saw was *True Grit*. Folks gave me a hard time about that. John Wayne swore up a storm in that. They said . . . 'A preacher goin' to see a movie with swear words in it!' I didn't tell them that a preacher can cuss with the best of 'em, 'specially one that served in the Navy."

"Well, in *Jaws*," I explained, "Shaw . . . his character, that is . . . talks about it briefly, about the sinking of the *Indianapolis*, the sharks attacking the men. . . . I'm sorry, you were in the Navy?"

"Yes, Ray, I was."

"I was in the Army." I hesitated before adding: "Vietnam."

"I was in the big one." He pointed to the book. "On that ship."

I almost dropped my tumbler. "You were on the *Indianapolis?* When she sank?"

Nodding, he continued: "We were torpedoed by a Jap sub. Sank in the blink of an eye. Nine hundred men went into the Pacific. It was four days and five nights before they pulled us out. There is a hell, Ray Price, for I have seen it."

So have I. I didn't, however, say this. Instead, my journalist curiosity speaking, I asked: "You delivered the A-bomb, right? And that's why no one knew you were out there. It was a secret mission?"

"Not really," McIntyre said with a sad smile. "We didn't

know what we were carryin', and it wasn't the entire bomb. Just the uranium they put in Little Boy, which they dropped on Hiroshima. And they knew where we were goin' after we left. Typical Navy snafu. But I've often dreamed about it . . . that God was punishin' us for Hiroshima." He shook his head and sipped his tea. "Crazy thought, ain't it?"

"Maybe not. I. . . ." Instead of continuing, I shrugged. I had often thought God had been punishing me. Maybe that's why I had worked for eight newspapers in twelve years, throughout the South, parts of the Midwest, and now Texas. I had become a cliché: Thirty-three-year-old Vietnam vet, restless, can't really hold a job or a relationship. Maybe I wanted to open up, confess my sins to a man of God. More than likely, I didn't want to say anything else because I was glad when the reverend changed the subject.

"I don't talk about this much," he said. "I'm sure you got your own secrets from Vietnam. We all do. That's why I study the Revolution. Most folks here like the Civil War . . . after all, we Sandlappers started it. But I like the Revolution. Lot of it was fought in the South."

"Yorktown," I suggested.

"No, that's Virginia, and these days we consider Virginia a Yankee state. I mean Patriots like Sumter, Marion, Pickens and . . ."—he gestured outside—"I guess even Augustin Drummond."

I mentioned that I had worked for fourteen months in Charleston so knew a little about Francis Marion.

"But I bet you had never heard tell of Augustin Drummond until today."

"True."

"Not much is really known about him. I'm kinda an amateur historian, and his bein' local only piques my interest."

"What do you know about those 'Despoilers'?"

"Nothin'. Let's face it. Drummond's a mystery. Even his gravestone has disappeared. But I'm a stubborn old coot. Next time you come by here, I might have the history of Augustin Drummond and The Despoilers, waitin' for your comments."

I finished the tea, waiting for the sugar buzz to kick in. "I'd like that very much," I said. "Well, I'd best take off."

"Good luck, Ray."

"Thank you." After shaking hands, the preacher walked me back to my car. I tossed the camera inside, shook his hand again, climbed in the rental car, then rolled down the window. "One more thing, Reverend. Just how do I get to the speedway?"

"Simple as pie," he said, cackling. "Just follow this road a couple miles till you come to the crossroads. Take a right, and drive till you reach the end of the earth."

I covered the events that weekend, filed my stories, and caught a flight back to Dallas. What I wrote, I couldn't tell you, although the driver won that million dollar bonus, but I vividly recall the dream I had Saturday night. I was the Japanese submarine commander who torpedoed the *U.S.S. Indianapolis*, only the destroyer's crew was all women, and I watched, laughing, as sharks picked them off. I woke up in a sweat, and hurried to the motel bar, packed with race fans. I knew what the dream meant. I wanted to forget.

For the next two years, I stayed in Dallas before moving on to a paper in Colorado—then another—and another— ever the drifter. I pretty much forgot about the Reverend Stan McIntyre, Cameron Branch, Augustin Drummond, The Despoilers, and the sinking cannon barrel, until fourteen years later when my fifteenth newspaper, the *Kansas City Star*, sent me back to Darlington, South Carolina. It was the fiftieth running of the Labor Day race, and, since Kansas City was in the process of building its own speedway, my boss sent me to cover the event.

My colleague from Charleston had left Sumter and was somewhere in Florida, or he had been five years earlier; we simply lost touch. I flew in to Columbia, rented some mystery green Dodge, and drove up Interstate 20 to Florence, just past Darlington, where I checked into a Howard Johnson. On Friday morning, I took Highway 76 to the sole stoplight in Timmonsville. This was the long way to Darlington, but I wondered if Stan McIntyre still preached at Cameron Branch. The railroad tracks had been ripped up, the livery stable torn down, but the country road that led to Darlington hadn't changed. I saw the county sign, and pulled into the church parking lot beside a relatively new Chevy Tahoe, a far cry from the old Impala I had seen there fourteen years ago. The historical marker still stood in front of the cemetery and appeared to have been used for target practice a few times since 1985.

I walked around the chapel, down the gravel walkway to what had been Stan McIntyre's office, and knocked on the door. The minister didn't greet me. I had expected this—he could have moved down the road, retired, or even died— but I couldn't hide my disappointment.

Before me stood a woman in her early forties, wearing a cotton print dress and too much make-up. She asked in a nasal Southern accent if she could help me.

"I was looking for Stan McIntyre," I told her.

"Did you know him?"

"Met him only once," I said. "Back here in 'Eighty-Five. He might not even remember me, and I knew this was a long shot. Just wanted to say hello and ask him if he had ever finished his history book."

She invited me inside, but didn't ask if I cared for any iced tea. "I'm Amy Gee," she said. "Reverend Harker's secretary. I hate to inform you, but Reverend McIntyre passed away last year." Her voice fell to a whisper. "Cancer. The doctors cut him open, and then sewed him back up. I'm sorry to break this news to you."

"It's all right," I said. "I imagine he was getting up in years." That I knew for certain for I would soon be bucking fifty.

"He retired, oh, I guess eight or nine years ago. Went to work on his manuscript. You knew about this, you say?"

"He had mentioned it."

"Worked on it almost till the day he died. I even typed some of it. Reverend Harker and I have been trying to figure out what to do with it. We really don't know anything about publishing."

"You have it?" This amazed me.

"Why, yes."

"I'm a writer," I told her, and handed her my business card. "I'd certainly like to read it if that's all right with you."

She hesitated. "I don't know. . . ." Then she read my name.

"You're Ray Price."

"Not the singer," I said lightly.

She wasn't amused. "Yes, I know that. But Reverend McIntyre spoke of you often. He even dedicated his book to you."

"To me?"

"Yes. Well, I guess you most certainly could read it. You should even have it. You'd probably know more about getting it published than us."

Amy Gee walked to a file cabinet, opened the top

drawer, and pulled out a manila folder. Too thin to be a long manuscript. Maybe a hundred or so pages. Well, McIntyre had said that Drummond was a mystery. She handed me the folder.

"I. . . ."

"You take it," she said.

"This should go to his family."

"He didn't have anyone. Betty, that's his wife, she died back in 'Eighty-Two. Had always suffered from emphysema. Their only child, Gretchen, was killed in a car accident in Charlotte seven years ago. She had never married." The voice dropped again. "I think she was a Lesbian."

I took the folder awkwardly. "Do you have a card? In case I can find a publisher for this?"

"I don't, but I have one of Reverend Harker's." She went to her desk, returned, and handed me his business card.

Maybe I had given them false hopes. I couldn't think of a publisher, even a regional one, that would take on this subject, a slim account from an amateur historian. A vanity press, perhaps, or maybe I could boil it down and offer it to a history magazine, *American History*, or something along those lines.

After thanking Mrs. Gee, I drove to Darlington, picked up my credentials, and got to work. One story for Saturday's paper, two for Sunday's, and two for Monday's, plus plenty of material to use later. I didn't even open Stan McIntyre's folder until I was seated in coach on a Delta flight, bound for Atlanta, where I'd catch another plane to Missouri.

One shaky take-off and Diet Coke later, I reached under my seat, unzipped a compartment to my laptop case, where I had filed McIntyre's manuscript shortly before checking

16

out of the Florence motel, and withdrew the folder. The title page read: *A Short History of Augustin Drummond, Forgotten Hero of the American Revolution. By Stanson J. McIntyre.*

I turned the page. . . .

FROM THE MANUSCRIPT
OF THE REVEREND STAN MCINTYRE,
PAGES 1–3

My interest in writing a history on Augustin Drummond comes naturally. I'm pastor at the Cameron Branch Baptist Church, and he is buried in our little cemetery. A historical marker out front notes his final resting place. Revolutionary War records can be scarce, I've learned, especially when dealing with a militia, ~~but~~ basically a guerrilla group, like the one where Augustin Drummond served.

Below is a clipping from a 1958 article in the *Florence Morning News.*

Revolutionary War Hero's Grave
Marked By Rusty Cannon Barrel

By Sturbin Pedley
Morning News Reporter
TIMMONSVILLE—One of the oldest memorials in South Carolina marks the grave of a Revolutionary War veteran who rode with Francis "Swamp Fox" Marion.

Augustin Drummond, who died in 1829, fought in the Colonial Army. Originally a resident of North Carolina, he moved south in the late 1770s and settled near Cameron Branch. A historical marker at the tiny church cemetery claims that he once had an Indian wife and that he also fought against a gang of renegades. The Daughters of the American Revolution put up the marker in 1938.

But another marker draws more interest. At the head of the old veteran's grave is part of a cannon that saw action in the Revolution and War of 1812. The cannon was brought to the church for an Independence Day celebration, apparently in the early 1920s. But while the church-goers were enjoying a chicken bog, a group of carpenters working on the church roof is said to have removed the barrel and placed it at the head of Drummond's grave.

For some reason, perhaps patriotism, the owner decided to leave it there.

The cannon barrel has sunk deeper into the ground over the past 30 years. "I think it'll be gone soon," the Rev. H. G. Chandler said. "And then Augustin Drummond will disappear—like the Swamp Fox vanishing in his lair after a raid against Cornwallis."

How prophetic.

The barrel's now gone, and this newspaper clipping is all I had to go on to begin my search. But I shall persist. Scouring the state archives in both Carolinas and even the National Archives in Washington, church records, old histories, pension files, journals and letters, a brief history of this mysterious man follows as best as I can tell it.

Little is know about Augustin Drummond's early life. He was born in North Carolina. Where exactly has never been determined. Various reports and church records give his year of birth as 1753, although some say 1747 and others 1754. His death occurred on December 29, 1839

1829. He settled near Cameron Branch in late 1779. This must have been after the Battle of Kettle Creek, Georgia, in Feb. of that year, between Tory and Patriot forces. Although our Patriots, led by Andrew "The Wizard Owl" Pickens, won that engagement, our subject was not so lucky. The name "Augustin Drummond" appears on a list of Patriot soldiers captured and paroled. Actually, his name is the only one on the list involving the action at Kettle Creek, Ga. Five Tory prisoners were executed after that affair, and it's a wonder our subject wasn't hung in retaliation by the Loyalists. Of course, the war at that time was slightly more civil than the Hades it would become.

CHAPTER ONE

February, 1779

"Look at them," Paddy McGee whispered in disgust. "Act like a mess of starving crows, not soldiers." He spat, wiped his dry lips with the back of his hand, and added: "Swine."

Augustin Drummond quietly pushed aside a growth of brambles with the barrel of his long rifle for a better look. The way those Tories cackled and sang, he didn't need to be that careful. They weren't about to hear anything short of a six-pounder's blast. In the muddy pasture ahead, Colonel John Boyd's Loyalists hacked away at two bloody carcasses that once had been cows, cutting out hunks of meat to be speared with bayonets and roasted over fires. Maybe they weren't first-class butchers, but the aroma of roasting beef made Drummond's mouth water and stomach cramp. Neither he nor McGee had taken a bite to eat since supper two nights ago when Colonel Pickens sent them on a scout to find Boyd's men.

"I best run, fetch the boys," McGee said, and began backing his way into the thick forest that bordered the Georgia pasture. "Stay put, and you bloody well better not let them see you, bub. If they move, trail them, and we'll catch up."

"They won't be goin' nowhere for a spell," Drummond said as he pulled back his flintlock.

"Aye," McGee agreed, glanced once more at the ravenous Tories, and was gone.

After McGee left, Drummond inched deeper into the woods until he found a good vantage point to spy on Boyd's men. He propped the long rifle against a fallen pine, rested his back against a live one, and rubbed his hands to fight off the winter morning chill. The wind had changed directions, so he no longer could smell the food, for which he was thankful, but Drummond could still detect the strains of "I've Kissed and I've Prattled". It was his wife's favorite song, and he hummed along.

Salâli would be feeding the chickens about now, talking to them in a mix of Cherokee and Back Country English, maybe singing "I've Kissed and I've Prattled"—at least the parts she remembered and could handle without choking on the English words. He smiled as he pictured this, thought of their cabin on Long Canes Creek, but the smile vanished. *If* she still lived at Long Canes, *if* she hadn't gotten tired of waiting for her husband to stop playing soldier and come home. For all Drummond knew, Salâli could be back at Kanasta, the Cherokee settlement on the headwaters of the French Broad River in North Carolina where he had first met her while working for Pickens.

Poor husband he had turned out to be. Almost two years he had been gone, fighting with Andrew Pickens's militia. Drummond could neither read nor write—Salâli couldn't, either—but now he thought he should have asked the parson or another one of the educated backwoodsmen he served with to put down in words how much he missed her, how much he wanted to see her again. Salâli was smart. She'd know it was from him, know to take the letter to the Witching Snake Tavern, where Zack Gibbs would read it to her. Old Zack had written the letter to Drummond's father and brother over in the North Carolina sandhills, the letter that told them he had settled on Long Canes Creek, had up and married Salâli, and they could accept that or go to hell. They hadn't written back.

Actually Salâli had been the one to persuade him to join Pickens. When talk of rebellion and independence first reached the South Carolina Back Country, Drummond didn't care one way or the other. He didn't plan on serving His Majesty or the Continentals. He would just keep working for Pickens, trading with the Cherokees when not hunting or fishing. It wasn't a bad way to live, although few folks in the Long Canes District straddled the fence like that. Drummond had witnessed many a fistfight at the Witching Snake between Loyalist and Patriot. He declined Pickens's request that he embrace the rebel cause, said he didn't feel much like fighting his neighbors and friends, that he and Salâli hoped to try for a baby. Pickens understood, and Drummond understood Pickens. The trader, farmer, and justice of the peace whom the Cherokees called Skyagunsta, the Wizard Owl, lived up to his name. He was a wise businessman, and as such couldn't afford to be taxed to death in the name of King George III. Most of Pickens's militiamen felt the same way. Others had suffered at the hands of fire-breathing Tories, and joined for vengeance. Some, men like Paddy McGee, simply hated the English and/or loved a good fight.

Drummond and Salâli tried to ignore the war. After British agents had coaxed the Cherokees into making trouble back in 1776, however, raiding farms and murdering Patriots, Zack Gibbs had paid Drummond a visit. "This war is not going to let anyone not pick a side," the innkeeper had said. "Folks already seem to think you might be a part of this Cherokee deviltry. Red devils butchered Tom Langston two nights ago no more than a Dutch mile from here but left ye place alone. I come here as a friend, Augustin Drummond. Everyone knows I pledge me loyalty to His Majesty, and I pray this conflict ends soon, but till it ends, son, ye must choose a side, and it pains me to say this, but ye must join Pickens. For if ye side with the Loyalists and me, those seditionists will burn ye cabin to the ground, and likely tar and feather ye and Squirrel. Or worst."

It seemed a silly argument at first. If anything, Drummond told Salâli, Zack Gibbs had made a pretty good argument why he should join the Loyalists. Why would he want to fight with Pickens's rebels when they were the ones threatening his wife and home? Salâli had been sitting in her nightgown by the fireplace, her black hair glistening. He could picture her just that way now, a portrait of Cherokee beauty in store-bought garments. She had walked to him, kissed his forehead, took his hand, and said: "You know, my husband, friend Zack Gibbs speaks true. In your heart, you always stand against King. You live free all your life . . . King threatens this freedom. You go to Skyagunsta. I wait."

"An' what about you?"

"I safe. Rebels not harm me for they know you fight with Skyagunsta. Others not harm me for they fear Yûñwiya, my people. Take your long rifle and be gone." She gave him a bewitching smile. "We try for baby when you back."

That had been in March of 1777, a couple of months before the Cherokees signed the Treaty of DeWitts Corner and ceded all their land in South Carolina.

A shot grabbed his attention. His head jerked up as he reached for the heavy flintlock, thinking Boyd's men had spotted him, and were about to pick him apart, yet, as the echoes of the blast died, he could hear the Loyalists laughing. Drummond crept closer to the clearing to see

26

what had happened. Another cow had wandered into the pasture, and the hungry Tories had shot it down. Almost immediately a handful of the soldiers had started butchering the animal.

Pickens's militia had been wandering about the South Carolina-Georgia border, preparing for a scrape with British Colonel Archibald Campbell's redcoats when word came that John Boyd's Tories were plowing through the Ninety Six District of South Carolina, burning homes and killing Whigs. Campbell could wait, Pickens ordered, and began hunting the marauding army. Boyd had some eight hundred men, all itching to tangle with Pickens. Here, near Kettle Creek, they'd get their chance.

Drummond knew Boyd, not well, but they had shared a few drinks. The Loyalist lived on the Upper Saluda River, had done business with Pickens here and there, and stopped in at the Witching Snake for a chopin of apple brandy or rum when business took him to Long Canes. A good man, Drummond thought, but his recruits? McGee was right. Rather than soldiers, these were nothing more than *banditti* and plunderers. Drummond withdrew into the woods as a Tory broke out his tin whistle and played a bawdy tune while others started another fire closer to the latest dead cow.

Yes, Drummond thought, *Colonel Pickens could take his time.*

"Anything happen after I left?" McGee asked.

"Killed another cow," Drummond answered. "Turned their horses out to graze."

The Irishman from Ninety Six licked his lips. "Won't be much bloody sport in this. But I'll enjoy meself."

Drummond turned his attention to the frowning

Pickens. The colonel was a dour man with a long face, thick chin, and bird-beak nose. In his late thirties or early forties, Skyagunsta was already losing his hair, and no one would call him handsome, nor would anyone ever accuse him of having a sense of humor. No, Andrew Pickens was a pious Presbyterian elder who never swore, drank, smoked or cursed, and frowned upon those who did partake—which meant he frowned on just about everyone in his army, including the good parson who was known to take a drag on a pipe or pull on a jug when he thought no one was looking.

"They act like despoilers," Pickens said as he drew his sword from its scabbard. "I would have thought a Christian man like John Boyd would have better discipline over his troops." He swung around to address the officers who had joined him with McGee and Drummond at the edge of the woods. "We attack at once. I shall command the center . . . Colonel Dooley the right, and Colonel Clarke the left. To your posts, gentlemen. May God have mercy on our souls." Pickens's eyes cut to Boyd's Tories, and he added with quiet reluctance: "And theirs as well."

Drummond never grasped the reasoning behind civilized battle tactics. To his way of thinking, the best way to fight a battle was to hide behind a good thick pine tree, and fire. That's the way the Cherokees fought, and the way the Back Country men, even Andrew Pickens, had learned. This war, on the other hand, wasn't fought that way. Instead, row after row of soldiers walked in a straight line in an open clearing to face row after row of more soldiers while lads beat out commands by tapping drums, others tooted on fifes, and banners flapped in the wind. "Glorious. Simply glorious," the parson said. *Stupid,* Drummond thought.

Tory sentries sent a few shots before falling back to the

unorganized camp as Drummond marched in the center line, Paddy McGee to his left, and Long John Norris on the right. He heard Pickens's calm voice—"Steady men. Steady."—Lieutenant William Evans keeping his company in line—drums and fifes—his moccasins slogging through the muddy pasture—McGee praying in Gaelic—his labored breathing.

His mouth turned to sand. Drummond hadn't been in a battle, a real battle, before, but rather Back Country skirmishes and night raids against poorly equipped Tories. The rifle felt strange in his hands, and he had been shooting it for eight years. He had a clear view of everything: Loyalist officers screaming out commands, trying to get their men in battle formation. Others kicking out the fires, their shirt-sleeves stained with blood from the butchered cows. Men chasing down skittish horses, cursing the animals as they loped across the pasture, finally dropping their saddles, and running for the woods—and a line of Tories finally marching out to meet the approaching enemy.

"Poise firelock!" a Tory officer cried.

They were behind in this game. Drummond had already readied his rifle. When the Loyalist officer shouted the command—"Cock firelock!"—Evans was yelling: "Fire!"

His rifle kicked his shoulder, and thick smoke clouded his line of vision. Drummond stepped aside and began to reload as the Tories returned fire. A bullet whistled overhead while the second line of Pickens's militia got its first turn at Boyd's men. Drummond moved as if in a trance, jerking back the steel frizzen to open the pan on his rifle—shutting the pan after priming it with fine powder—finding the powder horn at his side—filling the tip charger, and pouring sixty grains down the barrel—pulling a greasy patch from the box carved into the rifle stock—placing patch and

.50-caliber ball on the center of the rifle bore—drawing out
the ramrod—ramming down patch and ball—returning the
rammer underneath the barrel—shouldering the weapon
just as Evans shouted another command.

They fought as they had been drilled, front and rear
ranks synchronizing their movements. Fire. Reload. Aim.
Fire. Reload. Aim. Fire. Advancing all the while.

Now he could hear the deadly toll of the militia's fire.
Boyd's men came armed with fowling pieces, maybe a few
trade firelocks, some pistols and shotguns, effective at close
quarters, but not at this distance. Most of Pickens's men,
like Drummond, shot long rifles—Drummond had bought
his, a handsome piece almost five feet long and weighing
eight and a half pounds, from a Quaker gunsmith named
Langendorf up at Fort Prince George—and could kill at
four hundred yards.

"Front rank, make ready!"

Fire. Reload. Aim. Fire. Reload. Aim. Fire. Advancing
all the while. Smoke stung his eyes. He could taste black
powder, thought he could even smell blood.

A blast stung his right cheek, and Long John Norris
screamed in agony. Drummond glanced, saw the McAlpin's
Creek farmer on his knees, the smoking ruins of a rifle at his
side. The man held two bloody stumps in front of an astonished face. Fingers on both hands had been blown off, and
Drummond knew what had happened. Through the din and
excitement of battle, Norris had failed to notice his rifle
kept misfiring. He would pull the trigger, the pan would
flash but not fire the charge in the barrel. Unaware, he
would reload and shoot again until finally the pan ignited
the charge in the barrel, that, jammed with several patches,
ball and powder, exploded in the militiaman's arms.

Drummond looked away, hoped his rifle had not misfired. It was a miracle Norris hadn't been killed—or Drummond as well.

"Fix bayonets!" Evans screamed. The Tories had to be on the verge of retreat. Drummond couldn't tell. He could barely see. Besides, his rifle did not take a bayonet, so he ignored the order. "Charge bayonets!"

A cry of *Huzza!* echoed down the ranks as the lines of Patriots lunged forward. Drummond ran as well, hoping his vision would clear, but he tripped and went sprawling into the mud as the Patriot forces swam past him. He grabbed the rifle, checked it carefully while spooning off globs of mud, and located what had caused him to fall. A Tory boy, no more than thirteen or fourteen, lay staring at the overcast winter sky, still clutching a battered and bloodied drum, a bloody hole in the lad's forehead.

Rising, Drummond saw the Patriot line swarming the disorganized Tories, a few of them fighting but most loping for the woods, then he glimpsed another figure on his left flank staggering toward the woods, calling after his fleeing men. A splotch of red stained the back of his white waistcoat, and he grunted and turned. Another bullet shattered the man's arm, and he collapsed. Recognizing the face, Drummond couldn't stop himself as he ran to his wounded enemy's aid.

The battle had turned into a rout. Some of the militia had stopped to feast on the remains of the butchered cows. Others chased down the fleeing Tories, gunning them down, hacking them with sabers, spearing them senselessly with bayonets as Pickens, Clarke, and Dooley pleaded for a cease fire. Drummond set his rifle aside, and gently rolled over the mud- and blood-stained Loyalist officer.

"Colonel Boyd, sir," he said softly.

The man's eyes fluttered, finally focused. "I know you,"

Boyd murmured, and coughed.

"Augustin Drummond from Long Canes. Used to scout for Colonel Pickens."

Blood trickled from both corners of Boyd's mouth, but he managed to say: "Yes, I remember. I bought you a noggin of rum at the Witching Snake."

"That you did, sir. You bought several."

"Aye. Demon rum. I was never a skinflint when in my cups." He grimaced and shuddered. For a moment, Drummond thought the man dead, but he reopened his eyes and controlled his breathing. "I know I'm dying," he said, reached into his coat pocket, pulled out a gold broach, and lifted it weakly toward Drummond, who took it as Boyd's hand collapsed onto his chest. "My wife's. You will see she gets it?"

"Yes, sir."

"Your men have won the field on this dark day, and I do not wish to be buried by traitors. Could you leave two Loyalists with me . . . to see that I am buried?"

Drummond could still hear shots and screams. Finding two living Tories might be impossible once the butchery stopped. He was trying to figure out how he should answer when he realized John Boyd was dead.

Footsteps sounded, and he turned just in time to catch the blur of brown, and feel something hard crash against his forehead. He dropped beside the dead body, groaning, tasting blood, hearing someone scream: "He's killed the colonel!" Another: "And, damn his rebel soul, I shall kill him for it."

A rifle fired, followed by a grunt and the crumpling of a body as it collapsed into the mud, and, suddenly, several more shots. "Grab him. Take him and be damned quick."

He felt himself being lifted, then nothing.

CHAPTER TWO

He didn't have to read the sign in front of the brick building to know where he was headed. A redcoat sergeant opened the front door, and Drummond's Tory captors roughly shoved him inside. Another Royal soldier opened the door to an iron-barred cell, grabbed a handful of Drummond's stained linen hunting frock, and shoved him inside. He slammed against the brick wall· and collapsed on the damp floor, overturning a slop bucket that, thankfully, was empty. Slowly Drummond pulled himself up to lean against the back of the jail cell, staring through iron bars at unfriendly faces.

"Where is Colonel Boyd?" a British sergeant asked one of the Tories.

"Dead," the skinny, pockmarked redhead answered, and thrust a bony finger at Drummond. "Murdered by this fiend."

The ugly runt had been one of the Tories who dragged Drummond into the forest and across Kettle Creek, barely escaping capture or death only to be beaten senselessly by his captain. "You imbecile!" the officer had shouted as he lashed the private with his cocked hat. "When I said 'Grab him', I meant Colonel Boyd, not this rebel traitor."

· "But the colonel was dead."

The captain had kept beating the pockmarked gent until

a Welsh sergeant suggested they take Drummond prisoner and hurry on to Augusta before they all wound up like Colonel Boyd.

A shadow filled the outer area of the jail, and Drummond looked past the men. The Tory captain, a sunburned man with thick arms and unruly red beard, filled the door frame as he cleaned his fingernails with a jackknife. He wore canvas breeches, the calves protected by muddy spatterdashes, gray hunting shirt, and gray cocked hat still speckled with the pockmarked private's dried blood. A powder horn and leather hunting bag hung at his side.

The Royal soldiers turned to face the newcomer while the Tory soldiers backed away a few paces. After a moment, the sunlight returned as the captain stepped to the stove to warm himself. He folded the knife's blade, and looked the men over before speaking to the sergeant in charge.

"How long before this prisoner can be executed?"

"Sir," the soldier answered stiffly, "I know not what charges this man faces. Nor do I know you, but I assume you are with the Loyalist recruits under Colonel Boyd's command."

"That I am, Sergeant. And . . ."—he pointed at Drummond—"he's a murdering rebel. Killed John Boyd."

That staggered the Englishman. "Colonel Boyd . . . is dead?"

"Aye. And a lot of other good North Carolinians who stayed true to His Majesty. We were ambushed by Pickens's ruffians at Kettle Creek. Major Lancaster is dead or captured as well. Guess I'm left in charge. I'm Captain James Jernegan."

A nod from the jail's sergeant sent a Royal private scurrying out of the building. The scared Tories took advantage of this and left with him. Jernegan briefly told his version of what had happened at Kettle Creek, only he left out the parts about slaughtering three cows, drinking, gambling, and being caught by surprise and routed by an army half the size of Boyd's force.

Ten minutes later, another man hurried inside the jail. His wig looked crooked, his red coat and tan breeches wrinkled, and he carried a black boiled leather helmet tucked underneath his left arm. Jernegan's towering hulk startled him, and several seconds passed before the British officer could speak. His accent was Scottish.

"I am Colonel Archibald Campbell of His Majesty's Second Battalion, Fraser Highlanders. I am told that Colonel Boyd is . . . dead?"

"You were told right, Colonel." Jernegan cocked his head toward the jail cell. "The rat in there did the deed. I figured you would want to question him, then hang him, so I had my boys bring him along. I'm Captain James Jernegan . . . Jim to my friends. In command of all that's left of my boys."

Campbell looked around. "How many men have you?"

Jernegan replied with a frown: "Three hundred, I figure."

The leather helmet dropped and bounced across the wooden floor. "Three hundred! Captain, I was told Colonel Boyd had a thousand Loyalists with him. You cannot tell me that rebels have killed or captured seven hundred men."

"Nah. Boyd never had no thousand men. More like seven hundred. But Pickens had a thousand, likely fifteen hundred with him, and we never stood a chance. They hit us at Kettle Creek. I'd guess we lost one, two hundred killed, wounded, or captured. The rest turned gutless on me, be halfway home by now."

"What were the rebel losses?"

35

"Can't say. The boys I have are fighters. We cut down a couple hundred killed, and wounded a good share as well."

Drummond laughed, but no one heard him. Boyd's men had not come close to inflicting that many casualties. If Pickens lost more than forty men, killed and wounded, he would be astonished.

"Prisoners?" the officer asked.

"Just him." He spit in Drummond's direction.

Campbell shook his head. "One prisoner, Captain? You lose half your regiment and bring me one damned prisoner?"

"Well, sir, this is the one that killed Colonel Boyd himself. Murdered him. Shot him down like he was nothing more than a mongrel dog."

"That's a lie."

This time, Campbell, Jernegan, and the sergeant heard. The Tory captain grunted something, trying to ignore Drummond, but Colonel Campbell walked to the cell, and knelt, gripping the bars with his gloved hands and staring at Drummond. "What did you say?"

"Said I didn't kill Colonel Boyd."

"And you were not with those treasonous barbarians, right? That this is a mistake? Do you take me for a fool?"

"No, sir. I was with Colonel Pickens. An' Colonel Boyd died in battle, but I didn't kill him. I was with him when he died, seein' if I could do anything for him. That's how I got caught."

"So you would have me believe you are some sort of noble backwoodsman gentleman?" Campbell laughed, and Jernegan joined in.

With a shake of his head, Drummond went on. "Don't know nothin' about bein' no gentleman. You can hang me, Colonel. Don't look like I can do much about that. I just don't wanna see John Boyd's gold broach wind up in the hands of some brigand like Jernegan there."

Campbell released his hold on the bars, and spun around. "What is he talking about, Captain?"

"Hell if I know. . . ."

"Boyd gave me a gold broach right before he died."

"He stole it!"

It was the most emotion Drummond had heard from Jernegan. The sergeant had to hold the big man back.

"Stand at ease, Captain," Campbell said, and looked again at Drummond. "Go on."

Talking pained Drummond's dry throat. The Tories hadn't given him any water since his capture, but he forced himself to continue, his voice fading as he spoke. "A gold broach. It was his wife's. Boyd asked me to see that she got it. He lives on the Upper Saluda River in South Carolina, not more'n two days from my place. Shared a drink with Boyd a time or two when he came down to Long Canes. I bet Jernegan's got that broach now. Likely took it off the pigs who took it off me." He fell back, exhausted.

Campbell stood and took two steps toward Jernegan. "What of this accusation, Captain?"

"He's a traitor and a liar."

"Traitor, yes. Liar . . . I doubt it. I pride myself on being an excellent judge of character." He held out his right hand, palm up. "The broach, Captain. Hand it to me now or I shall throw you in the cell with our prisoner."

Jernegan looked like a bear ready to charge. He was big enough that he could crush Archibald Campbell in his hands, and Drummond momentarily thought that's what the Tory would do. The captain finally sagged, reached into his hunting bag, pulled out the piece of jewelry, and dropped it into Campbell's hand.

"The man's a thief and a murderer, Colonel. I planned on returning the broach to Boyd's widow myself."

"Of course, you were, Captain," the Scot said. "Now get out of me sight."

When Jernegan slammed the door behind him, Campbell spoke again. "Sergeant, see to it that the prisoner gets food and water, and clean his face."

Paroled. Drummond found it hard to fathom. He fully expected to be hanged, especially after hearing that Pickens had executed five Loyalist prisoners at Kettle Creek, but Colonel Archibald Campbell had signed the papers himself and explained everything to Drummond. He need not proclaim his loyalty to King George III, only vow never to raise arms against His Majesty's army. He could go back to his cabin on Long Canes Creek and live in peace, but join the rebel cause again and the Royal army would see Drummond hanged for high treason.

Sick of war anyhow, he wanted to get home to Salâli. The way he saw things, he had proved himself, had fought for the Patriot cause, did his best. There was no shame in being captured, being paroled. Over the past year or two, he had met several paroled farmers-turned-partisans-turned-prisoners-turned-farmers. So far, this rebellion had cost him a good long rifle, some cuts and bruises, sore feet, and several pounds—maybe a marriage as well. He would find out soon enough, after he delivered the broach to John Boyd's widow.

That wasn't Drummond's idea. Campbell had insisted that Drummond return the jewelry. Perhaps it was a form of punishment, or perhaps the Scot simply trusted the backwoods rifleman more than his own men. Drummond didn't know, didn't care really. Sure, he would have rather gone home first, kissed Salâli, told her how much he loved her and missed her before heading up the Saluda to visit the Boyd estate and explain to Mrs. Boyd that her husband had died in battle. Maybe that wouldn't have been such a good plan, after all, Drummond thought, because, once he held Salâli in his arms, he wasn't likely to let her go for a long spell.

Drummond had no choice in the matter. Campbell was sending a patrol of redcoat cavalry to the Tory stronghold at Ninety Six, and the Royal soldiers could escort the paroled rebel there. Drummond didn't really mind. He had been walking for just about two years now, so riding a horse would be a welcome luxury.

After leaving the British regulars at Ninety Six, he traveled up the west bank of the Saluda River afoot. With no weapon except a pocket knife, he stripped a sapling branch, pulled a wrought-iron hook and twine out of his hunting pouch, dug up some earthworms, caught a fish for supper, and slept on the ground a few rods from the river. By midmorning, he had reached the Boyd estate. His stomach fluttered—much as it had while marching into battle at Kettle Creek—and a chill raced down his backbone as he walked down the damp path.

Although it dwarfed Drummond's cabin, the house seemed fairly modest for a rich Tory like John Boyd. It was an old two-story hall-and-parlor made of pine crucks and red oak shingles, with large windows, towering brick chimneys on each side, and a fenced garden out back. Behind the main house, he spotted the kitchens and privies, wood shed, stables, barn, granary, and what he guessed would be a bathhouse. Beyond that stood the ramshackle quarters for Boyd's slaves. Still, this couldn't compare to Colonel Pickens's estate, although Drummond heard that Boyd also had homes in New York and Savannah, so perhaps those were fancy and this one simply functional.

He knocked, removed his battered low-crown, flat-brimmed hat, and waited. An elderly black man with white mustache and goatee but shaved head answered the door. He looked Drummond up and down as if he were examining a measly string of bony fish.

"May I help you?" the man asked.

"Come to see Miz Boyd," Drummond replied.

The slave just stared. Drummond was well aware that he certainly didn't look like any gentleman caller, with his ragged clothes that smelled of fish, smoke, and dried mud, and forehead still bruised and scabbed after getting knocked cold by those Tories. "I bring word of her husband, Colonel John Boyd," Drummond said. "An' this." He opened his pouch, removed a calico rag, and unwrapped it, revealing the broach.

Eyes widening, the slave told him to wait. Drummond could detect heavy footsteps as the man hurried up the stairs. A few minutes later, he heard the slave returning. The door opened, and the old-timer invited Drummond inside. He took Drummond's hat, hung it on a rack on the hall wall, and escorted him into a parlor. "You may wait here," the slave said. "Miz Boyd will see you shortly."

His nerves worsened, and he cursed Archibald Campbell. The colonel should have been doing this, or one of his officers—certainly not that lout Jernegan, though. Drummond warmed himself by the fireplace, tired of this, and walked across the large room to a mirror on the wall, accented by a pewter frame and candle holders. His appearance shocked him. Dirty, battered face and thick beard, hollow eyes and an unruly mane. He tried combing his dark hair, but tangled knots stopped his fingers. He was still pulling, biting his lip against the pain, when a voice surprised him, and he spun around, dropping his hands at his side. The fingers on his right hand remained cupped into the makeshift comb; his right hand held the jewelry.

"I am told you bring word of John," the woman said. She was a pretty woman, much younger than the colonel, with sparkling blue eyes, and blonde hair hanging in curls. She wore fingerless brown lace gloves, and a layered green linen dress trimmed with lace and three rose taffeta ribbons.

When he just stood there like a coat rack, she added testily: "Well?"

He nodded, cleared his throat, and said softly: "Yes, ma'am." His eyes dropped to his right hand. He started to lift it, hesitated, and looked up at the woman who didn't know she had been a widow for a few weeks now.

"Is it bad news?" The woman stepped toward him, gaping at the calico rag. He wanted her to stop, but she didn't until she stood close to him.

Nodding again, Drummond unfolded the cloth, picked up the broach, and handed it to her. She took it in her delicate hands. A lone tear rolled down her left cheek, then was gone. Again she looked at Drummond.

After slowly exhaling, he said nervously: "He was at Kettle Creek, not far from Augusta with his army when . . . we . . . attacked him. I saw him fall an' rushed to see if I could be of help. He give me the broach, asked me to see that you got it." Drummond paused, decided this was not enough, so he added: "He said to tell you he loved you." He tried to swallow, but found his mouth too dry. "He died quickly. Didn't suffer. He died a soldier. All of his wounds were in front." Another lie, but a small one. Boyd had been trying to rally his men, not retreat, when shot in the back.

41

Mrs. Boyd looked up. "You . . . you said when *we* attacked."

Drummond stared at his soiled moccasins, closed his eyes. "Yes, ma'am. I was with Colonel Pickens. I'm a paroled rebel."

The mirror cracked. His eyes shot open, and he realized Mrs. Boyd had flung the broach across the room at the mirror. Her face was flushed, her eyes angry. "You are a damned liar!" she snapped. "No damned rebel could kill my husband!" She slapped him hard, a stinging blow, although his coarse beard likely hurt her gloved hand worse than she hurt him. "Out! Get out of my house, you filthy brigand, rebel trash. How dare you. . . ."

She was still shouting at him, hurling words he had never heard from a lady's mouth as he crossed the parlor, grabbed his hat, and walked out the front door. The old slave waited for him on the front porch. Inside, Mrs. Boyd's curses had turned into choking sobs. Drummond wanted to throw up but figured that would have to wait until the slave, Mrs. Boyd's protector, was finished with him.

"Is it true?" the old man asked softly. "The master . . . he dead?"

"Yeah," Drummond answered. "I'm afraid so."

The slave shook his head sadly. "What she gonna do now?" he asked. "What to become of us?"

"I don't know," Drummond answered, pulled on his hat, and walked past the servant while tears streamed down the black man's face.

"This war," Drummond heard the slave saying as he walked down the road. "This war . . . this war . . . this damnable war."

A few days later, he had pushed John Boyd's widow to

the back of his mind. His pace quickened as he entered the Long Canes District, and hurried down the road, yet he saw no one, just the charred remains of a few cabins, now marked by blackened chimneys. This scared him, and he broke into a sprint for the last two miles, splashed across the creek, and headed up the overgrown path to his place. He stopped and stared dully, lungs burning from the cold air, stomach churning, heart laboring.

The cabin and barn were mere skeletal shells, blackened like the burned-out homes he had seen along the Ninety Six Pike. No hens, no roosters, not even the coop, no horse or cow, just a few scattered bones in the pasture. No Salâli. Cherokees? No, they wouldn't have done this, not to Salâli. Partisans or Tories likely, maybe *banditti*. Of course, by now he found it hard to differentiate between Loyalists and outlaws, or Patriots and outlaws for that matter. Where was Salâli? Maybe she had gone back to Kanasta. He would try there, but first he would head to the Witching Snake, learn what he could from Zack Gibbs.

He felt better till he detected the mound and cross underneath the sweetgum tree near where the chicken coop once stood. Drummond moved slowly to the edge of the grave. Someone had scratched into the wooden cross: **Squirrel**. Dead flowers lay rotting underneath the cross. He fell to his knees, fingering the cold earth, shaking his head, hearing the words of the Boyd slave: *This damnable war*.

Drummond had no recollection of how long he stayed there. Hours? A day? He couldn't remember crying, yet he knew he had. Blinking, he realized he was soaking wet, and cold. Only then did he notice the pouring rain. Drummond rose stiffly, mouthed a "Good bye, Salâli," and walked away, up the Long Canes banks, and through the woods until it grew too dark, and, somehow, he slept. At dawn, he walked again, reaching the Witching Snake at mid-morning. There was little left of it, as well.

The rain had stopped—when, Drummond couldn't remember—and he didn't feel cold, just numb. Broken glass and smashed furniture and kegs littered the yard in front of the tavern, while other kegs had been stacked neatly behind the burned ruins of Zack Gibbs's storage shed. The tavern itself had also been torched, but through the skeletal ruins he saw movement and heard a haunting voice. "Rum ye want, and rum ye shall have. A guinea and a pence have ye? Well, that's a sight to behold. Hard money. Aye, I'd be glad to join ye, friend, and put ye purse away. This is me inn, so I shall buy the first mugs. Don't worry, though, for I shall be glad to take ye money in due time."

Drummond rested his right hand on a blackened stud. Inside the wreckage, Zack Gibbs tipped a charred pewter mug as he sat in a rickety chair—he must have managed to save some furniture during the blaze, for the chair and a battered but unburned table were the only pieces standing in the rain-soaked ashes—and talked about rounds for the house and his preference for good old applejack over Madeira. The innkeeper pushed a jug across the table and continued his conversation. He sat alone.

Drummond picked a path through the fallen rafters, shards of pottery, charred tin, and soggy ash until he stood at the old man's side. The innkeeper ignored him, carrying on a conversation with his imaginary customer, and Drummond knelt, reached gently, and touched Zack's arm. The man turned slowly, stared blankly. "Aye," he said, and his mouth wreaked of apple brandy—the liquor wasn't imaginary—and smiled. "Join us, friend. Ol' Zack is buying tonight."

"Zack," Drummond said. "It's me, Augustin

Drummond. I need to talk to you 'bout Salâli, find out what happened."

The innkeeper reached across the table and slid the jug toward Drummond. "Ye don't mind sharing, not on a cold night like tonight, do ye, stranger? Aye, I figured ye for a good man. Any man who brings hard coin to the Witching Snake is a fine gentleman." His vacant gaze fell on Drummond again. "Help yeself, laddie. It'll take the chill off."

He closed his eyes, shook his head, and said, looking up at Gibbs again: "Zack, what happened here? To my place? I have to know. Who killed Salâli?"

"Drink! Drink! Drink!"

Drummond complied, thinking maybe that would help bring Gibbs to his senses. The brandy burned a fiery path, warmed him, and he placed the jug back on the table. "Now, Zack. . . ."

"Good!" The innkeeper laughed, and slapped his knee. "I like a man who can drink, and no one says Zack Gibbs serves bad essence of lockjaw. Not Zack Gibbs. Have another drink, stranger. . . ."

Hot blood rushed to his head, and Drummond exploded in rage, rising, lifting the innkeeper from his chair in the same movement, kicking the table over, and throwing the haggard man through all that remained of the far wall, snapping the burned wood. Drummond charged as Gibbs slammed into the mud near the shed's remains. Before the man could rise, Drummond straddled his chest, pinning his arms, slapping his face senselessly. This wasn't Augustin Drummond. He had never acted this way. Lost his temper, certainly, refused to speak to father and brother, been in a fistfight here and there, and fought at Kettle Creek. But this? He had become an animal.

45

"Damn you, old man! Listen to me! Who killed Salâli? What the hell happened? Answer me, by God, or I'll send you to Hades!"

Gibbs muttered something, sobbed.

Drummond stopped his assault. "What?" he shouted.

"I . . . I . . . I don't . . . can't recall."

He struck again. Blood gushed from both nostrils, staining the innkeeper's white mustache and beard. Drummond couldn't stop. He hit, hit, and screamed. "Salâli! Damn it, you buried her. You had to. No one else would have done that. Not here. Not put flowers on her grave!" Well, maybe Andrew Pickens, but Pickens hadn't been here. "Salâli, you fool. Your mind can't be all the way gone! Salâli. Squirrel. Damn it, Squirrel!"

"Squirrel?" the man blubbered, and again Drummond quit striking the man.

"Squirrel, Zack." His voice softened. "What happened?"

The innkeeper's eyes focused. "Augustin? Is that you?"

"Yes." Sighing, he rolled off his friend, tried to stand but couldn't, and sank into the mud beside the bloodied tavern owner.

Slowly Zack Gibbs sat up, crying now, looking across the ruins of his once profitable business. "Look what they done, Augustin. Look what they done to me."

"Salâli," Drummond said in a hoarse whisper. "Squirrel. I have to know."

"They murdered her, Augustin. I run over soon as I saw the smoke. Too late. They burned out lots of people. Killed the German, Dietrich. I found Squirrel." He wiped his bloody nose. "They . . . oh, Gus!" Gibbs wailed now, and Drummond realized he was crying as well. Neither spoke again until the old man's sobs quieted.

"Who did it?" Drummond then asked.

"*Banditti*. We tracked them, found them along the Keowee. Killed them to the last man."

All dead. He should be glad but felt betrayed. He had hoped to exact his own vengeance. "When?"

"Not quite a year ago. June, I think."

That long. Where had he been in June? He couldn't remember, and it didn't matter much. Salâli was dead, and he blamed himself. If he had stayed home, let the war go on without him, none of this. . . .

"An' your place? Bandits do this?" Drummond asked a minute later.

"No, rebel militia. Few weeks ago. Payback after John Boyd's Loyalists marched through, flogged that blow-hard Roland Harker and hung Jack Corbett from the oak tree in front of his house, then burned it to the ground. Boyd had too many with him, so the treasonous Whig cowards burned me out instead." He pointed to the stacked kegs. "Those were delivered less than a week ago, paid for already, as if I have use of them now." He started bawling again.

Drummond felt exhausted, lost. He leaned over an oaken keg and cried for a while, then straightened. He discovered the blackened ladle in the mud, the rock just beside it. Gibbs, his mind afflicted again, had returned to the shell of his tavern and was picking up the overturned chair and table, complaining about any foofaraw in his establishment, screaming that: "By thunder, Aaron Taylor would pay for the damage or be run out of here on a rail!"

Yes, Drummond thought, staring at the rock and ladle. With both hands, he snatched the rock, lifted it over his head, and sent it crashing against the top of the keg, again and again until the rock splashed after he lost his grip. His hands were bleeding, but he didn't care. He scooped up the ladle, lowered it into the rum, lifted it, and drank.

FROM THE MANUSCRIPT
OF THE REVEREND STAN MCINTYRE,
PAGE 7

One does not hear again of Drummond until the following year, after he had built or bought a cabin and began clearing fields. One of the earliest recollections of our subject can be found in a book, *An Early History of Florence and Darlington Counties* by Jas. DeWitt, self-published, date unknown, a dusty copy of which I discovered at the Society Hill Public Library. According to Mr. DeWitt, part of a letter from one Dr. Oliver, written on the 3rd of April to his wife, waiting out the Revolution in Jamaica, reads: *"Will drop by Drummond's to-morrow before embarking for Georgetown. He is a fine fellow, although taciturn. My darling, would you believe even our Rosemary seems to have taken a fancy to him? I do not think she shall admit this, however. Her pain is still too great."*

Drummond's cabin probably lay west of Cameron Branch.

CHAPTER THREE

Winter, 1779 – 1780

The day after Christmas always burdened Rosemary Madison. For two days and nights she would paint on her best face, laugh with her father, daughter, and friends, attend church, sing carols, and help the servants prepare a feast of mutton, potatoes, corn, sweetbreads, sheep tongues, Sally Lunn bread, and—Rachel's favorite—Queen's cake. Now, once more, Christmas had passed, and the world turned dreary. Over the faint notes of a small harpsichord, which Rachel was playing downstairs, a clock chimed as Rosemary stared out the window, gazing down on the magnolia-lined road that led to her father's estate. Noon, and she had not left her bedroom, although she had dressed.

Hard to believe, Richard would have turned thirty today. Thirty! They had married on his birthday seven years ago. Wedding anniversary, birthday, day after Christmas . . . too much for one day, especially with him being gone three and a half years now. Corporal Richard Madison of the 2nd Regiment had fallen at the palmetto fort on Sullivan's Island on June 28, 1776, when Colonel William Moultrie's Patriot forces had repelled the British fleet. A great day for those who cried for liberty. A dark day for her father, Dr. John Oliver, a Loyalist who had simply frowned when his son-in-law joined the move for independence, and gotten d⸱ when word came of his death. A heartbreaking day f⸱

51

chel and a stunned widow.

Major Francis Marion, a soft-spoken Huguenot planter near Eutaw Springs, had written her a touching letter that Ebenezer Moore had delivered personally. During the furious bombardment, Richard had volunteered with Marion and several others to resupply the Patriot forces with powder for their cannons. They rowed out to the *Defence*, a schooner at anchor in a cove on the other side of the island, loaded up, and brought three hundred pounds of vital powder to Colonel Moultrie's defenders. Richard and another soldier were carrying the last keg when a shell from His Majesty's *Bristol* exploded several rods away and sent fiery débris penetrating the powder keg. Richard and the other soldier never knew what killed them.

"Richard was a true patriot," Moore had said as he took her hand in his own. "More than that, he was my friend as you have always been. I am here for you. I will always be here for you." He had kissed her hand, kissed her forehead, and left.

Colonel Moultrie had written later, saying it might make her feel better to know that "our Patriots peppered the *Bristol* with grapeshot, shell, and musketry until her decks ran red with the blood of the men who killed your gallant husband." It didn't make her feel better at all, for it didn't change anything. She was still a widow; Rachel would never know her father.

South Carolinians and Whigs throughout the colonies celebrated Sergeant William Jasper, who had rescued the fallen colors, waved the flag furiously at the British ships, nd, with Captain Peter Horry's help, tied the flag to a ff, and speared it into the palmetto log fort's rampart to ot cheers. No one, however, remembered Corporal d Madison or the other 2nd Regiment soldier blown to oblivion. Rosemary didn't even know his name, and no one sang songs about the others who had died defending Charlestown.

Therefore Rosemary Madison had made a shrine of her own, fashioning a blue flag out of an old dress, sewing a white crescent moon in the upper left corner and **LIBERTY** emblazoned across the crescent—-like the flag Jasper had rescued. She hung it on the wall of their home. Loneliness and gloom permeated the cabin though, so they had moved in with her father in March of 1777, yet she still visited the cabin once a year. That's all she could stand. Once a year—on December 26.

Quit putting this off. After grabbing a black linen cape from her wardrobe, she hurried out the room, and down the stairs. "Where's Mommie going?" Rachel asked Jezebel, the house servant who had been with her father since Rosemary was a child.

"She be back, chil'e," Jezebel told the six-year-old. "You jus' keep practicin' your playin'."

Ezekiel must have heard the front door slam for he hurried out of the barn, shouting if she wanted him to saddle her mare. "I will walk, Zeke," she told the slave, and made a beeline for the Salem Road, passing underneath the wintry magnolias, through the front gate, and turning right, walking with a purpose, ignoring the bitter wind and her tears.

Shortly after leaving the road and turning on the path that followed alongside Cameron Branch, Rosemary Madison thought she heard the dull thud of an axe. She stopped to listen. Yes, it did sound like someone chopping wood, but a minute or so later the noise stopped. Something else then, or maybe activity from a nearby homestead. Sounds could travel far in this country. She continued, caught the scent of smoke, and felt her heart racing. She was not imagining this. Someone had to be using her cabin.

Instincts told her to run as hard as she could back to her father's mansion—*Get help!*—yet she moved forward, cautiously, making as little noise as possible until she reached the clearing. Last December, a stiff wind could have knocked over the corral, but it had been repaired. A pine had fallen across the cabin's roof, collapsing part of the chimney, yet smoke now floated gently from the freshly cut logs rising from the stone base, and firewood had been neatly stacked on the porch. The mud chocking between the cabin's logs had also been replaced, and a deerskin was pegged outside to dry. Someone had been here for a while.

It should not have surprised her. The cabin lay well off the Salem Road in the thick forests and near the swamps. The only person who ever ventured here was Rosemary Madison, and she only came once a year. Fear gave way to anger. Someone had moved into her home, the place she and Richard had built—over her father's protests; he had wanted them to live closer to civilization.

Civilization such as his mansion: a square, two-story brick building at the end of a magnolia-lined road, a two-tier portico lined with whitewashed pillars of Portland stone. Four rocking chairs resting on the flagstone floor of the lower portico, and the woodwork on both sides of the front door holding etchings of bears, deer, geese, and other wildlife scenes. Stained glass above the door, and an ornate interior with beautiful chandelier, marble mantels, black cypress wainscoting, brightly painted walls with lots of stenciling, and heart pine floors.

Richard and Rosemary needed only the drafty log cabin with a leaking roof and fireplace that seemed to suck heat out of the house rather than warm it, yet it had been home. This is where she had given birth to Rachel with only

Jezebel, serving as a midwife, to help because her father was in Georgetown, and Richard was laid up with a broken leg. Her face flushed, and she had half a mind to charge up there, open the door, throw the scoundrel out.

Common sense returned. Whoever occupied the house might be on the run from the law, a runaway slave or some sort of *banditti*. She spun around and ran down the path— straight into his arms.

She screamed, and he pushed her away. She fell on her backside, heard the sound of a flintlock being cocked, and looked up as the hood of her cape fell back and sent her auburn curls flowing.

The hideous monster gaped. He wore wretched clothes that she could smell from where she sat. A behemoth beard and thick brown hair hid most of his face as his eyes moved from her to the Queen Anne pistol—Richard's pistol!—in his right hand. He quickly shoved it into his belt and stepped forward, mumbling an apology as he extended his hand.

"Do not touch me!" she said, and both jumped back.

He remembered his hat, a motley black thing that must have been used for a pillow when it wasn't serving as head protection or a snack for some rat, and pulled it off.

"Didn't mean to startle you, ma'am," he said. "Just heard you, an' thought you might be a highwayman."

"Highwayman!" she scoffed. "That would be you."

"No, ma'am," he said.

"No. You just barge into my house and make yourself at home!" She pulled herself up. Her dress was damp and stained from the mud, and she felt like slapping him.

"Your house?" The man looked thunderstruck.

"Yes. I live here!"

"*Live here?* Ma'am, the only creatures livin' here when I

happened by was rats an' a 'possum."

"*Lived* here. Till my husband was killed."

His eyes shot to the cabin behind them, back to her. "Killed? At Sullivan's Island?"

How did he know that? She stared at him.

"Saw the flag in the cabin. It's still there. I haven't taken nothin'."

"That is *his* pistol."

He glanced at the weapon, pulled it out with his left hand, took the barrel, and handed it to her butt first. She took it hesitantly.

"Just borrowed it, ma'am. Name's Drummond. Augustin Drummond. Served with Colonel Pickens till I was captured at Kettle Creek an' paroled."

"I suppose you borrowed his rifle as well."

He gaped at his feet. "Yes, ma'am."

She couldn't believe the impudent brute. "You just barge into abandoned cabins and make them your homes?"

"Long story," he said, looking up. "I'll take my leave, ma'am, and be out of your way. Apologize for the intrusion, for squattin' on your place, for scarin' you witless."

Her anger subsided as she realized he was harmless. The stranger walked past her to the cabin. She looked at the pistol once, tossed it to the ground, and followed him. Inside, he packed his belongings—not much—in a knapsack. He said nothing, and she went to the far wall, where her flag still hung. Rats had chewed on the bottom edge—she remembered that from last year—but this squatter had raised the flag higher, out of the pests' reach, even washed the home-made flag, and mended a rip beneath the crescent moon.

The cabin itself had been cleaned by this filthy vagabond. *Shrine,* she thought, not hardly. This cabin, her husband's home, would be a rotting ruin by now if not for this

Drummond. "Good bye, ma'am," he said, and headed outside. He was halfway to the path when she stepped onto the
porch to call out his name.

"Been livin' off brandy an' rum," he said, tossing another log on the fire. "Driftin' as far as I could from the
Long Canes, drinkin'. Couldn't exactly recall the last time
I'd been sober. Anyway, one day I was staggerin' down that
road, stumbled down the trail to empty my gut of rotten applejack, an', instead of goin' back to the main road, I just
come here. Passed out, I reckon. An' when I woke up, when
I sobered up, I dunno. . . .

"This cabin reminded me an awful lot of the one me an'
Salâli had built. I suddenly realized that bein' a drunkard
wasn't no befittin' tribute to pay her, not what she would
want. I saw that flag, had seen drawings of it before, knew
what it meant. I just figured this cabin was about as far
from the war as I was likely to get, so I started fixin' her
up." He looked into her eyes. "Don't reckon it makes much
sense. Don't reckon I make much sense."

Strange, she thought with a smile, *how two strangers could
open up to each other when neither could talk to their own
family.* She had told him all about Richard, most of her feelings, and he had spoken of Salâli, Squirrel, he said it meant,
in Cherokee. Dreams cut short by a revolution.

First, she had asked for proof that he was, indeed, a paroled rebel, and he had pulled out the letter, trying to hide
with his thumb the wavy scrawl that resembled three side-
ways S's strung together. Neither his illiteracy nor his pride
surprised her. She liked this gentle, haunted man. She felt a
bond between them, one of pain and regret.

"I must be going," she said, and rose. " 'Tis getting
late."

57

"I enjoyed the talk," he said. "It was nice meetin' you, Miz Rosemary. I'll be off as well."

Her eyes shot up. "No." She heard the word before realizing she had spoken it, almost shouted it. "I mean, you may stay as long as you like, Mister Drummond. This cabin would be nothing more than rotten timbers if not for you."

She returned two days later, and they talked for another hour. On her third trip, the following week, he gave her a jar of something called pemmican. She had heard of it, some sort of Indian food. "Rent," he told her, and she had laughed. When she came back the following Saturday, she brought him gifts. "Scissors," she said mischievously, pulling the pair from a bag. He took them, and her hand disappeared into the bag again. "Razor . . . comb . . . and soap." She also opened the trunk she had left behind, the one containing Richard's clothes, which the rats had yet to destroy. Drummond had the same build as Richard. She hadn't shed a tear upon opening the trunk. Maybe she was getting better.

When she returned the next weekend, his appearance shocked her. Gone was the thick beard, and his wavy locks had been trimmed. He looked presentable, although she had to touch up his haircut, slicking his brown locks with bear grease, and fingering a braid. She used green ribbons from her own hair to tie the long plait.

After that, she made it a habit to see him once a week. Fearing her father would wander by the cabin, she told him about Augustin Drummond. He didn't seem upset. Maybe he had known, what with her sneaking off regularly. "Well, what kind of rent can I expect from this paroled rebel?" he demanded, although the twinkle in his eye told her he was joking. "Pemmican," she answered, and presented him with a jar.

In March, she invited Drummond to her father's house. "His birthday is tomorrow," she told the backwoodsman, "and I want you to come. It is time for you to meet him, and my daughter Rachel."

"You know any games?" Rachel asked.

"Hustle-cap," Drummond answered. "That's 'bout it."

"How do you play it?"

"Little girls don't play it. Nor do gentlemen. Wisht I never learned."

"Oh, it's a naughty game."

"That's right."

Rachel dropped her voice: "Grandpa plays naughty games sometimes."

Rosemary burst out laughing. She couldn't remember when she had laughed so hard, but Drummond, sitting stiffly in a purple ottoman coat and trousers, lavender vest with silver brocade, and stand-up collar that had to be choking him, looked hilarious as he talked to curly-headed Rachel.

Jezebel brought out the birthday cake and placed it on the dining room table, whispering to Rosemary as she passed: "That Massah Drummon', he be a right handsome man. You be a lucky gal."

"Fiddlesticks," Rosemary said. "We are just friends." Still, she found herself looking at the backwoodsman. There was a ruggedness about him, the scarred forehead, crooked nose, cleft in his chin. He wasn't nearly as handsome as Richard, but. . . .

The front door swung open, and Dr. John Oliver stormed inside, looking dashing in his powdered wig and formal suit of red velvet, silver braid, and silver buttons. He loosened his cravat, handed Jezebel his bag, and sprinted down the hall. Rachel screamed—"Grandpa!"—and ran to him, leaping into his arms.

"That's my baby!" Oliver said, tossing her into the air and catching her as the girl screamed in delight.

Drummond entered the hall, and Rachel was lowered over her protests. "Later, my love," Oliver said, and walked to Drummond. "So," he said, his eyes still twinkling, "this is the gentleman who pays rent with pemmican."

"He brought a hindquarter of venison with him today, Father," Rosemary said.

"Indeed. Well, we sha'n't starve as long as he is around." Her father towered a good head over Drummond. They shook hands formally, then the doctor slapped Drummond's shoulder. "Care for a snifter of peach brandy on this fine day, my lad?"

Rosemary shook her head. "I think you've already had a few snifters today, Father," she said, trying to sound teasing but being serious.

"Yes, I have, at Weaver's Settlement. 'Tis my fifty-fifth birthday and a glorious one, indeed. Worthy of celebration."

Drummond smiled politely, while Rosemary just stared. Rachel asked when could they eat cake.

"You have not heard," Oliver said to the blank faces.

"Heard what?" Rosemary asked.

"The British have laid siege to Charlestown. General Lincoln and the Continentals are all but trapped." He clapped his hands and darted for the cabinet holding his stock of brandy and rum. "Yes, by all means, we should celebrate, but not just your father's day of birth. This awful rebellion will soon be squashed."

FROM THE MANUSCRIPT
OF THE REVEREND STAN MCINTYRE,
PAGE 16

Historians know well that on May 12, 1780, General Benjamin Lincoln surrendered his Continental Army forces to British General Henry Clinton. Patriot losses at Freeman's Farm, Brandywine, Germantown, and Philadelphia could not lite a candle to this defeat. The British army had just captured 5,500 soldiers, close to four hundred cannon, nearly six thousand muskets, and scores of ammunition and powder.

By all rights, the American Revolution should have ended shortly thereafter. And after the bloody disaster at the Waxhaws, and later Camden, the British would have the run of the South.

Speaking of the Waxhaws, this writer has had no luck tracking down Augustin Drummond's parents and siblings or any of his ancestors. I have looked through files after files in southern archives. Interestingly enough, I did come across a strange petition for a pension in the National Archives, filed in 1818 by one Prudence Drummond where she cites her husband's service with Colonel Abraham Buford's Continentals. Kin? Who knows?

Chapter Four

Spring, 1780

"Yes, suh, Mistah Drummon', these catfish'll fry up jus' fine." Ezekiel held up the string of fish Drummond had presented him, and grinned in admiration. "We be eatin' high on the hog since you showed up. Too bad Mastah John not be here to enjoy 'em. He shore likes his fish fries."

"We'd put 'em in a stew in Long Canes," Drummond told the slave.

"You don't say. What all you put in it?"

"Bacon, onions, tomatoes. . . ."

"Tomatoes? You et them things?"

"We sure do."

"Huh. Never heard no white folk eatin' tomatoes." His eyes looked past Drummond's shoulders, and he lowered the mess of fish. "Riders comin'," he said, but Drummond was already turning, instinctively stepping closer to the long rifle leaning against the open barn door.

"Why that be Capt'n Moore," Ezekiel said, and sprinted to greet the two riders.

Drummond picked up the rifle anyway, tucking it in a non-threatening position under his right arm, and walked to the front yard. He stopped near the doorsteps as Ezekiel told the taller rider that it certainly was good to have him back, that he had feared the "capt'n" had been captured by the redcoats, and maybe even killed.

"They certainly have tried, Zeke," the rider said. He swung off his roan and handed the reins to the slave. "You shall take good care of Charger, won't you, boy? Look after the colonel's horse, too."

"Yes, suh. Yes, suh."

Favoring his right leg, the other rider slowly dismounted, and had to be helped by the taller man.

"I'm all right, Captain," the injured man said, and, using a cane, limped toward the Oliver mansion as Ezekiel led both horses to the barn. The first man had been staring at Drummond the whole time. Now he hooked his thumbs in his wide belt, close to the pistol tucked inside, and began walking, never taking his eyes off Drummond.

He looked to be about three inches taller than Drummond, maybe the same age, although he needed to shave. His face was lean but firm, like something chiseled out of granite, his blue eyes hollow yet intense. Handsome, a woman might say, in a strange sort of way. A difficult man to read, or know. Cautious. On edge.

The other man carried a dignity despite his painful limp. He was much shorter than the captain, and at first glance seemed rather meek and uninspiring, weak and sickly, and not just because of his injury. A slight, middle-aged man with a high forehead and pale complexion, who likewise needed a bath, haircut, and a shave, to whom most people wouldn't give a second look. That would be their mistake. His nose resembled a hawk's beak, but, when he looked up, Drummond detected a ceaseless drive in those brooding black eyes, did a quick reëvaluation, and decided this was a man to be reckoned with.

Both wore bedraggled uniforms of South Carolina's 2nd Regiment. They had been riding hard, hiding out it appeared.

"I am Lieutenant Colonel Francis Marion," the injured man told Drummond, "and this is my adjutant, Captain Ebenezer Moore." His English had a trace of French. Huguenot, Drummond guessed, and tried to place the names. Yes, this is the officer who had written a kind letter to Rosemary after her husband's death, and Moore had delivered the note. Colonel Pickens, too, had spoken favorably of Francis Marion. "I do not believe I have had the pleasure."

Drummond leaned the rifle against the banister, and offered his hand. "Augustin Drummond," he said. "It's an honor to meet you, Colonel. Can I help you up the stairs?"

Marion had a tremendous grip, and his laugh put Drummond at ease. "I think not that I have strength to mount Doctor Oliver's stairs, sir," Marion said. "I shall rest on these bottom steps if you do not mind." He lowered himself gently and stretched out his right foot with a grimace.

"Is not that Richard's rifle?"

Drummond looked back at Moore, saw the captain staring at the long rifle. It was similar to Drummond's old weapon, the one Tories had stolen after Kettle Creek, of the same caliber and length, but slightly heavier and with a different style of stock.

"Was," Drummond answered. "I been livin' at his old cabin."

"And wearing his clothes." Moore's voice had an icy nastiness to it. The comfort Drummond had felt evaporated.

Instead of responding, Drummond walked up the steps and knocked on the door. When Jezebel answered, he whispered the names of the visitors, and asked the servant to fetch Rosemary. He also asked Jezebel if she would bring a pitcher of water and some glasses. He thought about going back down the steps, but decided against it. That would mean engaging Moore in conversation, which he expected might lead to some sort of fight. Jealous. Drummond clucked his tongue. Don't that beat all? Moore was jealous of him. Misplaced jealousy, he told himself, because a woman of Rosemary Oliver Madison's class wouldn't have anything to do with a Back Country ruffian like Augustin Drummond.

The front door opened, and Drummond took the tray from Jezebel, and eased his way down the steps. Marion poured a glass with heartfelt thanks. Moore declined any water, so Drummond set the tray on the ground. A hard frown had been carved into Moore's stony face, and Drummond figured it was permanent until the door swung open again, Rosemary screamed his name, bounded down the steps, and leaped into his arms. They spun around underneath the magnolias.

Why, hell, Drummond told himself, *who's jealous now?*

Hard-faced Ebenezer Moore became a grinning schoolboy, and, when Rosemary asked if he cared for any water, he accepted, and she poured him a glass. "I was worried sick about you," she told him, and, turning to Marion, quickly added, "and you, as well." Her eyes dropped to the wrapped ankle. "Oh, my, Colonel, you have been injured. How rude of me. . . ."

"Nonsense, my child. It does my heart good to see you laughing. Where is Rachel?"

"Taking her nap." She dropped to her knees and began unwrapping the dirty osnaburg. "I see no blood. Tell me, Colonel, that you have not been shot."

"No, Rosemary, I have not been shot." He chuckled in spite of himself. "Although I may wish I had been after I tell you how I broke this ankle."

Marion had been in Charlestown, preparing the city's

defense when General Moultrie's adjutant general, Captain Alexander McQueen, invited several officers to a party at John Stuart's wonderful home at the corner of Tradd and Orange streets. The guests consumed wine and rum with abandon, except Marion, and, when everyone, especially Captain McQueen, had become sufficiently intoxicated, except Marion, the host demanded that no one could leave his home until everyone was drunker than he. Which prompted applause and more drinks. McQueen even filled a mug, and handed it to Marion, insisting that he imbibe. When Marion politely declined, McQueen told his servants to lock the house and that no one should leave until Francis Marion satisfied the host.

Marion had walked upstairs—prompting a drunken laugh from McQueen, who said there was no escape, that he could run but not hide, and that he better quit his fussing and start drinking or there would be no liquor left. Little chance of that, Marion had thought. They had more wine and rum than a dozen taverns in Charlestown.

Frustrated, he opened a window in a second-story drawing room and jumped, breaking his ankle, but getting out of McQueen's house without taking a drink. At least, he said, he had found an open window on the second story, instead of being forced to leap off the third story or captain's walk.

"I needed a litter to be carried across the Cooper River," recalled Marion, shaking his head, "and am now quite the laughingstock of Charlestown. A doctor worked on it at Moncks Corner, but I fear I have reinjured it. Rosemary, I know your father's Loyalist leanings, but I was praying he would tend to my ankle. I shall be glad to pay him for his troubles."

"You are no trouble, Colonel Marion," she said, "but

Father is not home, nor at Weaver's Settlement. He received word two days ago that Elizabeth Langston's two boys have malaria, perhaps even yellow fever, and left for their home on the Black River."

Drummond noticed the sweat beads on Marion's forehead when the colonel sagged at the news.

"I've had some dealin's with broken bones, Colonel," Drummond said as he knelt beside Rosemary, "an' can take a look at your injury."

Marion's eyes met Drummond's briefly, and the colonel nodded. Rosemary had finished unwrapping the soiled bandage, so Drummond pulled his skinning knife, cut away the bottom of the shabby breeches, then pulled off Marion's stocking. The Huguenot clenched his jaw and clamped his eyes shut but uttered not a sound. The swollen ankle was black and blue. Drummond took a firm hold of the man's foot and told Rosemary to pin his legs. He could have, probably should have, asked Moore to do this but didn't feel like it. Moore didn't like Drummond, and Drummond would rather have Rosemary close to him than the haughty captain. "It's gonna hurt, Colonel," Drummond said before setting the break.

This time, Marion grunted and swore.

Ezekiel supplied a makeshift splint, and Jezebel tore strips of an old bed sheet, which Rosemary Madison used to rewrap the broken ankle.

"It feels good as new," Marion proclaimed, refilled his glass with water, and drank thirstily.

"I doubt that, sir," Drummond said. "You probably should stay off that leg a spell. An' I'd definitely pay another visit to Doc Oliver soon. I am no sawbones."

"I fear I cannot follow your orders, Doctor Drummond,"

Marion said with a wink. "I have a war to fight. If I had not acted so impishly at Captain McQueen's, I would be much better off."

"Nonsense," Rosemary shot back. "If more officers had your morality and convictions, Colonel, our cause would not be hopeless."

" 'Tis not hopeless, Rosemary," Moore said stiffly.

Her mouth fell open as she turned to him. "You . . . you have not heard."

"Heard what?" Moore asked.

"About Charlestown." She chanced a glance to Marion, who looked just as puzzled.

"Dear God, must I be the one to tell?" Clasping her hands, she spoke to Marion. "General Lincoln surrendered his entire forces to Sir Henry Clinton in Charlestown on the Twelfth."

"Rubbish!" Moore exclaimed. "A damned Tory lie. Rosemary. . . ."

"No, Ebenezer, couriers have been bringing word since yesterday." Her eyes welled with tears. "I'm so sorry," she said softly.

The news staggered Moore, who collapsed heavily on the ground, pushed back his leather helmet, and shook his head. "It cannot be," he said to no one in particular. "It cannot be."

Marion pulled himself up, handled his cane, and tested his ankle. " 'Tis all right, Rosemary," he said. "We are used to bad news. Dark days for liberty, but the fight will go on. Ezekiel, I would be obliged if you would bring our horses."

Drummond followed the slave, helped saddle the roan and chestnut, and told Ezekiel that he would bring the guests their horses. Rosemary had apparently already bid her farewell to Marion and Moore because she had gone inside with Jezebel when Drummond led the mounts out of the barn. Moore, having recovered, stood beside his commanding officer, both faces firm, mouths tight. They took the reins, and Drummond helped Marion into the saddle. He stepped back from both men.

"Good luck," he said.

Moore started to tug on the reins, but stopped and stared at Drummond. "Pardon me for being rude, sir, but where do you stand in this war, for the King or for liberty?"

"I served with Colonel Pickens," Drummond answered. "Was captured at Kettle Creek an' paroled. I have the paper."

"Your paper will not be worth a tinker's damn. . . ."

"Captain," Marion said in soft rebuke.

The captain started to argue, stopped himself, angrily jerked the reins, turned Charger, and kicked the roan into a gallop. Marion controlled his own horse, which wanted to run after Moore's, and stared at Drummond.

"Thanks for helping with my ankle, Drummond," he said. A long pause followed during which the only noise came from the fading hoof beats of Moore's roan. Finding his words, Marion continued. "This war is not over. On the contrary, victory is still sure. The enemy, 'tis true, have all the trumps, but they lack the spirit of generosity. They shall treat people cruelly, and that is the one thing that shall ruin them and save us. I could use a man like you, Drummond."

"I signed that paper, Colonel. Give my word I wouldn't fight Royals or Tories no more."

The Huguenot planter nodded. "I find your honor admirable, sir, but your judgment damnable. Good day."

Whipping his horse, Marion galloped underneath the magnolias, and chased Moore down the Salem Road. He didn't ride like a man with a broken ankle.

CHAPTER FIVE

Magnolia leaves rustled in the sudden gust, and Rosemary Madison shuddered, although not from the wind. The breeze felt refreshingly cool on this muggy afternoon. *A premonition?* she wondered. Spring had been short this year, and dark. Several dogwoods failed to bloom, and few magnolias flowered. Bad signs, Jezebel had said. Be a bad year. Unlike the elderly servant, Rosemary had never been superstitious. Still. . . .

Rosemary stopped rocking. She had been sitting on the portico, reading the Bible to Rachel, when her father returned. Looking tired, he was heading toward the house, but a rider called his name. The galloper reined in his lathered horse, and John Oliver changed course to meet the newcomer. The rider talked excitedly, but she couldn't catch his words. Her father asked a few questions—again, she couldn't hear—and finally nodded his head. "Don't tarry, for the love of Christ!" the rider shouted, and galloped down the Salem Road from where he had come. Shaking his head wearily, her father walked underneath the magnolias like a man headed for the guillotine.

"What's that word, Mommie?" Rachel asked.

She glanced down quickly. "Danites," she said absently.

"What's it mean?"

"Nothing." She closed the Bible, handed it to her

daughter, and told her to take the book inside. The girl pouted but did as she was told, and Rosemary stood to greet her father as he climbed the steps.

"Bad news?" she asked.

Her voice startled him, but he quickly recovered, only he didn't smile. A bad sign. With a sigh, he said: "I am needed at the Waxhaws. There has been . . . a fight . . . many wounded. Many. . . ." His head shook sorrowfully.

"The Waxhaws? Father, that is too far. There are doctors in Charlotte, and that is much closer. Why should you . . . ?"

"Because I have been asked. Because I am a doctor. Because the British soldier who led this attack did not leave a surgeon to tend the wounded he left behind, and the poor rebels. . . . No matter, I must leave at once."

She followed him inside. "I shall go with you," she said. "I can help as your nurse." He slowly turned to her, his face mixed with pride and fear, and shook his head.

"The roads are too dangerous, Rosemary. I fear what this Colonel Tarleton has done will lead to much more bloodshed." By disappearing into the library, he dismissed her offer. When she followed him into the room, he was pouring himself a brandy. He must have expected her, because he said without looking up: "I thought once General Lincoln surrendered, and then the rebels at Ninety Six and Kershaw's band at Camden, peace would return to Carolina, but this. . . ." He gulped down the liquor and refilled his glass. "This portends revenge and anarchy." Another drink. He looked at his daughter. "The courier told me the rebels tried to surrender, but this Tarleton ignored the white flag, and put them to the sword. More than a hundred dead. A hundred and fifty left to die."

She was proud of him at that moment, more than she

had been in quite some time, at least since the rebellion began. The Waxhaws lay some seventy miles, perhaps more, northwest, yet Dr. John Oliver would go. He would treat the Patriot soldiers—he called them rebels—despite his loyalty to England and King George III, because he was a doctor, and it was his oath. Most Loyalists cried God, King, and Country, but not Dr. John Oliver. His priorities had always been Family, Profession, King, Country. God, she lamented, had been lost years ago.

They had not seen eye-to-eye over the past five years, and never talked politics. Besides, it wasn't a woman's place, or so her parents, her minister, Richard, even old Jezebel and Ezekiel, had tried to teach her. Even when Richard joined the Continental Army, even after he had been killed, they never talked about her feelings. She believed in the cause of Revolution—her father knew this, if he never said it—but she could not bring it up. After all, this was his house. Although her beliefs in the cause of liberty had strengthened even after Richard's death, she remained silent. Strengthened, yet what had she done but mope around in her gloom and wear black? *Time to change,* she thought. *Time to act.*

"I was thinking about sending you and Rachel to Jamaica to stay with your mother," he told her. "Until this rebellion is crushed. Until peace returns to Carolina." He closed his eyes. "I had prayed so hard for this war not to come to the Back Country."

That her father had prayed surprised her, yet she would not back down. "I am not going to live with Mother," she said firmly. "I am going to the Waxhaws. If you will not take me, I shall go on my own. You have trained me as a nurse, or have you forgotten? I have helped you when the sick came here."

"This is different," he said. "You are not prepared for. . . ."

"I was not prepared for Richard's death." Her voice trembled as it rose. Anger. It felt rejuvenating. She cried out, saw Jezebel and Rachel standing in the open doorway, their mouths open, but she did not care. "I was not prepared to raise a daughter without a husband. I have done nothing since Richard's death. I am your daughter, Father. I am a nurse, and I have more reason to go treat those poor soldiers than you. It is I who believes in their cause, not you, sir."

His eyes glared, and a quick look at Jezebel made her close the library's door, and lead Rachel away. "You shall stay here or sail to Jamaica," he said, clenching his fists. "That is my command. Who would look after Rachel if you went traipsing to the border with me? Certainly, you would not bring her into this cauldron of blood."

"Jezebel can look after Rachel."

"I forbid it."

"With you or alone, Father, I am going. It is time I did something with my life again."

With his face turning crimson, he slammed a fist against the desk top so hard the entire room seemingly shuddered. "You have helped me treat malaria, given doses of mercury and Jesuit's bark, yet you told me yourself you did not set Squire Marion's broken ankle when he happened by. Drummond did." He lowered his voice. "Rosemary, do you honestly believe you could help hold down a screaming man while I sawed off his leg? I do not mean to be grotesque, Daughter, but this will be a most ghastly business."

"I am going to the Waxhaws. I am tired of acting weak and scared, longing for what cannot be, blind to the future. You and Mother raised me better than that."

His shoulders sagged, and she knew she had won. He drained the last of the brandy before sinking into his chair. "You may come with me, but do not forget I warned you. If you flinch just once, I shall send you home immediately. This will be bloody hell. Have Ezekiel ride to Drummond's, ask him if he would serve as an escort for us. I shall pay him for his services, furnish him with horse, saddle, and provisions."

"I doubt if Augustin will take your money, Father."

The pews had been carried out of the Presbyterian church and stacked along the side of the building next to the dead bodies being prepared for burial. Those fortunate enough to have been slain by Banastre Tarleton's Green Dragoons had been lowered in a mass grave at the massacre site. These men at the Waxhaws church had taken a week to die. Others, deemed hopeless cases by Oliver and other doctors, lay shaded by the pines several rods from the chapel.

At least the unholy screaming had stopped. No more amputations, Drummond hoped, although now he could hear the sound of spades breaking the earth as Back Country volunteers dug fresh graves in the church cemetery. He wondered how Rosemary was holding up.

Body after body, row after row of moaning men covered the church floor, already stained with blood. *Like a dream,* Drummond thought. *Not real. The bodies, the gore.* Doctors, nurses and other volunteers moved quickly, working frantically, all watched by the painting of Jesus above the altar.

A day had passed, and neither Oliver nor his daughter had stepped outside other than to attend nature's call or fetch water. Drummond busied himself as well, bringing out litters of the dead and hauling water to the dying beneath the pines. A black man in a cocked hat—freedman, Drummond guessed—knelt by each soldier, reading scripture, sprinkling water over each ashen face, and then, looking skyward, making the sign of the cross and begging the Lord God to take this poor soul to heaven. It did not matter if the soldier, or the preacher, were Presbyterian, Anglican, Baptist, or sinner.

"Water," a voice cried weakly.

The man had been sabered in his stomach. Water would only hasten his death, make it even worse. "For Christ's sake, just a sip of water." Drummond moved quickly past him, trying to shut off the pitiful moans.

"Water."

The next man was dead. A quick glance told Drummond the gravediggers were too busy to notice him, so he continued on. A ladle of water, smoke on a pipe, or just a few words of comfort, some of regret. He worked his way down one line, started back down the next.

"Water, please, water."

The soldier had lost his right arm below the elbow, had been hacked or bayoneted repeatedly in both legs, and a bloody bandage covered his forehead and left eye. The right eye, dull and brown, locked on Drummond as he sat down and dipped the ladle into the oaken keg. The smell from the man's wounds almost gagged him.

Lifting the soldier's head, Drummond let him drink, although most of the water cascaded down the dirty face. The lone eye never left Drummond. He whispered something, so Drummond bent closer, and the man tried again. "God answered my prayer. My brother, my brother, I love you."

Drummond simply patted the delirious man's shoulder before turning away. He dropped the ladle in the water, picked up the bucket, and started to move on.

"Augustin."

He froze. The pines creaked in a strong breeze, the black minister recited a psalm, and shovels struck the earth. "Augustin," the soldier repeated, and Drummond knew he had not imagined this. He lowered the bucket, turned slowly. The dying man smiled. Drummond walked on his knees to his brother, sank beside him, and squeezed his left hand. A tear rolled down his cheek. His emotions surprised him. This was his brother, the one who had never answered his letter, the one who, like their father, ceased all contact with him because he had married a Cherokee. Yet he was blood.

They said nothing, just stared at each other.

"I sent letters," said Michael, his voice barely audible. "You never wrote back."

Guilt sliced him like a razor. "I never got 'em," he said, grabbed the bucket and ladle, and gave his brother another drink.

"Friend?"

Drummond saw the preacher, waiting his turn to give Michael Drummond his last rites. "There are others, friend, who need water," the freedman said somberly.

"This," Drummond heard himself saying, "this is my brother."

With a solemn nod, the preacher picked up the bucket of water and left without another word.

He didn't know where Michael found his strength. "You used to be the peace-keeper," his brother said hoarsely, licking his lips, swallowing before he continued. "Never a fighter. I always scrapped with Papa, not you. Never took a stand till you married Salâli." Michael remembered her name, which surprised him. "So," his brother asked, "are you loyal to King George or George Washington?"

"Served with Pickens," he answered with a shrug, "got captured at Kettle Creek an' paroled."

"War's over for you, then?"

"Reckon so."

"Good. No matter what happens . . . you promise me to stick by your parole." Drummond felt his brother's grip tighten. Like his voice, his strength had improved, maybe from the water, probably from seeing his brother and wanting to say everything that needed to be said. Drummond's head bobbed ever so slightly, and Michael looked relieved. "Feel better. Don't want you to die. War's over. The King's won."

Some ladies had gathered outside the church and were singing hymns. A soldier nearby tried to sing along but soon passed out. "Papa's dead," Michael said suddenly.

"What?"

His brother tried to nod but couldn't. He didn't seem able to move at all now, just talk. "Cherokees finally got him. English bastards put the Injuns up to those raids, damn them, but Papa's neighbors tracked down them red devils, killed most of them. After hearing that, what the King's soldiers was willing to do, stirring up Injuns to scalp us all, I joined Colonel Buford. Now I am killed."

Drummond had pictured his father many times over the past few years. Pictured him as the bitter old Indian fighter he surely had become. Estranged from his youngest son, living a hard-scrabble life in the North Carolina sandhills. Pictured him alone, drinking his peach brandy, pulling back his gray hair to reveal the scar on his neck the Cherokees gave him in 1760, only no one was there to see him show off his badge of honor, or the Cherokee scalps he had taken in revenge. Pictured him at the grave of his wife, who died

in the smallpox outbreak of 1758. Pictured him in many
ways.

But never dead.

"Don't judge him harshly, Brother. He tried. . . ."

"I don't," Drummond lied.

"You don't know . . . traders . . . he had traders from
Long Canes . . . tell him how . . . you and Squirrel . . . were
doing . . . hoped . . . for a grandchild. Proud. Our father . . .
would you believe?"

Eyes clamped shut, Drummond shook his head.

"So . . . any children?"

"No," he answered, catching a sob.

"Me either. Live . . . in Virginia now . . . wife is Prudence. You'll tell her . . . about me?" His voice was fading
again. He could no longer feel his brother's grip.

Drummond said he would return quickly with water. Instead of finding the preacher, he ran to the church, snagged
his canteen off the saddle Oliver had loaned him, lifted it
over his head to let the water splash his face. He breathed
heavily, sorting out his feelings, and briefly thought he
might vomit.

"You must be strong," a gravedigger told him. "Those
boys up there need your help."

Nodding, Drummond hurried to the well.

She felt drained, too tired to sleep, too stunned to cry,
and nothing in her stomach to throw up. They had saved
some lives, and her father and others continued to work inside but had demanded that she sleep now, get out of the
stifling church, and breathe fresh air. They would call when
they needed her.

The night air felt cool, the moon as bright as dawn. A
black man in a cocked hat offered her water, and she drank

greedily, almost forgetting to thank him. He nodded politely and walked to the well. "Sir!" she called out, and, when he turned, she saw he also carried a tattered Bible. "I am looking for my friend, who escorted my father and me here." He shook his head slowly. "His name is Drummond, Augustin Drummond." The head shook again. "He has been helping out here. Dark hair in a plait and darker eyes, wearing a green hunting frock and black hat?"

"Up there," said the man, pointing to the pines.

She maneuvered carefully among the rows of men, her eyes welling with tears as she heard their lamentable cries for water, for their mothers, for their deaths. She felt thankful that Richard had not perished this way, had not suffered. Drummond's accent carried above the sobs, and she spotted him in the moonlight, leaning against a pine and holding a Continental soldier's hand. His voice caused her to shiver.

"Remember after Mama died, an' you told Papa we wasn't fetchin' his jug no more . . . that Mama never taken to his drinkin' on the Sabbath. Remember that, Michael? After whippin' the tarnation out of us, he locked us in the wood shed. Remember? I was cryin', but you wasn't. You told me to be a man, that we had to stick together. An' you opened your jackknife an' we made that blood oath, said no matter what, we was brothers an' would stick together, an' Papa could go to the devil." He shook his head. "What happened to us, Michael? You stood up to Papa, then. Why couldn't you stand up to him when I married Salâli? An' now you tell me Papa was spyin' on me all that time, proud of me? He never could show it, though, could he?" He sipped from his canteen, corked it, and set it aside.

She felt like an intruder but didn't want to leave. She wanted to be with Drummond now, to comfort him. She cleared her throat and moved closer. Drunk? No, the canteen held water. She would have smelled liquor.

"Salâli's dead, Michael. Bandits murdered her while I was fightin' with Pickens. Zack an' the others killed the ones that killed her. Now Papa's dead, an' his killers as well, Tarleton's murdered you, an' I'm on parole an' bound to my word. To you an' Colonel Campbell. That's the one thing Papa an' Mama taught us good. Live by your word." He was crying now, letting the canteen fall to the ground, releasing his brother's white hand, and crawling toward her. "I tried my best, Rosemary, to run away from the war, an' run smack-dab into it again."

She reached for him, pulled him close, let him cry on her shoulder. She was crying, too, stroking his hair, apologizing for bringing him to this awful place. "We shall return to Cameron Branch," she told him. "We will go back where there is no war. I promise you that, Augustin."

His tears finally stopped, and he shuddered once and straightened, wiping his nose on his sleeve. She told him again that everything would be all right, that they would go home.

"I know," he said. "But first I gotta bury my brother."

FROM THE MANUSCRIPT
OF THE REVEREND STAN MCINTYRE,
PAGES 21–22

Like the Alamo, the Buford Massacre became a rallying cry for the Patriots. If William Sherman is the South's most hated enemy, then Colonel Banastre Tarleton must surely be first runner-up. The incident at the Waxhaws led to more butchery, and we must surely deduce that many Patriot hands, perhaps even Augustin Drummond's, likely ran red with the blood of British and Tory.

The summer of 1780 was one of the bloodiest years of the American Revolution, and most of the blood would be spilled in South Carolina's Back Country.

Retaliation came quickly. Thomas Sumter, who became known as the "Gamecock," and Francis Marion, who we all know as the "Swamp Fox," started forming small militia units to combat the evil forces. After a few small engagements in the Back Country, minor ambushes and not major battles, whenever Loyalist or British regular soldier tried to surrender, the Partisans would cry—"Tarleton's quarter!" or "Bloody Tarleton!"—and take no prisoners. It truly became a civil war.

This prompted an even tougher response from Lord Charles Cornwallis, who had taken over command of British operations in the South after Sir Henry Clinton returned to New York upon Charleston's surrender.

All across South Carolina, but especially in the frontier

regions from the High Hills of the Santee to the mountains and North Carolina border, two other names became hated as equally as that of Banastre Tarleton by that terrible and tragic summer of 1780:

Major James Wemyss of Britain's 63rd Regiment.

And a Tory outlaw called "Bloody Jim" Jernegan.

CHAPTER SIX

August, 1780

Thick smoke swept through the piney woods like a black fog, carrying with it the sickening smell of burning flesh. Kneeling, Captain Ebenezer Moore touched the stained pine needles with the tips of his fingers, and lifted his left hand. Blood. A lot of it, too. The redcoat wouldn't get far. Moore's eyes burned from the smoke and sweat, and he longed to get out of the confines of the dark forest, return to his men, and leave the road before Cornwallis's regulars investigated the smoke. No need in taking risks. His patrol had accomplished its mission.

As he turned to leave, however, he heard coughing. He checked the Pennsylvania pistol in his right hand, ducked behind a pine, and listened. The hacking worsened, and Moore crept through the forest until he saw the British officer lying in a sunken trough, his face a mask of agony, left leg soaked in blood, weakly trying to stanch the flow with a ruffled neck sock. A pistol lay at the top of the sinkhole, well out of the lieutenant's reach.

Moore stepped into the open, trained his pistol on the soldier, and walked forward.

The lieutenant started for his weapon, realized the futility of everything, and sank back against the soft ground. "I am your prisoner," the Englishman said. "Have you a surgeon?"

"No," Moore answered, leveled the pistol, and pulled the trigger.

It misfired.

"Bloody hell!" the redcoat shrieked, and tried to crawl out of the trough, his grave, screaming for mercy and the rules of warfare. Moore cursed as well, tossed his pistol aside, and leaped into the sinkhole, pulling the weak Briton down by his legs. The lieutenant flailed at him, but he was too weak from the loss of blood. "For the love of God," the officer began as Moore unsheathed his bayonet. The redcoat fell silent, his blue eyes frozen as Moore lifted the bayonet, and brought it down savagely into the chest of his enemy.

The eyes fogged over quickly in death. Staring at the corpse, Moore found himself shivering uncontrollably. He vomited, hurried out of the hole, stumbled through the woods, leaving his bayonet behind. He tripped, slammed into a maple, shuddered.

"Captain Moore?" someone called. He waited until his breathing found its proper rhythm, wiped his mouth with the back of his hand, struggled to his feet, and walked to the sound of the voice, forcing himself to look strong.

He was a soldier, an officer in the Continental Army now leading a militia unit since there was no longer any Continental Army in Carolina. He had killed men before, but never like this, never face-to-face with a bayonet, never when the enemy had tried to surrender. There was nothing he could do. They couldn't take prisoners; how could they care for them? This man was wounded, bleeding like a stuck pig, and Moore had no surgeon with him, nor did Colonel Marion. The redcoat would have likely bled to death, anyway. He had done him a favor, put him out of his misery. Besides, what mercy had Banastre Tarleton shown those Continentals with Colonel Buford? Granted, this redcoat had been with the Royal Welch, not the Green Dragoons, but that didn't matter. Killing the lieutenant had been just. He had to do it.

The Catawba Indian first let out a sigh when he saw Moore, but his expression changed to concern. "Captain," the militiaman said as he rushed to him. "You hurt?"

"No, Tom."

"You covered with blood."

Moore hadn't noticed his hands. Even his sleeves dripped with the redcoat's blood, and stains had spattered against his breeches. His left hand was balled into a fist, and, when he relaxed, something dropped into the straw. Moore stared at the button he must have pulled off the dead redcoat.

"What that?" Catawba Tom asked.

Be strong. Be an officer. Make this heathen respect you, fear you.

"A trophy," he said, and knelt to pick up the small piece of pewter. "I shall collect these, one for each man I kill, until I can outfit Colonel Marion's entire militia." The Indian just stared. "I'm all right, Tom, and 'tis not my blood, as you shall discover when you head back in the woods."

"Huh?"

He forced out a chuckle. "I seem to have forgotten my pistol back there, Tom. Fetch it for me, as well as my bayonet, and there is another weapon for us, too. That redcoat won't have need of it any more." He walked out of the woods and onto the road, feeling the heat from the burning wagons.

British dead littered the road. Most of his men had already mounted, but a few plundered the bodies for booty. A wiry freedman handed Moore the reins to Charger, but, before mounting, he wiped his bloody hands on the legs of his breeches, uncorked his canteen, and drank thirstily, longing for something stronger than tepid Lynches Creek water.

"Where's Tom?" asked the freedman, a man called Dobie.

"Running an errand for me," he answered, and swung into the saddle. He thought he might throw up again, but, somehow, steadied himself despite the awful smell from the wagons and the face of the dead lieutenant that he could not shake.

"As soon as he returns, we ride." He needed to do something, get his men's attention, make them think he was just as poorly lettered, as cold-blooded as they, so he laughed aloud as he looked across the road. "I guess General Gates will not laugh at us any more," he said. "Right, men?"

They let out a cry of *Huzza!*

"And," Moore added, "I am sure Colonel Marion will send General Cornwallis our thanks for giving us these supplies."

"*Huzza! Huzza!* Hurray for Captain Moore!"

His smile turned genuine, and he realized he would do anything to protect this uncouth multitude of Patriots.

"Marion," Drummond whispered as he stared at the carnage blocking the Salem Road.

"What that you say?" Ezekiel asked.

"Nothin', Zeke." He flicked the reins, and the mules began pulling the wagon toward the smoking ruins of wagons. Royal and Tory soldiers scurried about the ambush site like ants, and maybe ten bodies, all in redcoat uniforms—except those burned beyond recognition—had been lined out in a row alongside the shoulder. In a clearing on the left, a dozen Continental prisoners were digging a mass grave—for the British soldiers, Drummond hoped.

The mules became skittish at the smell of smoke and blood, but kept going until a British captain raised his hand, and Drummond pulled on the reins, stopping in front of the officer and several nervous soldiers armed with Brown Bess firelocks.

"I am Captain Hall of the Royal Twenty-Third Regiment," the Englishman spoke in a high-toned, nasal accent. "Who are you and what business have you on this road?"

"Name's Drummond. Augustin Drummond, an' this here's Ezekiel, Doctor John Oliver's . . . hand." He didn't want to insult his friend by calling him a slave. Drummond liked Ezekiel and never really considered him Doc Oliver's property. He hadn't been around slaves much. You came across few in Long Canes, and not too many elsewhere in the Back Country. Certainly they were plentiful on the Low Country plantations, but not on the frontier. Colonel Pickens owned some, as had John Boyd, while Dr. Oliver had two. Most Back Country folks, however, did their own work, and liked it that way.

The captain barely considered either occupant of the wagon. "What is your business?"

"Comin' from Camden. We took Doc Oliver there, an' his daughter. She's a nurse. To help treat your wounded."

A red-headed sergeant nodded, and lowered his firelock. "I remember these men, Captain. Saw them with the doctor and a striking young woman. Oliver's a loyal servant to His Majesty, sir. These men are all right, I think."

"Very well, Sergeant, but where are the good doctor and his nurse?"

The question had been addressed to Drummond, so he answered. "Still at Camden, sir. Sent us on home to tend to the crops an' stock." He jutted his jaw down the pike. "The doc's house is only a few miles down the road. If you need any help. . . ."

"Thank you for the offer, Mister Drummond, but there is nothing to be done for these poor lads. Butchered at the hands of rebel cowards." He stared at the bodies, shook his head, and looked back at Drummond as an afterthought. "What of you, Drummond? Why are not you serving in one of the Loyalist regiments?"

He licked his lips before answering. "Got captured at Kettle Creek. Paroled. War's over for me."

It was the truth; he just didn't tell Captain Hall whose side he had been on at the time. The redcoat stared, perhaps considering him a coward, maybe about to challenge him, but, at last, he shrugged and told Drummond to move on.

Once out of earshot, Ezekiel said: "I thought Mastah John said the war be over after them rebels got beat at Camden."

"He did."

"So, was he wrong?"

"I don't know, Zeke."

From what Drummond had pieced together, after arriving at the battlefield, General Horatio Gates had led his Continental Army and Virginia and Carolina militia against Cornwallis's regulars and Tory forces about five miles from the city near Gum Tree Swamp. The battle quickly became a rout, and the Patriot forces had been almost wiped out. Charged by British infantry, many rebel militiamen had fled without firing a shot. When the battle was over, Gates had lost eight hundred killed and wounded, and another thousand captured. Cornwallis lost just more than three hundred killed and wounded.

Doc Oliver had been right. The war should have been over.

It wasn't, though, not by a damned sight.

Drummond knew this, and also had a pretty good guess as to who had led the ambush against the British supply train. At Camden, he again had helped with wounded colonists left to die, giving them water, pipe tobacco, just an ear or kind word. He remembered a dying Continental major's story.

"Be glad you were not here, lad," the major had said. "Bet that Colonel Marion's glad the general sent him away, too."

"Marion?"

"Aye. You should have seen his . . . army, he called it. I swear we had never seen the likes. A couple dozen of the filthiest vagabonds you had ever seen. Even had Negroes and Indians with him, if you can imagine that. They stank to high heaven, armed with pitchforks, slingshots, a few battered old firelocks, long rifles, and fowling pieces. It was hard not to laugh at the very sight of them. An army, Marion called it. State militia ready to fight. General Gates did not want those paupers anywhere near our camp, so he sent them off on some fool's errand. Hit and run. Burn some boats, ferries. Keep the British at bay on the roads leading to Camden. God help me, though, now I wish I had ridden out with Marion and his army."

Jezebel asked if she wanted anything to eat or drink, but Rosemary Madison simply shook her head, glad to be back home with Rachel and the servants, glad to be far away from Camden and the Waxhaws. "All I want is to sleep for about thirty-six hours. Sleep without dreams." She had had enough dreams lately. She started climbing the staircase, turned to thank Jezebel for looking after Rachel, and headed for her room, where she climbed into bed without bothering to take off her clothes.

It had been a ghastly spring and summer. The Waxhaws and Camden, plus other battles as well, usually between small forces of partisan militia and Tories, and most of them northwest of Camden—Williamson's Plantation, Rocky Mount, Hanging Rock, Fishing Creek.

Her father thought the war would end after the lopsided Patriot defeat at Camden, but he was wrong. The war wasn't over. Thomas Sumter and his rebel militia had swatted a hornet's nest with raid after raid against Tories. So had Squire Marion, although she hadn't heard his name in a while. Had he been captured or killed? And what of Ebenezer Moore? Most likely, Moore and Marion had fled South Carolina and the immense British army. Go to North Carolina, she said to herself, go away from here. She wanted to keep the war from Cameron Branch, from her father, from Rachel, Jezebel, Ezekiel, Drummond. She wanted . . . wanted to sleep. Sleep. Sleep.

Chapter Seven

September, 1780

Staring at the hides, Adam Cusack began twisting and tugging on his Van Dyke. "I'll be outside," Drummond told the trader, picked up the mug of rum Cusack had poured, and stepped through the open doorway into the steamy afternoon. A bare-footed black man in linsey clothes and straw hat sat on one end of the porch, scratching a dog's ears. Two white men in summer hunting shirts and lightweight breeches sat idling on the opposite end, drinking, smoking, and shaking coins in an old sailor's cap and tossing the coins onto the wooden planks, playing hustle-cap. Recalling little Rachel's words, Drummond chortled. Hustle-cap was a *naughty* game. The white men were too occupied by their gambling, so Drummond ignored them, but nodded at the black man, who returned the greeting. Waiting on the rickety doorsteps while sipping his liquor, Drummond watched the dust rise above the treetops, down the road.

Just as Drummond finished his rum, Cusack stepped outside and lit his pipe. A middle-aged man with corn-colored hair, the trader had led a hard life at this Back Country crossroads. He had served in the Continental Army at Charlestown and had been there when General Lincoln surrendered. Scars marred his forehead, his nose was bent and crooked, and left earlobe missing, as well as a few front teeth. Dressed in dark homespun clothes, buckled shoes, and dingy white stockings, he didn't look the part of a wealthy trader.

Cusack walked down the steps, spit on the ground, and tapped his pipe against a wooden column. "Hides are fair," he told Drummond. "You got a trade in mind? Applejack? Grub? Tinware?"

"Hard money," Drummond answered.

The trader snickered and said—"Money's scarce. You new to these parts?"—before sticking the pipe reed in his mouth.

"Stayin' at Cameron Branch."

"Long walk for you, 'specially hauling them hides."

"I've walked farther."

"Aye. Well, sir, I'd rather barter than buy. To make a profit, I'd have to sell your hides in Georgetown or Charlestown, and I don't fancy dealing with Tories or redcoats."

"If I wanted to trade, I'd 'a' done my business at McAllister's near Sparrow Swamp."

"Aye, or Jimmie Gregg's over near Welsh Neck. He's a fair man. Weaver's Settlement is much closer to Cameron Branch, but not too much trading there, although that King-loving Abe Weaver does a bit at his tavern. Or . . . you see that road there? You walk one way to Cheraw, t'other to Georgetown." Noticing the dust, Cusack removed the pipe and added absently: "Could pack your hides to either settlement, friend, and sell them yourself."

"Figured I'd give you the business. You won't haul my hides to Georgetown, an' you know it. You'll sell it to some sloths," he said, nodding toward the two gamblers, "who be too lazy to skin their own an' need leather breeches for the winter. It's coolin' off," he said, although it remained quite warm.

Cusack tapped his pipe again, still staring down the stagecoach road but listening to Drummond. "Fancy yourself a haggler, do you, lad?"

With a smile, Drummond answered: "Well, sir, I did work for Andrew Pickens."

That caught the trader's attention. "Pickens, you say. I suspect he taught you well, then. Give you five guineas for your wares."

"Fifteen."

Cusack laughed, but kept his concentration on the dust. "Lad, I haven't held fifteen guineas in a 'coon's age. I'll give you seven, though, and that's my last offer."

"Twelve."

"Seven. You can't haggle a haggler, lad."

"McAllister offered me nine."

"McAllister! That Tory scoundrel. You told me you didn't stop off at his place, and where would he get his hands on nine guineas?"

"Said I could 'a' done business with McAllister. Didn't say I didn't stop at Sparrow Swamp. An' I didn't ask him where he got the money. He's a lot like you, Mister Cusack. Wanted to barter. Wanted to cheat me. Nine guineas for all those hides."

"Aye, McAllister's a cheat," the trader said with a smirk. "I guess you were not lying when you said you worked for Pickens. I'll give you eight guineas . . ."—he held up a hand to stop Drummond's protests—"plus a couple of blankets, sack of peaches, new handle for your hatchet, and I'll fill your powder flask and mug. And throw in a decent hat."

Drummond looked up at his battered hat. "Reckon I could use a new one."

"Aye."

"Let's do business, an' I'll buy you a drink as well."

They could hear the jingling of chains and snorting of horses now. Having stopped their game, the gamblers stood on the edge of the porch. The black man's dog began growling as an army of redcoats cleared the tree line on the road from Georgetown.

Cusack muttered an oath. "We'll finish our business after the air clears up, lad. British dung spoils the taste of good Jamaica rum."

"I am Major James Wemyss of His Majesty's Sixty-Third Regiment of Foot and shall have your names immediately." A dark-haired man with dull gray eyes, he stood in front of the post, slapping white gloves against the palm of his left hand. The gamblers mumbled their names, and Drummond and Cusack gave theirs. The black man said nothing, just held the growling dog tightly. Wemyss hadn't been addressing him anyway.

A few soldiers waited beside the major, but most stood by Cusack's well, slaking their thirsts while ignoring the horses and oxen. Across the road, four others escorted a fair-skinned woman and small boy about Rachel's age—Cusack's wife and son, Drummond guessed—out of a whitewashed house to the post.

"So you are Adam Cusack," the major said through a hollow smile. "You have been a nuisance."

"How so?" Cusack asked.

"I have been told that a month ago you refused to ferry the King's troops across the Black River."

The trader shrugged, saying: "Nothing says I have to keep your boys dry, Major."

"Indeed, sir? Are you forgetting your parole?"

"My parole says I won't shoot at you redcoats any more, and I haven't done that. Nothing says I have to do everything you boys ask me to do."

"That's where you are wrong, Cusack. Lieutenant Blackburn, if you will."

A blond-headed officer at the major's side-stepped forward, reached into his coat, pulled a paper from an inside pocket, and began reading: "By order of Sir Henry Clinton on this Third day of June in the year of our Lord Seventeen Hundred and Eighty . . . Be it known that because of the current state of rebellion all colonists in Georgia, South Carolina, and North Carolina will actively support His Majesty King George the Third and the Royal government. All who refuse this support will be considered traitors, outside the King's protection and subject to the most severe of penalties." He returned the paper, and stepped back.

"That's not what my paper says," said Cusack, frowning.

Drummond felt his stomach churning. Those weren't the terms of his parole, either.

"So you see," Wemyss said, "if I do not think you are aiding His Majesty, I have a free hand to do as I please with you vermin. I can burn your post and home."

"Touch my property and . . . ," Cusack challenged.

"What? You have no say in the matter, Cusack. I have been ordered by Lord Cornwallis to purge the Back Country of seditionists and traitors, and that is what I shall do." Hoof beats interrupted Wemyss's speech, and two riders galloped into the yard.

Drummond's mouth went dry as Captain James Jernegan and another man dismounted.

"Adam," Cusack's wife said in a trembling voice.

"It'll be all right."

Jernegan, his eyes trained on Cusack, had not recognized Drummond. He led the second man, a husky, balding gent in an ill-fitting coat, to Wemyss, who never acknowledged either.

"Is this the man?" the major asked.

"Yes, Major," the second man said.

When the trader spit, Wemyss said: "I take it you recognize John Brockington, Cusack."

"Aye. I smelled the troll long before he rode into view."

"Brockington says you fired at one of his slaves."

"I don't deny the charge. I'm only sorry I missed him."

"Then I take this as a guilty plea."

"You take it any way you please, Major. Brockington threatened my family, so I was just paying him back a little."

"You broke your parole, Cusack."

"Parole! I shot at a thieving Tory's slave, I never fired at no soldier."

"No matter. You fired at property belonging to a loyal subject of our King. We shall dispense with any tribunal, Cusack. You admitted your guilt, and so you shall hang."

His wife screamed, and the son began to cry. Drummond stepped forward, although he didn't know what he planned on doing. Maybe nothing. It was more of an involuntary reaction than anything else. Six firelocks were suddenly trained on his stomach, and he stopped. He should have stood still, for now Jernegan walked to him.

"Well, well, if it isn't the high and mighty rebel from Kettle Creek." Jernegan buried his right fist into Drummond's stomach. Drummond doubled over, and felt something hard slam into his head.

He came to, smelling thick smoke and feeling heat. Rolling over, Drummond saw Cusack's trading post swallowed by flames, the trader's body hanging from a rafter, fire licking the dangling feet, buckled shoes smoking. Gagging, he stumbled away, pulled himself to his feet while checking the pecan-size knot on his head. His hair was matted with blood, his vision blurred, and everything spun around for a few seconds. Somehow, he didn't throw up.

Fighting back pain and dizziness, he lifted his head. Flames engulfed the whitewashed house across the road, and British soldiers were driving horses and wagons through Cusack's garden. The two gamblers stood near the crossroads, watching, but the silent black man and his dog were gone. Drummond turned toward the hysterical screams of a woman. Mrs. Cusack stood in the center of the road, her son, balled up like an infant, sobbing at her feet. She pointed a finger at Wemyss, who sat mounted on his dun horse.

"Out of my way, you rebel strumpet, or I shall run you over," the major said as he started to touch his spurs against the horse's flanks.

Wemyss would have done it, too, would have trampled the widow and son without a second thought. Drummond didn't know where he found the energy, but he half ran, half staggered into the road, shouted, pushed Cusack's widow out of the path, and waved both hands over his aching head as Wemyss charged. Drummond closed his eyes, expecting to be torn apart by the horse and rider. Instead, he heard both man and animal scream, and, when his eyes opened, Wemyss was somersaulting over the rearing horse's back.

Another blow to his head dropped him into the dust beside Cusack's bawling boy. A minute later, someone kicked him hard in the ribs, and he rolled over and out of the road. Through the blackness, he heard Mrs. Cusack's screams.

"Silence that trollop!" Wemyss shouted.

A *thump* followed, and all he could hear were the boy's sobs, distant barks from soldiers destroying the Cusack garden, and the roaring fires. When the blackness passed, Wemyss and Jernegan stared down at Drummond.

"That is the second time you have interfered in the King's business," Wemyss said. "I have half a mind to hang you as well. Who is this man, Captain?"

With a wicked laugh, Jernegan replied: "A cowardly rebel we caught at Kettle Creek, after he cut down Colonel John Boyd in cold blood."

"Why was he not hanged?"

"Colonel Campbell give him a pardon."

"I see." Wemyss kicked Drummond's feet. "Where do you live?"

When he didn't answer, the major kicked harder. "Tell me, damn you. Where do you live?"

One of the gamblers stepped forward, saying: "Major, me an' Pete heard him an' Cusack talkin'. He told Cusack he lived over at Cameron Branch."

Wemyss faced the blond lieutenant, who had buried his face in a map.

"It's here, Major," the officer said at last. "Maybe twenty-five miles, just off the Salem Road."

The major nodded and knelt beside Drummond. "I shall not pass judgment on you yet. For the moment, I shall assume you were acting in the interests of Cusack's wench and imp, but should I find one sign of sedition at your home, you will pray for a death as merciful as the one I handed Cusack."

The major stood, dusted off his coat and pants, and kicked Drummond savagely in the ribs again.

He told them how to find the cabin. Drummond couldn't

remember telling Wemyss, but he must have done it. How else could the soldiers have found the place? His feet and wrists were raw, his clothes almost ripped off his dirty, bloody body. They had bound his hands, and pulled him behind the column, where he choked on dust. When he had grown too tired to walk and had fallen, they dragged him.

Wemyss and Jernegan probably would have let him die, but Blackburn, the blond-haired young lieutenant, brought soup and water, and sometimes rum, each night.

He lay beside the corral, too stiff to move, staring at the swaying pines and cloudless sky, sickened by the chattering and laughter from Wemyss's regulars and Jernegan's Tories as they ransacked his cabin. "Major!" a soldier shouted, and Drummond heard footsteps running across the clearing.

A short time later, Wemyss came into his vision. He held something in his hands, something blue, and a mirthless smile spread across his face. "Can you explain this?" the Englishman asked, and held the home-made flag, blue with the white crescent and **LIBERTY** written across the moon, high for him to see.

Drummond said nothing. If he told the truth, Wemyss would not believe him. He was too exhausted to speak or even shake his head, anyway.

"I thought so," said Wemyss, tossing the flag to a private. "Fire the cabin, and burn this rag with it."

"Yes, sir!"

"Shall we hang him?" Jernegan asked, and Drummond felt suddenly cold.

"I think not," Wemyss answered. "I think I shall make an example of him, but not by hanging him. Have Sergeant Talley bring his cat-o'-nine-tails, and, Captain, have some of your men tie this seditionist to the corral."

101

She had been checking the peach orchard when she spotted the smoke. Her heart skipped, she pulled off her cumbersome shoes, and ran as fast as she could down the Salem Road in her stockings. She ignored the burning in her lungs, the rapidly increasing fear, and forced herself, leaning into the wind as she ran and prayed.

Rosemary Madison couldn't believe it. Wagons, cannon, horses, and what seemed like hundreds of redcoats lined the road near the pathway to the cabin. Couldn't believe it, but she dared not stop running. Several men stared at her, but she ignored them, and, when a blond officer raised his hand and asked her to stop, she sprinted past him and turned down the path.

"In the King's name, halt!" the soldier cried out before taking off after her.

After stumbling into the clearing, she tried to scream, but had no breath for it. Towers of orange flame leaped skyward from the cabin, lighting treetops like candles. Men had trouble controlling the skittish horses that knew—much better than the soldiers, it appeared—that this whole patch of forest would soon be an inferno.

One barrel-chested, red-bearded man in frontier dress lunged for her, but wound up slipping on horse droppings and crashing to the ground. Another redcoat reached out to grab her, but she avoided him. She only stopped once, and that was briefly when she spotted a one-armed soldier, his hair and uniform wet with sweat, send a short leather whip popping against the bloody bare back of a man lashed to the corral.

Augustin! Sprinting, she tackled the soldier as he prepared to use the whip again. Rosemary clawed the man's face, heard him curse, and kicked at him. Hands reached for her, and she found her voice, screamed, kicked, and bit at least one thumb, fighting like a demon, but there were too many. Someone yanked her hair. Men pinned her arms and legs. She squirmed and fought, but finally shuddered and began sobbing.

The one-armed man with the whip jumped to his feet, placed his left hand against his bloody cheek, and started to strike her, despite the fact he would have lashed his own men as well. He stopped in mid-stride upon realizing his attacker was a woman.

"Damned rebel whores," another voice said. She turned to the newcomer, a dark-haired officer with unblemished face who stood over her, slapping white gloves against his left palm. "Are you all right, Sergeant Talley."

The bloodied sergeant nodded.

"Tie her beside Drummond," the man ordered. "We shall give her a taste of the cat-o'-nine-tails as well. Sergeant, you shall give Drummond twenty-one more lashes, then flog this one ten times if you are not too weakened."

The sergeant blinked, comprehending the order. "No, sir," he said after a moment, gathering the cat-o'-nine-tails and tucking it underneath his one arm.

"What's that, Sergeant?"

"I shall not lay a hand on a woman, rebel or not, and never a whip, sir."

Trees began popping from the flames. A horse bolted down the path.

"We should leave, sir," another soldier suggested timidly.

"When we are done. We are downwind, safe for the moment. Sergeant, finish your orders. I shall find someone else to flog this. . . ." He shook his head, and his eyes blazed as he stared at the other soldiers. "I said tie her beside Drummond."

No one moved.

"You have your orders!" he screamed, and the men holding her down obeyed. "Strip off her dress and chemise so her back will taste the leather. Damn you, do it!"

She was too tired to feel anything. "Sergeant," she heard the officer say, "carry on."

"I'm too tired," the man called Talley answered. "Get someone to finish it, *sir*."

Another voice: "I'll spell you, Sergeant. And I'll whip the bitch as well. If you don't mind, Major."

"I do not mind. Carry on, Captain Jernegan. Be quick, though. This fire is starting to look rather nasty."

CHAPTER EIGHT

"The woman you had whipped, sir," Lieutenant Jason Blackburn told Wemyss, "is the daughter of Doctor John Oliver, a Loyalist of high standing here in the Peedee."

"She interfered with the King's business, Lieutenant," Wemyss said in quick dismissal before blinking. "Is she still alive?"

"Yes, sir. A Loyalist by the name of Abernathy visited Doctor Oliver yesterday. You left her and the rebel to burn in that forest fire, Major, but someone found them and took them to Doctor Oliver."

Wemyss shrugged and sipped his tea. "*Them?* The rebel's alive as well."

"He was, sir, barely."

They had camped between Lynches Creek and the Peedee River just off the Georgetown-Cheraw stagecoach road. As far as Blackburn was concerned, the rebels were welcome to keep this deplorable colony full of ticks, mosquitoes, and snakes. He had probably lost fifteen pounds just from sweating and longed to be with his wife and daughter back in West Suffolk. He had told Susan that he would write her once a week, but he knew he would not live up to his promise. How could he tell her what he had been a part of, what Major Wemyss and Captain Jernegan were doing? Orders, he kept telling himself, are orders. His wife, however, didn't have to know.

"No matter," Wemyss said. "I assume the loyal doctor is angry at me."

"To say the least, Major," Blackburn answered. "He has written letters to Lord Cornwallis and Sir Clinton."

The major sniggered as he finished his drink and handed the empty cup to his striker. "I can handle Cornwallis and Clinton," he told Blackburn. "We will follow my orders, burning these houses of sedition and making these heathen think twice before bearing arms against His Majesty. The colonists will not be so quick to join those rogues led by Sumter and Marion. You shall see, Lieutenant, that I am right."

"I hope so, Major, but I fear you underestimate these backwoodsmen."

"I think not, but, to appease you, carry my compliments and apologies to Doctor Oliver. Bring him some brandy we liberated from Cusack. Tell him I would not have had his daughter flogged had I known of his loyalty to King George. Tell him I shall pray for her quick recovery. Perhaps that shall pacify the good doctor. If not. . . ." He shrugged and laughed. "If he becomes a boil on my neck, I shall have him lanced . . . as I had Drummond."

As he turned to leave, Blackburn said: "You should have hanged Drummond, or left him alone."

He didn't mean for Wemyss to hear, but the major's ears missed nothing. "Explain yourself, Lieutenant."

Blackburn let out a sigh. The last "house of sedition" Wemyss ordered torched had been a church. That wasn't the way to make these colonists loyal to King George, and whipping a woman was abhorrent. The major had alienated many of his officers and men—the real soldiers, not the rabble riding with Jernegan. Blackburn didn't care much for

Major Wemyss's warfare. If Wemyss continued his burning, pillaging, and murder, men loyal to the crown would be joining Sumter and Marion, and so would paroled soldiers. Something in the rebel Drummond's eyes had made Blackburn take notice. "Are you familiar with Chaucer, sir?" he asked Wemyss.

Chuckling, the major said: "Quote your verse, Lieutenant, and carry out your orders, and get out of my sight."

" 'It is nought good a slepyng hound to wake, ne yeve a wight a cause to devyne'."

Images and smells came to him, but never clearly. Broken, disjointed, like something in a dream. He remembered the first blows from the whip, the heavy smoke from the cabin, the burning of his back, grinding his teeth against excruciating pain. He had passed out for a long while, but knew he woke up briefly, hearing the *pop* of the knotted leather tails but feeling no pain, and a scream tore at his heart. He knew it had been Rosemary Madison, realized the callous Major Wemyss had ordered her flogged as well, and he roared in anger, hopelessly tearing at the bindings that bit into his wrists. The cat-o'-nine-tails lashed his back again and again, and Jernegan's laughter echoed inside his mind. Darkness enveloped him again, and he welcomed death.

Another image—the face of a man, a black face, mouthing something, but Drummond couldn't understand. Being lifted and carried out of the woods, now thick with smoke, feeling the heat, sweat burning his mangled back like whisky poured over a knife wound. The face? Who was it? An angel? Ezekiel? The apparition vanished. His father appeared again, and Michael, even his mother beckoning to him. There was Salâli, sitting by the fireplace, so lovely. He felt at peace then, but the image of Wemyss replaced Salâli, and he watched him ball his parole paper into his fist and ram it into the remaining rags that once had been Drummond's breeches.

He opened his eyes to focus on another face, waiting for his vision to clear. Red curls and small lips, a face smeared with . . . blood?

"Jezebel made a rhubarb pie. Want some?"

"No." Drummond barely recognized his own voice.

Rachel shook her head, and took another bite. She spoke with her mouth full of pie. "Grandpa told me to watch you. Sure you don't want some?"

"No, thanks." His back felt as if someone had set it on fire. He tried to move, realized his mistake, and settled into the bed. He lay on his stomach in a comfortable, huge bed, soft, not like the straw and ticky blankets he usually slept on. The walls were bright yellow with dark wainscoting, meaning he had to be at the Oliver mansion. "Maybe some water," he told the child.

Rachel smiled as she polished off the last of her pie. "I'll get Grandpa. He's fixing Mommie's back right now."

He remembered Rosemary's screams. At least, he thought it had been her. He wanted to ask Rachel about her mother, but she was gone in an instant. No matter, he would be better off getting the story from Doc Oliver. Exhaustion overtook him again, and he fought to keep his eyes open. *Don't sleep,* he ordered himself. *Don't sleep until you have spoken to the doctor.*

The tall man entered the room, and peered down at Drummond. Oliver hadn't slept in days, looked worn out, like he had after the unending treatments at the Waxhaws and Camden, only worse. He lifted something off Drummond's back, and Drummond flinched as every muscle in his body tightened and thousands of knives pricked his back.

"Better," Oliver said. "No infection . . . yet. I shall change the dressing. How many times were you lashed, a hundred?"

"One-fifty."

"My God." Oliver dropped into the chair Rachel had been sitting in, faltered before continuing. "Rosemary had ten lashes. She's improving. Won't be sleeping on her back for a while. Nor will you. No, do not talk. Save your strength, son. I shall do all the talking. Rosemary said she saw the smoke and ran to the cabin, where they were whipping you. They had her flogged as well. This Major Wemyss and Captain Jernegan are cutting a swath from Georgetown to Cheraw. Destroying fields, looms, and Lord knows how many ewes and rams they have butchered! They burned the Indiantown Presbyterian Church, John Wilson's house on Willow Creek, John James's house near Witherspoon's Ferry, Adam Cusack's trading post and home. They hanged Cusack and burned his body in front of his wife and child."

"I know," Drummond said. "Was there."

Oliver stared at him momentarily. "I see," he said. "Well, Wemyss will not lay a hand on Rosemary again, or you. I will see to that. I have written to Lord Cornwallis and Sir Henry Clinton protesting this outrageous, uncivilized act of barbarity. The cabin was burned to the ground. Almost the entire patch of woods between Cameron Branch and the swamp is charred timber. Wemyss will pay. He had no right. . . ."

Drummond swallowed. "How did I get here?"

"Someone knocked on the door, and Jezebel found you and Rosemary lying on the portico, your wounds covered with some sort of mud poultice. She saw a man riding away, but it was dark, and she could not recognize him."

"Zeke?"

"Heavens, no. Ezekiel would not have left you like that, and he was here. He helped carry you both upstairs. No more talking, Augustin. Doctor's orders. You rest. I shall bring you some water and fresh dressing. You are not out of the woods yet, son. That major had you lashed until your skin was hanging on by threads."

After knocking lightly on the door, a grinning Jezebel stuck her head inside the room to say: "You gots a visitor."

At first, Rosemary thought it might be Drummond, but she knew he couldn't be out of bed yet. She remained on her stomach in her own room, and that Tory pig had given her only ten lashes; her father said Drummond had been whipped one hundred and fifty times. Her mouth fell open as Ebenezer Moore dashed into the room, pulled up a chair, and sat beside her, immediately taking her right hand into his. He smelled of horsehair and sweat. Chuckling, Jezebel left them alone.

He must have worn out several mounts to get here as fast as he had, and looked a fright, his uniform threadbare, hair matted in sweat, in need of a shave. Some sort of necklace caught her eye: a piece of sinew looped through three buttons. The Ebenezer Moore she knew, the one who always visited her and Richard when he traveled to Weaver's Settlement, had been a vain man, pleasant and charming, not one to wear something like that. She briefly considered asking about it, but found herself addressing something far more urgent, and immediately forgot about the three buttons dangling from his neck.

"You should not be here," Rosemary said.

"Of course, I should."

"There are Loyalists and British everywhere."

"If I find them, my dear, they shall taste my steel or be shot for laying a whip against your precious skin." He almost spit out the words, and the glare in his eyes frightened her. Moore smiled, and the tension left his face immediately. He patted her hand and leaned back. "I came as soon as I heard. I left Colonel Marion in North Carolina, but he plans on ending his exile soon. We shall fight back. Enough of men's talk. How are you?"

"Better," she told him. She felt embarrassed like this, helpless. She wanted to sit up, and she certainly didn't enjoy entertaining a gentleman caller in her bedchamber, in her sleeping garments, and only white cotton covering the welts on her back. What had Jezebel been thinking? Where was her father?

"I'm glad." He leaned over, kissed her cheek, and her face flushed. Part of her wanted him to stay, but she also wanted him to leave. It wasn't safe here, and she didn't like him seeing her like this. He whispered her name three or four times. "I feared you had died. I feared those cowardly pillagers had killed you. I am sorry about your friend Drummond, but I shall avenge his death as I have Richard's."

"Augustin is not dead," she told him, but her heart skipped. Or was he? Had her father kept this secret from her for her own well-being?

"I was told he had been whipped to death by the demons that dared strike you."

Shaking her head, she explained: "Whipped, yes. Savagely. One hundred and fifty lashes, but he is recovering, so Jezebel and Father tell me. Two doors down. You should visit him."

She couldn't read Moore's face. She thought she detected a slight shaking of his head. "I think not," he said softly.

"Ebenezer," she said lightly. "You would like him. Augustin has been a great friend to me."

"To you, perhaps," he said, his voice rising, "but not to liberty. He is a coward, Rosemary."

"He is not." Her voice rose as well. "He was captured and paroled. There is nothing cowardly about that."

"You do not know the whole story, dear. I do. No, he is, at the best, merely a coward. At the worst, he is a traitor to our cause and a spy for the British army."

"That is a lie."

Moore's face hardened, and the glare in his blue eyes did not dissipate. A faint knock sounded again, and the door swung open. This time, Ezekiel stepped inside, hat in hand, and whispered: "Capt'n, a British officer be downstairs callin' on Mastah John. Jezebel says you best get out while he's inside. I got your hoss ready. We go out the back way."

Standing swiftly, Moore placed his hand on the butt of his pistol. "Who is this officer, Zeke?"

"Calls hisself Blackburn. Here to see Miss Rosemary. Brought Mastah John some brandy. Says he's apologizin' for what them others done to Miss Rosemary and Mistah Drummond."

"Then he shall die." He pulled the pistol, but Rosemary cried out: "No!" She had flung her covers aside, lunged as best she could from a prone position—more like flopping as a fish on a bank—and gripped Moore's arm with her left hand. She wound up with her torso hanging off the bed, and probably would have tumbled onto the floor if not for her grip on Moore's arm. Her dressing fell to the floor. "No," she said again, holding back tears. Her back burned fiercely, and she felt dizzy.

He melted, staring at her back, lips trembling, and couldn't move. Ezekiel reacted first, grabbing Rosemary gently, and covering her wounded back with the cloth. Moore recovered, shoved the pistol inside his belt, and helped Ezekiel move her back on the pillows. As Moore covered her with the cotton coverlet, Ezekiel was telling him that Rosemary was right, that the officer likely had a bunch of other soldiers just down the road, that he'd guide Captain Moore through the woods behind the garden, that they'd get out of here without no trouble.

"All right, Rosemary," Moore said. His eyes welled with tears. "I shall go, for your sake." He kissed her cheek again. "But these fiends will pay for their crimes. I promise you this, my love." He spun around, and was gone.

"My love," she said to the closed door. "*My love.* Oh, Ebenezer, what have I done?"

"You have to eat," she told him, but Drummond shook his head.

He had been spoon-fed by Jezebel, Zeke, Doc Oliver, even Rachel, and now, for the past three days, Rosemary, and was plenty sick of it. He didn't like being fretted over and cared for like some cripple. At least he was sitting up now, although his back still blazed even when resting against a wall of pillows on the bed. "Rosemary, you give me so much soup it's 'bout to come out my nose."

"All right," she said with a laugh, "be that way." Fatigued but still beautiful Rosemary Madison handed the tray to Jezebel, who took it downstairs. When the servant had gone, she stared at him, and didn't look happy any more. "Jezebel said you were trying to walk yesterday, and you fell," she admonished him. "She had to call on Zeke to get you back in bed."

He shrugged, saying: "Legs quit workin' for me."

"I see. We will have no more of that, Augustin. You are too weak to get out of bed now."

"You're up an' around."

"And still mighty sore, but I only got ten lashes. You almost died."

He looked away.

"Augustin," she said, her voice softening, full of concern. "Everything is all right now. Father has written to the authorities, so do not worry. Wemyss and Jernegan will not be back. They are up in Cheraw, I hear, and you still have your parole." With a smile, she reached into her apron, pulled out the crumpled paper, and handed it to him. He stared at the fancy lettering, the ink smeared and faded.

The vision returned: *Major Wemyss balling up the paper, stuffing it inside his breeches, then nodding at the sergeant before stepping out of the cat-o'-nine-tail's path.*

"Augustin," she went on. "You did your duty. I've lost my husband. You lost your family. The war has passed us by, at last." She paused, shook her head, and stared at the ceiling, trying to collect her thoughts. "You are a good friend," she eventually said. "I do not want to lose you, too. Forget about Wemyss and Jernegan. All right?"

After he nodded, she left, promising to return later. Drummond didn't move after the door closed; he just looked at the paper, a parole for a militia private. Only, he wasn't a soldier. He had always been the peace-keeper. Isn't that what Michael had told him? Live by your word, his brother had also said, and Drummond had given his word, to his dead brother and Colonel Archibald Campbell. Don't fight. Take all of this, the hundred and fifty lashes, the murders, everything. That's what Rosemary wanted. Forget about the welts on her back, too. He thought of Colonel

Marion's words. *I find your honor admirable, sir, but your judgment damnable.* What had his stupid parole gotten him? One hundred and fifty lashes, and Rosemary whipped.

It galled him as he realized he *had* been a coward, had been running away from the war since Salâli's death. By thunder, he had carried that piece of paper with him for a year and a half, pulling it out like some sort of medal. Well, he had lived up to his end of the bargain, had not broken his parole, but what Wemyss and Jernegan had done . . . that was a violation.

He hated war, would never forget Kettle Creek as long as he lived. Sure, Rosemary wanted him to stay, and that would be so easy, spoiling Rachel and helping Rosemary and Doc Oliver, but a man couldn't do that. She had to know that as well as he did. Doc Oliver was a good soul, but he believed he could close the doors at home, simply shut out the tumult in the Peedee and rest of the Back Country. Oliver thought sending letters to Clinton and Cornwallis would bring lawfulness, but Drummond knew better. Maybe he couldn't read or write, but he was a man, and he knew what was right. More than three years ago, when he had sided with the rebels, Salâli had told him that in his heart he knew the Patriots were right, but he wasn't sure, back then, if he really believed in their cause, their cries of liberty and justice, only now he did.

He wouldn't be able to sleep on his back for a year, maybe never. Rosemary would carry her scars for the rest of her life. The sons-of-bitches would pay.

Drummond began shredding his parole paper.

FROM THE MANUSCRIPT
OF THE REVEREND STAN MCINTYRE,
PAGE 33

Just when Augustin Drummond returned to Patriotism's cause is unclear. He could have joined Thomas Sumter's forces. After all, the Gamecock had been putting a damper in Banastre Tarleton's and James Wemyss's reigns of terror in the Peedee basin. But perhaps it is no surprise that he enlisted in the militia led by the man history came to know as The Swamp Fox. His was a motley crew, and Drummond no doubt fit in well.

I have read many accounts of Francis Marion, from what historians have wrote to what his contemporaries had to say. I think the best quote about the Swamp Fox and the men he commanded came from Marion's friend and fellow Patriot, Col. Peter Horry: *"No officer in the Union was better calculated to command them, and to have done more than he did."*

CHAPTER NINE

Fall, 1780

The easiest thing would have been to sneak out in the middle of the night. Just get up, dress, and be gone before Rosemary or Doc Oliver woke up. Drummond considered it—in fact, almost talked himself into doing it—but he owed his doctor and nurse more than that. So, for the fourth consecutive day, he came downstairs for breakfast, and he blurted it out.

"I'll be takin' my leave soon as I et," he said to a plate of lye-soaked hominy, ham, eggs, and rice pudding. The chatter around the breakfast table stopped instantly, followed by the dim pitch from a dropped fork or spoon. Drummond lifted his eyes.

"What does he mean, Mommie?" Rachel asked.

Rosemary just stared across the table, her mouth open slightly. The doctor cleared his throat and continued stirring his coffee.

"Did you only now decide this?" Rosemary asked.

His head shook slowly and he reached for his cup. "Been thinkin' on it."

"Mommie?" Rachel asked.

"Mister Drummond has to go somewhere," she told the girl, who mouthed an *oh,* dropped her head, and began picking at her food. After a couple of seconds, she mumbled: "Will he be back for my birthday?"

"I'll try," Drummond answered.

"How does your back feel?" Oliver asked.

"Itches."

"That is a good sign." He took a sip of coffee. "Try not to scratch it."

More silence. Drummond, having lost his appetite, tried to think of something else to say, to thank the doctor and Rosemary for their kindness, but every time he thought he had picked the right words and opened his mouth, he just sat there like an oaf.

"Well," Oliver said, "I should pack you some fresh dressings for your back, medicine as well. Mayhap you will not find these where you are going, and Jezebel will not hear of me sending you on your journey without food, so I had best tell her. Come, Rachel." He stood, walked over to the girl, and held out his arms. "Come give your grandfather a hand."

Rachel didn't want to go, but she obeyed, and Doc Oliver closed the door to the dining room behind them. Rosemary Madison and Augustin Drummond just stared at each other.

Finally she asked: "Back to Long Canes?"

He shook his head.

"I guessed as much. You are still too weak to travel." It came out as a pitiful argument, and both knew it.

"I'll make it. Can't stay here forever."

"I wish. . . ."

He forced himself to finish his coffee. The chair legs scraped the floor as he stood. Rosemary remained seated, but her eyes, now misting over with tears, never left him.

"They shall kill you," she said at last.

Words of bravado came to mind, but he didn't speak these, knowing they would ring false to both of them. Instead, he asked: "When's Rachel's birthday?"

She smiled sadly, knowing days and months would be lost where he was headed. "November Eleventh."

"You've been. . . ." His head dropped again, and he knew if he didn't leave now he might never have the courage to try this again. He crossed the room and put his hand on the door.

She sprang out of the chair, and called out his name, but didn't move away from the table. "If you are doing this for me . . . ," she began.

"Good bye, Rosemary," he told her, and hurried out of the room.

Outside, he shook Ezekiel's hand, and walked underneath the magnolias, where Doc Oliver waited for him at the gate, holding two knapsacks, one containing bandages and medicine for his back, and the other food prepared by Jezebel. That would be all he had to his name, except for the clothes he wore—brown cocked hat, osnaburg shirt, gray breeches, and stockings, all of which had been purchased by Oliver at McAllister's post, and a pair of moccasins Drummond had made while in bed with nothing else to do. No weapon of any kind, not even a knife. A fine fighter he would make.

The doctor handed him both bags, and Drummond draped them over his shoulders, grimacing at the pain when the straps touched his back. He thanked Oliver, waiting.

"I wish you would reconsider," the doctor told him.

"Can't do it."

"Sumter or Marion?"

"Best you don't know."

Oliver nodded sympathetically. "I understand. I can descry your reasoning, Augustin, but you know my allegiance is with the King."

Even after the King's troops lashed Rosemary, Drummond thought, but kept his views private.

With a sigh, Oliver gazed down the Salem Road and said: "I never thought I would live to see this, Augustin. Neighbors fighting neighbors. The lawlessness. Murder and plunder. Good men I have known since settling here turning into raging animals, mere despoilers. I think, when this rebellion finally ends, peace will remain a long time coming to the Back Country. There has been too much hatred, too much bloodshed. If the King wins, and I think he will, we will all be better off, but I foretell rancor between Loyalist and rebel for perhaps another generation. If the rebels win, I ask myself if they will let me, and other Loyalists, remain in our homes. Yours is not a forgiving bunch."

"Nor is yours," Drummond said.

Setting his jaw, Oliver gave a slight nod of dismissal, and Drummond stepped through the entry, turned right, and started down the road.

"Augustin."

Drummond stopped but stared straight ahead.

"Let us part as friends, yet know this . . . if you join Marion, Sumter, or any other gang of rebel ruffians, you are no longer welcome in this house. I say this not because of my personal politics, but for the well-being of my daughter and granddaughter, as well as my slaves. I cannot risk being accused of aiding the rebellion, cannot risk having my home burned out of revenge. If you care for Rosemary and Rachel, and, I believe you do, you shall honor my request."

Drummond had no idea where he could find Francis Marion, nor did the British and Tories. That's what made the little Huguenot so successful in his hit-and-run raids. What Drummond did know was that Marion had defeated a small force of Tories on Black Mingo Creek in late September and, once again, vanished in the forests and swamps. Marion had left his wounded at Dollard's Inn, but those men were either prisoners by now or had long fled the forces of Tarleton, Wemyss, and Jernegan.

He stopped at McAllister's post near Sparrow Swamp to rest. McAllister was a Tory as well, so Drummond kept his mouth shut and just listened while pretending to examine fishing hooks, tin candle holders, and sacks of Orangeburg-ground flour, much cheaper than flour hauled in from Philadelphia down the Wagon Road. Drummond had not even a pence to spend and nothing to trade, but the building was packed, and no one paid much attention to him.

That's how he heard that a Loyalist colonel named Tynes was assembling a force near Tearcoat Swamp, and why he left McAllister's and headed southwest. If a Tory army was being assembled near the swamp between the Pocotaligo and Black Rivers, Marion would be there soon.

His path took him past the ruins of Adam Cusack's property, and Drummond forced himself to dig through the muddy ash with the toes of his moccasins. He hated himself for this, kept thinking he smelled the burned flesh of the partisan merchant who had been murdered here, but he knew this was just his imagination. He wasn't imagining the fact that he had turned into a scavenger, rooting among the dead for something he could use. He came away with a few charred wrought-iron fish hooks and blackened blades to a long knife and tomahawk. Both handles had been burned off, but he could replace them as well as fashion a fishing pole and line. The food Jezebel had packed him was almost gone, although he had made off with a few overripe peaches from an orchard at another abandoned home, but now he wouldn't starve to death.

Ebenezer Moore positioned his hands to keep Charger quiet. "You shall get your wish in a moment, my friend," he whispered, knowing the stallion wanted to run. His own heart pounded, and the forest sounded alive with crickets, frogs, and the occasional owl's hoot and nighthawk's cry. In the clearing ahead came even more sounds: snores of men, snorting horses, shouts and laughs from gamblers, and some jester trying to play "Barbara Allen" on the bagpipes. Marion had worried that Colonel Tynes would flee Tearcoat Swamp before the partisans could attack, but they were still here, about to die.

"Rider come," Catawba Tom whispered.

Turning to the Indian scout, Moore listened but couldn't hear a horse. He knew not to doubt Catawba Tom, whose ears detected more than the hound that accompanied him everywhere. Soon enough came a cry from the Tory camp.

"What news, Alastair?"

"Bad news, I fear, Colonel. Major Ferguson is dead, his troops routed, killed, or captured at Kings Mountain two weeks ago."

The bagpipes stopped, but the next few exchanges were lost. Moore's own eyes had widened at the news, and he glanced down the line, looking for similar expressions in the faint moonlight, only he couldn't make out the faces of the waiting warriors. Another question from the camp grabbed his attention.

"Any word of Marion?"

"Aye, Colonel. I hear he is on his way to torment Harrison at McCallum's Ferry."

A smile spread across Moore's face. Not only had the

cause of liberty scored a massive victory at Kings Mountain, but the rumors spread intentionally by Colonel Marion had been believed by these fools. That's why they had not fled the Tearcoat. The fires from the camp grew larger as word spread of Ferguson's disaster, and men began rising from their slumber to discuss the ill news.

Damn the luck. It had to be around midnight, but these Tories didn't seem to want or need sleep, and more and more would rise because of the news. He heard the whispers coming down the line, knew Marion had given the order to mount, but waited until Catawba Tom's confirmation. He passed the word, swung into the saddle, cocked the massive Jägerbusche rifle he had taken off a dead Hessian grenadier, along with a button, and licked his lips.

"Huzza! At them boys! Huzza!"

Charger didn't need to feel the spurs to explode into a gallop. Ducking low to avoid branches until clearing the forest, Moore felt the exhilaration of battle. He guided Charger toward the nearest campfire, saw silhouettes of men scurrying about the camp, heard screams, orders being shouted, dogs barking, and suddenly the roar of musketry.

The stallion slammed into one Tory, knocked the man aside, and Moore yanked on the reins, sending Charger spinning as Moore looked for a target, ears ringing from the cacophony of battle. Howard's pack of vicious dogs brought down one screaming enemy, and tore at his gut and throat. Moore finally spotted the Tory who had been knocked aside by his strong mount, but, before he could raise the German rifle, another militiaman speared the man with a makeshift spontoon.

Swearing, Moore reined Charger to a complete stop, and just happened to look down as a man started to crawl from underneath his blankets. The Tory, so close he could have

125

reached up and grabbed Moore's right boot, froze as fire-light danced in his eyes. Happily Moore lowered the cocked Jägerbusche until the barrel almost touched the soldier's face, and fired.

A stupid act. He knew that even before he pulled the trigger, still he couldn't stop himself. One did not fire a fully charged .65-caliber rifle with one hand. The kick from the blast almost tore Moore's arm from the socket and snapped off his wrist. He felt himself being pulled over the side of the horse, and landed hard, his right arm crushed between his own weight and the Jägerbusche's barrel, hearing, but not feeling, the bones in his lower arm snap.

The fight was over in fifteen minutes. Marion came away with total victory, killing three, wounding fourteen, and capturing more than twenty. Most of the Tories fled into the swamp and woods, while Colonel Samuel Tynes climbed up behind the courier named Alastair, and loped toward the Santee River. The Patriots captured eighty horses, saddle and tack, firelocks, powder, shot, food, and clothes. Marion's losses totaled only three wounded, the most serious being Ebenezer Moore's broken arm.

Pain came now that the rush of battle had passed. Biting his lower lip, the captain rose, his mangled arm dangling loosely at his side, and staggered to the body of the Tory he had killed beneath the blankets. The lad's face had been blown off, but Moore ignored the grisly sight, snatched off a wooden button from the blood-soaked linsey shirt, and slipped it into his waistcoat pocket.

He careened through camp, saw a Tory captain, with a neat hole in his temple, stretched out on a blanket. The dead man's hands grasped three cards, and Moore leaned over and jerked the paste cards. Ace, deuce, and jack. A good hand, and he had been reaching for his winnings when the bullet killed him. "You lose," Moore said, tossing the cards to the ground on top of the coin. He would leave the money for his men, but contemplated removing one of this man's buttons. He didn't, however, for he had not killed the captain personally.

It was getting easier, the killing, the collecting of buttons. He felt chilled suddenly as he tried to move on, and gripped his broken arm gently.

"Captain Moore!" shouted Catawba Tom, leaping off his mount. Moore almost collapsed in the scout's arms.

"My arm," he said weakly, and passed out.

When his eyes fluttered open, Colonel Marion was kneeling over him, offering his most reassuring smile. "You rest, Captain," Marion said softly. "I have sent Captain Snipes after Colonel Tynes. We shall tidy up here and be gone."

Another voice called out to Marion, and the colonel straightened. "We f-f-found this . . . this man along the road, C-Co-Co-Colonel," Peter Horry stammered. "He says . . . he has been look-look-looking to join . . . our . . . c-c-c-cause, and says you will re-re-remem-ber him."

Horry and another man stepped into the firelight. Moore managed to catch the choking in his throat as he recognized Augustin Drummond.

Their eyes locked momentarily before Moore looked away. Drummond glanced at the broken arm before turning toward Francis Marion. Several men had surrounded the colonel, and Drummond could feel more gathering behind him. In the firelight, he didn't notice one friendly face, including Marion's. A couple of dogs growled at Drummond. The hounds of hell looked as friendly as their owners.

"So you have decided to give liberty a chance?" the Huguenot said.

"Yes, sir."

"Trust him not, Colonel," Moore said through his pain. "We know of his treachery."

Drummond looked puzzled. *What are they talking about?*

"I have received reports, Drummond," Marion told him, "of your cowardice at the Battle of Kettle Creek."

"Cowardice?" His stomach knotted. How could that be? Who would accuse him of such? Certainly not Colonel Pickens. Who would brand him a coward, and why? Because he had been captured?

Marion's gaze fell on Ebenezer Moore.

"A coward and traitor," the captain said bitterly.

His back began to throb, and Drummond longed for something to drink. Marion's dark eyes revealed nothing, and, when the partisans behind Drummond began whispering, a quick rebuke from their colonel silenced them.

"You mind explainin', Colonel?" Drummond said.

Another voice called out to Drummond's left, and Paddy McGee stepped into the light. The Irishman's blue eyes blazed with hate as he stepped into the circle, pointing a finger at Drummond's chest.

"This is the man, Colonel. Augustin Drummond. Marched with him with Colonel Pickens, I did, and was at Kettle Creek right beside him. Mind you, I didn't notice him much after the ruckus commenced, but two men saw him running away during the fight . . . Colonel Elijah Clarke himself and a true fighting man named Long John Norris. Norris, by the saints, is now a cripple, lost both of his hands in the fight while this bub fled the field."

Drummond looked back at Marion.

"Most men I have, when their honor has been insulted, would issue a challenge," Marion said calmly.

Drummond didn't take the bait. "Paddy's mistaken." He tried to figure out what McGee was doing here, but that didn't take much of a guess. Once Pickens had disbanded his militia after the fall of Charlestown, McGee would have gone looking for another band of rebels to join.

McGee spat and stepped forward. He had to be restrained by Peter Horry and two others. "I'll not hear this swine besmirching the good names of Colonel Clarke and John Norris! I'll kill the wretch."

"Quiet, Sergeant," Marion said, and the Irishman obeyed. "Colonel Clarke also reported seeing you riding with a patrol of redcoats on the road from Augusta to Ninety Six. Traitors are summarily executed, Drummond. I advise you to defend yourself."

With a sigh, he answered: "I saw Colonel Boyd shot down, an' went to see if I could help him."

" 'Twas not . . . your d-d-duty," Horry argued. "Your . . . duty was to f-f-f-fight."

"Hell, you wasn't there. The fight was over. An' John Boyd was a brave man. I knew him. Used to trade with Pickens some. Figured, Tory or not, Boyd deserved some comfort. That's how I got captured. An' I rode with them redcoats to Ninety Six to deliver a broach Boyd give me to see that his wife got."

McGee cursed again. "I don't believe you."

"Nor do I," Moore added.

"I do not care one whit what you think."

"Turncoats are w-wor-worthless to our c-c-cause," Horry said. "Samuel Tynes f-f-fought f-for liberty once. Now he . . . leads Tories . . . against us."

Drummond fell silent, thinking how it would be just his luck to try to join Marion only to be hanged by him, instead. He felt like a dunderhead.

"Why did not you remain at your home once you were paroled?" Marion asked.

Anger suddenly clouded his face, and his reply was barely audible. "That's my business."

"Hang him, Colonel!" McGee said. "He won't fight. He's betrayed us once. A coward and a traitor, he is. Hang him!"

"Sergeant McGee," Marion said. "One more word from you, and I shall have you put in stocks. Do you have anything else to say in your defense, Drummond?"

He shook his head, surprised when someone else piped in: "He ain't no coward, Colonel, and I dare say he got as much reason to fight as any of us."

A black man pushed his way through the crowd. Drummond didn't recognize him, at first, but finally placed the face. This had been the man at Cusack's, the one with the growling dog, and, later, at the cabin. His was the face of the angel, the man who had carried Drummond and Rosemary through the burning forest, dressed their backs with a mixture of mud and moss, and carried them to Doc Oliver's house.

"Explain yourself, Dobie," Marion ordered.

Smiling, the Negro walked around and gently lifted the back of Drummond's shirt. Drummond grunted in pain, and men gasped and whispered upon seeing the scabbed wounds and scars left by the cat-o'-nine-tails. "Delivered," Dobie said, lowering the shirt, "by Bloody Jim Jernegan and Major Wemyss after the Cusack affair. I seen it all."

No man spoke until Marion ordered: "Grab a horse for Drummond and a firelock as well." The dark eyes glimmered as he faced Drummond briefly and glanced at Moore. "I know how you are at setting broken limbs, Drummond. See if you cannot help the captain."

Chapter Ten

Six Tory prisoners gave their allegiance to Marion, and, to Drummond's amazement, the colonel returned their firelocks. Maybe it shouldn't have surprised him. The partisans numbered barely four dozen, and several of those fought only when summoned, then retired to their farms and families. Some militiamen had served in the Continental Army, but most had the discipline of an offensive puppy and temperament of a bee-stung bobcat. They were a filthy lot in threadbare, patched frontier clothing, supplemented with coats, shoes, and other garments taken off dead Tories.

"Turncoats are worthless to our cause," Peter Horry had said, but that wasn't true. Marion needed turncoats to fill his ranks, and the more he thought about it, the more Drummond realized the former Tories would likely make Marion's hardest fighters for they knew, if they were captured, they would be executed for high treason. If they deserted Marion, men like Paddy McGee let them know their throats would be cut. The remaining Tories, as well as Colonel Tynes and the horseman Alastair, who had been captured in the High Hills, were delivered to a North Carolina prison camp.

From the Tearcoat, the bulk of Marion's force headed southeast, crossing the Black River, skirting around Kingstree, and traveling over animal trails rather than the major pikes before fording Lynches Creek below Witherspoon's Ferry, which Wemyss had destroyed. Through the swamps, brambles, and thickets, Catawba Tom and Marion led the group a few more miles before the Indian stopped his horse and mimicked a crow's *kaw* six times, quickly answered with a panther's scream, the beat of a woodpecker, and splash of an otter or large fish—imitations as good as any Cherokee's. Catawba Tom *kawed* twice more, and they rode on to the banks of the Great Peedee River, where a half dozen waiting partisans ferried most of the men, horses, dogs, and spoils of war across the muddy water in large flat boats. Catawba Tom, Dobie, and two other soldiers herded the captured Tory horses into the river, swimming them across the current.

They landed on Snow's Island.

Perhaps a Dutch mile across, maybe a little more, the ridge climbed out of the moors at the confluence of Lynches Creek and the Big Peedee. At the center of the island, they arrived at camp, where they rubbed down, fed and watered their mounts, and dispersed captured weapons, powder, food, and clothing among the men who had been left to guard the stronghold. "Make sure the prisoners are fed as well," Marion ordered before retiring to a cabin.

The log building, called Goddard's cabin after the settler who had built it years ago, looked about as run-down as the Madisons' had been when Drummond first discovered it, although Dobie told him the roof didn't leak so the colonel stayed dry unless there came a blowing rain from the coast. "East wall's got more holes than my breeches," Dobie said.

Drummond scanned the rest of camp. Goddard's cabin looked like an upper-class Charlestown tavern compared to the rest of Marion's base. Most of the men slept on straw and blankets underneath shoddy lean-tos. A crude barn stood in the east corner, and storage bins pockmarked the rest of the grounds. The whole place, dark and forbidding, stank of stagnant water, manure, and the wretched odors of decay that permeated the surrounding bogs. Cypress, pines, elms, and briar patches surrounded the compound like a palisade, trapping stifling heat and humidity.

Sergeant Paddy McGee pointed to two sacks of rice a soldier had unloaded, and barked out an order: "Dobie, you and Drummond take those to the bull pen."

The bull pen turned out to be the barn. Two guards in hunting frocks and kilts lowered their blunderbusses, unbarred the doors, and swung them open as Drummond and Dobie approached. Dobie dropped his sack just inside the door and motioned Drummond to do the same. He did, and, when he looked up, he stared at the most lamentable creatures he had ever seen: perhaps a dozen gaunt Tory prisoners with haunted eyes and bleeding gums. No one spoke, and Drummond was glad to leave the foul-smelling barn. The Tearcoat Swamp prisoners would never know how lucky they were to have been escorted to North Carolina, and not brought here.

"This be your home for a spell," Dobie told him. "You can share a blanket and mess with Catawba Tom and me. We be pretty much the outcasts here. So are you, I warrant."

The men in camp came from different circles. A few, like Marion, were wealthy planters who brought along their manservants—the colonel's slave was named Oscar. Ebenezer Moore, Drummond learned, had been a barrister in North Carolina who often visited a sister at Weaver's

Settlement. Stuttering Peter Horry had fought alongside Marion since the war began, and his brother, Hugh, served as well. In fact, there were many pairs of brothers: John and Gavin Witherspoon, James and Roland DuRant, and Gary and Robert Joyner, plus Marion's brother, Gabriel. The colonel's nephew, also named Gabriel, had likewise served with the partisans only to be captured and executed earlier in the fall by Tories.

Others brought their dogs. Dobie and Catawba Tom owned wiry hounds, great tracking dogs that seldom barked but shed hair and, to Drummond's eternal discomfort, ticks and fleas. One-eyed Clarence Howard never uttered a kind word unless praising his six terrifying beasts that looked and acted like red wolves. There were loners as well: Captain Roche; a mulatto called Levi; towering, barrel-chested Miles Jensen; a half-Tularosa, half-Frenchman named Marcel; and Paddy McGee. Lettered soldiers, too: Paul Hamilton, Captains Snipes and Dozier, Lieutenant O'Donnell, Sergeant Pierce, and Timothy P. Stokes, men who kept journals and wrote letters, pleasant fellows quick with a smile or song.

Men with nothing in common with each other, except a scalding hatred of the crown.

Almost daily, the force grew stronger. Marion's victories at Black Mingo and Tearcoat Swamp, coupled with the plundering committed by Wemyss and Jernegan, had Back Country men taking to the swamps to join the militia. Even a few former Loyalists decided to take up the partisan cause. One of these was David Langston, a Georgetown doctor who cursed the British after Bloody Jim Jernegan flogged his son-in-law to death because the lad refused to shine the captain's boots. They weren't the only ones searching for Marion. As the colonel increased his ambushes and raids, Charles Cornwallis ordered Lieutenant Colonel Banastre Tarleton and his Green Dragoons to find and subdue Francis Marion.

Drummond spent all of his time on the island, guarding the prisoners in the bull pen, policing camp, fishing, or stationed at the redoubt near Dunham's Bluff. He didn't care much for these assignments, but Marion let him know it wasn't because of a lack of trust. "Your back must heal," he said kindly. "You shall have your vengeance upon the enemy. This I promise you." Ebenezer Moore, because of his badly broken arm, also found himself confined to Snow's Island.

Drummond had just returned to camp on a sunny November day with a string of bream for supper, when Marion and a raiding party rode in out of the woods. Drummond and the other militiamen heard them long before they saw them. Not the horses. Laughter.

Everyone appeared cheery, apparently at Marion's expense, because the colonel just shook his head, dismounted, and handed the reins to Oscar. He limped toward Goddard's cabin, opened the door, and started to enter, but turned when James Witherspoon, who had likewise stayed in camp, asked: "Come, lads, we could use a laugh. Let us in on your joke."

Leaning against the log walls, Marion removed his battered leather helmet from his Second South Carolina Regiment days, and waited. Every raiders' eye shot toward Marion, who nodded his consent.

Beaming, Peter Horry began: "Well . . . we were . . . ch-ch-chased by C-C-Co-Colonel Tarle-ton . . . himself. . . ."

"This could take all winter," muttered Clarence Howard, dropping to a knee to scratch the ears of one of his wolfhounds.

"Almost . . . th-thirty miles . . . we rode, f-fr-from the Po. . . ."

"Pocotaligo," Captain Hunter finished.

"Yes." Horry nodded, licked his lips, and went on. "To Ox Swamp. And f-f-f-final-ly . . . Ta-Tarle-ton c-c-cries out . . . 'C-c-come . . .'." He turned to Hunter, pleading: "You were the . . . c-clo-closest."

With a widening grin, Andrew Hunter straightened in the saddle and said: "Tarleton shouts to his men . . . 'Come, my boys. Let's go back, and we will find the Gamecock. But as for this damned old fox, the devil himself could not catch him'!" Raising his long rifle over his head, Hunter shouted: *"Huzza!"*

Everyone in camp roared back. Drummond glanced at Marion, and thought he found the trace of a smile before the tired leader disappeared inside the cabin.

"Huzza! Long live our *damned old fox!"* Hunter shouted. "Long live the Swamp Fox!"

Lieutenant O'Donnell was the first with the sickness. A week of unseasonal monsoons hit camp hard, a blessing at first as the weather cooled. As the camp became more and more crowded from volunteers and a few other Tory prisoners, and, as Marion limited the number of raids because of the weather, others came down with chills and fevers. Some of it Drummond recognized as malaria. Admitting his relapse, Captain Hunter retired to his lean-to to sweat it out. Many contracted dysentery, groaning from intense cramps and soiling themselves with a malodorous purge of blood- and pus-filled stool. Five days later, Mickey O'Donnell died.

Drummond helped David Langston with the sick, cleaning those too weak to lift their arms, covering those with chills with blankets, and giving others water while Langston would cut their arms to drain the bad blood. Drummond gagged frequently, vomited three times, but did his job the first day. The next morning, he still choked at the smell, only did not throw up. Three more died before Langston himself took ill. In less than a week, the Georgetown doctor departed for Glory.

Three men deserted the following night, and the next morning, when Drummond was ordered to feed the bull pen prisoners, he thought about fleeing himself. He backed out of the barn quickly, ordered the guards to close the doors, and dashed across the camp to the cabin, not even bothering to knock. He flung the door open, stepped inside, and stopped. Huddled over a map, Marion and a dozen officers glared at him.

Drummond found his voice. "A word, Colonel?"

Moore, his arm still in splints and sling, whirled. "You are a private, Drummond," he said. "You ask your sergeant for permission. . . ."

"Captain," Marion said in soft rebuke, "this is not the Continental Army. What is it, Drummond? I pray not another death."

"I don't think so, sir. Not yet. But. . . ." He caught his breath. "It's the Tory prisoners, Colonel." He had seen this before. In fact, many of the soldiers in camp bore the scars, but in Cherokee country he had heard the horror stories and seen with his own eyes the deadliness, death spreading like wildfire, entire Indian villages wiped out.

"Smallpox," Drummond said.

Dr. Oliver explained everything as he rushed about in his office, grabbing the bag of medicines he had bought from the Camden apothecary, to which he added the nearest

137

bottle of rum. He had dropped in at Weaver's Tavern for a dram of pumpkin ale and was gossiping with the proprietor about the state of affairs when two men barged in with news that Reginald McAllister, his wife and son, and a stranger had come down with the pox. They rushed the doctor home in a four-wheel phaëton to pick up his supplies.

"Do you want me to come with you?" Rosemary Madison asked.

"Yes," he replied, which staggered her. She didn't wait for him to change his mind. She grabbed her cloak, told Rachel to mind Jezebel and Ezekiel, and followed her father out the front door, down the steps, and to the road, where two men waited in front of the carriage.

She recognized neither the burly man with the whip nor the slight redhead. Both wore bedraggled clothes that, like the two men, had felt water only since the last rain, but their boots were new, and they carried pistols, knives, and hatchets in their belts, and firelocks at their sides.

"What is she doing?" the big man asked.

"She has been inoculated," said Oliver, climbing into the wagon. "Have either of you?"

The big man blinked. "Inoculated?"

"We shall take care of that at McAllister's," Oliver said as he helped his daughter into the carriage.

"I don't know," the big man said, pointing the end of the whip at Rosemary. "She. . . ."

"Miles," the young redhead said urgently, thrusting his chin down the road.

A redcoat patrol had just rounded the bend. Neither man said another word. The big fellow climbed aboard, let his whip fly, and the phaëton took off.

She suspected something then, but shrugged it off as imagination. A lot of Back Country folks remained leery of any redcoat after what Wemyss and Jernegan had done. She tried to steady herself in the bouncing, swaying carriage, and closed her eyes to fight the dizziness and fermenting stomach, which helped a little.

An hour later, Dr. Oliver exclaimed. "You have taken the wrong fork."

Rosemary's eyes shot open. "Stop and turn around. Time is imperative!"

The redhead pulled the team to a stop, but, instead of turning around or backing up, he set the brake and leaped out. The big fellow rolled up his whip, saying nothing, but, when he turned, he had pulled out his pistol and aimed it at the passengers.

"What is the meaning of this?" Oliver asked.

"Sorry, Doc," he said, "but we sha'n't be taking you to McAllister's this day. As far as I know, the Tory pig is in good health. Which is more than you shall be if you give us any trouble."

The smaller man had disappeared into a pine thicket. Now he returned with three other strangers. All four sat atop strong horses, with the redhead pulling three mounts, saddles empty, behind him.

"Shall we, Doc?" the big man said, waving his pistol slightly.

They rode throughout the night, traveling trails Rosemary never knew existed, and likely blazing a few of their own. By the next afternoon, she found herself hopelessly lost in the middle of some swamp. Her father had no idea where they were, either, but the kidnapper named Miles halted the group, reached into his knapsack, and handed two flour sacks to the redhead, whom she had heard called Stokes. He rode up and handed a sack to Rosemary and her father. "I am sorry," he said sincerely, "but you must put these over your heads now."

After tying them on, Stokes and another man took their reins, told the prisoners to grab fistfuls of mane, and began leading them through a maze. The sack itched and made breathing difficult. She heard the bubbling of water, cries of birds, and the occasional warning from Stokes: "Low branch. Duck please. You are clear now." "About to ford a creek. Hang on." "Up a hill. Lean forward." "Another branch. Watch your heads."

They halted a few hours later, but only briefly. A crow *kawed*—no, one of the men imitating the bird. Other animal cries answered, and they pushed on a couple more minutes before stopping again. Rough hands helped Rosemary out of the saddle. The blindfold remained on, but she knew they were at a river. She felt herself being led away from the horses, and her feet splashed in water and sank a few inches into mud. "Step high!" another voice called out, and she knew she had climbed into a boat or some sort of raft. They were ferried across, horses and all, to the opposite bank, taken ashore, and helped onto the horses. Maybe twenty minutes later, Stokes pulled off the sack.

She squinted her eyes at the light and breathed deeply, but the smell gagged her. Stokes helped her from the saddle, and, as her eyes adjusted to the sun, she looked in horror at the awful camp. The entire place reeked, and she covered her nose and mouth with both hands.

"Thank you for coming, Doctor," a kind voice said, "and you, as well, Rosemary."

Squire Marion stepped toward them and offered his hand.

Oliver stared at it, but did not extend his own. Instead, he said bitterly: "I did not have a say in the matter, sir."

140

Marion stepped back, his black eyes burning with an anger she had never seen. "Private Jensen, your orders were to send word that I desired Doctor Oliver's help."

"We thought he might not be so inclined to help us, Colonel," Miles Jensen explained. "Him bein' a Tory and all."

"Who gave you the right to think, Jensen, let alone kidnap an honorable man and bring his daughter to this abyss? I should have you flogged." Marion spun around, removed his battered helmet, and apologized. "If you wish to be taken home immediately, it shall be done."

"We are here," Oliver relented. "I am a doctor. Where are your sick?"

Marion bowed at them, and shouted a name that chilled her.

"Drummond!"

"All the prisoners have the pox in some form," Drummond said softly. "We thought it was jail fever, at first, but I seen smallpox before. Four of our men got it as well. We got our boys on the far end of camp, left the Tories locked in the bull pen."

"The bull pen?" Rosemary asked.

Drummond pointed at the shoddy barn. Her face flushed, and she turned angrily. "Those men are not animals, Augustin. They should. . . ."

"Rosemary," he said, "I been doin' all I can for 'em, an' our other sick, as well. Lots of our men, an' plenty officers, wanted to burn the barn with the Tories in it."

"You have other sick?" Oliver asked.

Drummond nodded.

"Not smallpox?"

"No, sir. Few got malaria. An' a bunch dysentery."

"How many have died?"

Sighing, he said softly: "Ten, includin' Doc Langston."

"David Langston?" Oliver was amazed. "Of Georgetown?"

Another nod.

"My, God. Did he treat these men before he was taken ill?"

"Yes, sir. Not the smallpox. He was dead before that come about. He give some calomel an' snake root, tried bleedin' most of 'em, but that did no good far as I saw."

"Certainly," Oliver said. "In thirty years practicing medicine, I have witnessed only a handful of patients improve by bloodletting. Still. . . ."

Rosemary had recovered, and she found herself concerned. "Augustin, how do you feel?"

"Fine," he answered.

Her father picked up the interrogation. "No headaches? No muscle pains?" Drummond shook his head. "No coughing? Sneezing?" Two more shakes. "Cramps?" Another negative. "How are your bowel movements?"

Drummond's face reddened, and he tilted his head slightly. "Doc?" he pleaded, and Rosemary felt her smile spreading.

"Roll up your sleeves," Oliver ordered, and Drummond obeyed. "No eruptions," the doctor said, after examining the backwoodsman's arms, and letting out a breath of relief. "God watches over you, Augustin. Have you been inoculated for smallpox?"

"I . . . I reckon not."

"Well, you should be. Everyone here, who has not, should be. It is the best fight against the pox, Augustin. We shall do this first, then see to the dysentery, save the malaria cases for last. I shall need your help, if you feel up to it."

CHAPTER ELEVEN

The treatment, Dr. Oliver explained, was quite simple. There was little he could do for those with bad cases of smallpox, just comfort them. They would live or die, and the survivors would carry the scars from the disease. No, the most important thing now was to prevent smallpox from spreading throughout the camp, and he would do this by inoculation. Two partisans and three Loyalist prisoners had contracted mild cases of smallpox. Oliver would remove the dried scabs from these men, and gather those uninfected with the disease in camp. He would lance each healthy man's left arm ever so slightly, and place a small portion of a smallpox scab over the wound.

"You mean give me the pox?" Drummond asked incredulously.

Taking his hand, Rosemary said gently: "It really is for the best. I have been inoculated. It builds your resistance."

" 'Tis quite true, Augustin," Oliver went on. "We shall then wait, giving you and the others we inoculate some of the late Doctor Langston's snake root to regulate any fever and purge your body of sickness. The odds of your contracting a bad case of the pox and dying are four hundred to one."

That didn't ease Drummond's nerves. There were about four hundred men on Snow's Island. "What if I happen to be that one?" he asked, not entirely jesting. They didn't give him an answer.

Those who had received smallpox vaccinations would care for the sick and rid the camp of much of the filth. Smallpox and malaria could be treated with a good chance of survival. Regarding the dysentery, Oliver added, it was a miracle they were not facing a cholera outbreak.

Marion, Major James, and Colonel Horry had the men gathered early the next morning, and they explained the smallpox vaccination procedure, the need to do it, and reassured the safety. They were met with skepticism.

"A Tory doctor give us the pox?" Paddy McGee shouted. "Tarleton can't kill us in battle, so he sends this bub to kill us with smallpox!"

"Aye," Clarence Howard agreed. "No one shall give me the pox."

"Gentlemen," Marion pleaded, "I assure you of the safety. Those of you who served in the Continental Army know these vaccinations are a necessity. Please, all of you that have been vaccinated, step forward."

Quite a few did, and Major James pointed out that these men, perhaps fifty in number, all looked fit. "The vaccine did not kill these men," he said, but McGee and others still shook their heads.

"Why should we trust this doc?" Miles Jensen argued. "A man who'd kiss King George's feet if his royal arse dared show his ugly face in South Carolina."

Peter Horry stamped his foot in the mud. "And what . . . ch-ch-chance will you have to f-f-fight . . . Britons and . . . T-Tories if you are too sick . . . to ride and shoot? To win thi-thi-this . . . war, we must have . . . our . . . health!"

They talked among themselves like rabble, and Marion asked for volunteers. Drummond stepped forward, and the crowd fell silent. They watched in awe as the doctor pricked his left arm, and placed something over the wound. A smiling Rosemary Madison led him away.

"Oh," Marion added, "after the vaccination, you are off duty for a week. Turnips, stew, hot tea, and coffee. Those of us who have been vaccinated will divide latrine duty, care for the sick, and bury the dead."

Catawba Tom followed. Next came Dobie and Timothy Stokes. One by one, they filed in line.

The bull pen was torn down and stacked with the belongings of the dead, straw beds, and other filth that could burn, while the Tory prisoners, many of whom also suffered from scurvy, were placed in large, clean lean-tos next to the sick partisans. Marion was not pleased with the idea of a pyre, fearing the smoke would bring Royal forces to the island, but he relented. Dr. Oliver told him the smoke would purify the bad air. The dead were dug up from the graves near camp, and reburied on the far side of Snow's Island. Two Tory prisoners died of smallpox, and three of Marion's militia succumbed to dysentery or another sickness. Their clothing, bedding, and personal items were burned, and their bodies carried across the island for unhallowed internment.

"You should never have come here," Ebenezer Moore said on the afternoon of the bull pen fire.

Ignoring his comment, Rosemary Madison readjusted his splint and sling. "Your arm heals nicely, Ebenezer."

His resolve vanished, as it always did when she smiled at him. He wanted to reach out and touch her auburn hair, to brush the matted bangs off her forehead, to kiss her, and pledge his undying love. Instead, he just nodded.

She reached out and fingered the buttons hanging

around his neck. "What are these?" she asked.

His ears reddened, a reaction he wished he could control, if not eliminate, and he pushed her hand away, not angrily, for he certainly did not wish to offend Rosemary Oliver Madison. Her fingers should never touch such lurid trophies of war.

"They are nothing," he said, and grinned at her. "I have thought of you often. I am glad we finally have a chance to talk. You look well."

"You have lost too much weight. You are merely skin and bones."

"Fear not, Rosemary. I received my smallpox vaccination in Charlestown and have not had so much as a slight fever." His eyes burned from the thick smoke, and he stifled a cough. "I think this smoke your father desires has rid us and the air of any putridness. Shall we walk to the river?"

He stood, offering his good arm, and helped her to her feet. He led her past Goddard's cabin and down a dark path canopied by the tops of cypress trees. They talked of nothing important, of old stories retold for the hundredth time, of songs and fashions, of minor courtroom cases and Rosemary's first experiences as a nurse, of Moore's sister and Rachel. Never of Richard, or the war. Never of the whip marks on Rosemary's back. Never of Drummond.

Traces of winter had finally arrived, far later than normal, bringing the first frost to the Peedee basin and much welcomed cooler temperatures. The weather had helped the sick soldiers as much as John Oliver's treatments and directions for cleanliness. No longer did the mosquitoes buzz and bite. Snow's Island had turned peaceful.

He stopped her before stepping into the clearing. Having been a soldier for almost six years now, he knew always to remain on alert. Moore stepped forward and studied the tree-lined banks on the opposite side of the Great Peedee. He did not move for five full minutes, until he was certain there was no danger. Then he took Rosemary's hand and led her to the landing.

She knelt and splashed cool water over her face. Rivulets streamed down her thin neck, and she sat on the muddy bank and stuck her feet in the river, laughing like a child. It had been so long since he had heard that laugh. He sat beside her, and placed his own boots in the Peedee. Moore didn't care much for the water. He feared the leather would shrink up so that he wouldn't be able to pull the boots on tomorrow morning. In fact, he found the river bloody cold. He dared not complain, not with Rosemary enjoying herself, so close to him. She kicked her feet, splashing cold water over them, giggling uncontrollably.

"I wish we could stay like this," he said. He didn't know why he said it, and certainly didn't mean it in his soggy stockings and numbing toes.

"It is nice," she said, and stopped kicking. "Beautiful. Alas, Father and I will take our leave tomorrow or the day after. We have done all we can here, and I miss Rachel terribly. I have not been a good mother since this war began."

War. She had finally brought it into the open.

Bitterness returned, and he couldn't control it. "This war has been costly for every Patriot," he said coldly. Rosemary pulled her feet out of the water, bringing her knees close to her body. She stared at Moore, her eyes filled with concern and, perhaps, fear.

He wanted to stop, yet couldn't. His rage inflamed out of control like his reddening ears. "I have not forgotten what Wemyss did to you, Rosemary." Absently he fingered his necklace of buttons. "He shall pay dearly."

She touched his good arm, and he stopped talking. She

gave him another smile, but he knew it was forced as he heard her say: "Wemyss has already paid, Ebenezer."

His look was one of bewilderment, so she explained. "He was gravely wounded and captured by Thomas Sumter somewhere earlier this month. The war is over for the major."

"Sumter! He hanged the devil, I hope."

She shook her head. "Paroled him, I am told. It matters not. My back feels fine, Ebenezer. Wemyss will harm me no more . . . he might never walk again, I hear . . . and Jernegan is in Cheraw, far from us."

His ears turned a brighter shade of red. Knowing he would not be able to cut down Major James Wemyss sickened his stomach.

Rosemary stood, still smiling that fake smile, and offered him her small hands. "Come," she said in mock cheerfulness. "We should return to camp. I want to see Augustin before I leave."

"Drummond!" he roared, rising angrily and shoving Rosemary aside. He did not mean to do this, but he had no control of his temper. It exploded like Charger in battle. Rosemary fell into the river, soaking her dress, and he longed to apologize, to help her out of the shallow water, to take her into his arms and beg for forgiveness. Instead, he cried out: "All you ever talk about is that uncouth, unlettered, unkempt imbecile! How could you love him, Rosemary, and not me?"

"I don't. . . ." Her mouth dropped open. Shock clouded her eyes.

"Shut up!" He clamped his eyes shut and shook his head violently. "I will not hear his name, will not hear your futile lies." His eyes shot open. Rosemary had not moved. "Look at this arm! I could have lost this arm because of you. Do not you remember anything, woman? Richard. Richard. Richard. All you ever spoke of was how brave your poor husband was. The first Patriot, according to you, but think back, Rosemary. It was not Richard. Damn him, when merchants and Patriots started coming to the Back Country speaking against King George, against his taxes, stumping for liberty and revolution, Richard did not care. All he spoke of was the need for a bridge over the Black River, of schools, but you heard and believed in the cause, as did I."

He thumped his chest. "It was I, Rosemary. I joined the Continental regiment first. I joined because of you, because it is what you believed. Richard came later. I never hated him. He was like a brother to me, but you talk of him and this Drummond until my ears almost burst." His eyes locked shut again. "Cannot you see that I love you, Rosemary? That I desire you to be my bride? That I have always loved you, long before Richard Madison and long before Drummond?" He was crying now, unabashedly, and dropped on his knees into the water beside her.

"Marry me, Rosemary. Marry me, for the love of God."

He opened his eyes and saw Rosemary crying as well. Moore cursed himself for rendering her to tears.

"Ebenezer," she said softly, "it has been too soon."

"No. You no longer wear black, I see. Three years, Rosemary. No, four. More than four long years since he died so valiantly defending Charlestown. *Years.* Rosemary, my sister Helen married just two *months* after Benjamin's death of white plague. Put Richard behind you, and forget Drummond. He is not for you, and this you know is true." He fingered his buttons. "These . . . I have killed for you, my dearest. For revenge. Count these buttons, Rosemary. They prove my love."

"I do not love Augustin, Ebenezer," she said, standing

149

quickly. "He is a friend. That is all." She touched his shoulder. "I care for you. Deeply, I do. But I do not love you, Ebenezer. Not that way. It breaks my heart to think I could have led you to believe this. Forgive me. Please. I cannot marry you." Her eyes stuck on his necklace. "And those . . . I. . . ."

He watched her run into the woods, heard her sobs, and he fell face down into the water, groaning, pounding the water with his left fist, cursing his own stupidity, cursing Rosemary Madison, cursing her father and late husband, cursing Drummond.

This time, Drummond knocked on the door at Goddard's cabin. "Come!" Marion called, and Drummond stepped inside, pulling the door shut behind him.

The colonel stood in front of his desk, holding a sword and scabbard in both hands. Major James, Colonel Horry and Captains Dozier, Wilson, Snipes, and—now recovered from his malaria—Hunter also stood on one side of the cabin. Across from them sat Dr. Oliver and Rosemary Madison.

"You wanted to see me, Colonel Marion, sir?"

"Indeed." Still holding the sword, Marion crossed the room and peered through the window. "Where is Captain Moore?" he asked no one in particular.

Drummond studied the officers' faces, realized they were without an answer, and replied himself. "Took a dozen boys on a scout late last night," he said. Marion looked at him skeptically. Drummond wished he had remained silent.

"A scout?" Marion shot out. "I did not authorize a scout."

Major James stamped his feet. "Damn that impertinent. . . ."

"No matter," said Marion, calming instantly and returning to his previous position. "Let Captain Moore have his raid. We shall address that matter upon his return. We have business at hand." Facing Drummond, he continued: "We lost Lieutenant O'Donnell."

Head bowed, Drummond muttered a respectful: "Yes, sir."

"We need to fill that vacancy," Marion added.

They couldn't be talking about him, but, when he looked up, Marion held out the sheathed sword.

"C-c-c-come on, Drum-mond," Horry stammered. "T-take it."

Rosemary whispered his name, and he stepped forward. It wasn't much of a sword, just an old blade from one of the nearby sawmills that the smithy Jensen had turned into a saber. He let Marion place the sling over his shoulder. The sword and scabbard rattled against the dirt floor and felt awkward, hanging over his left hip.

" 'Tis a brevet, Drummond," Marion said. "You have earned it in our eyes."

"But," Captain Hunter added, "you must prove it to many of our men. They still think you a coward, maybe a traitor. As an officer, you will have many more responsibilities, and some will resent you. As a private, you are climbing several grades in rank. More than a few sergeants will frown on this."

Drummond stared at the sword before leaning closer to Marion and whispering: "Sir, I can't read a lick. Can't write neither, not even my name. I ain't so rightly sure this is such a good idea, Colonel, beggin' your pardon."

With a smile, Marion placed a hand on Drummond's shoulder and gave it a reassuring squeeze. "You shall do fine, Lieutenant." They shook hands, and Marion stepped back. "Your first assignment, Mister Drummond, is to escort the remaining Tory prisoners to Britton's Neck."

"Sir?"

"The good doctor has convinced me that I should pardon those poor souls. We have taken the fight out of them, and we certainly cannot care adequately for them. This we have learned."

"Yes, sir."

"Then I desire you to escort John and Rosemary home. Take a half dozen men with you. Return to Snow's Island forthwith."

He stood there like a simpleton as the officers shook his hand and offered words of encouragement. Even Dr. Oliver smiled and gave him a wink. Rosemary kissed his cheek and whispered: "I am so proud of you."

He blushed a little. "Pick your men, Lieutenant," Marion ordered. "I dare say Rosemary and John long for home, and the Tories are certainly tiresome of our company."

"Yes, sir." Drummond saluted, spun around, almost tripping over the sword, and sped out of the cabin, not knowing really what he was supposed to do next. Ask for volunteers? Order a detail? Who would take him seriously? He cursed underneath his breath while seeking Catawba Tom and Dobie. They'd be a good start.

Squire Marion saw Rosemary off. His servant, Oscar, helped her into the saddle, and the colonel handed her the reins and patted her hands before tilting his head in Drummond's direction.

"He is a good man," Marion said. "A little troubled, but I think you two can work through that."

"Francis," she said, shaking her head. It was the first

time she had ever called the planter by his Christian name. "My heart still belongs to Richard. Augustin is a dear friend."

Marion's knowing grin shocked her. Stepping away from the sorrel, he said: "I am not blind, child."

"I. . . ." She paused, stared at the Huguenot for a second before quickly searching for Drummond. Mounted on a buckskin, he was whispering something to the swarthy partisan called Catawba Tom. The Indian nodded and took off ahead of the rest of the party, followed by his dog. Drummond pushed back his cocked hat and began a conversation with the freedman, Dobie.

"Oh, my," she caught herself saying. Was Marion right? Was she in love with Augustin Drummond? Friends, she had been telling everyone for months now, close to a year. Friends, friends, friends. She felt a catch in her throat, a quickening of her heartbeat, and dared not look again at Colonel Marion. She had been lying to herself. She was in love with Augustin Drummond, and had been for some time.

FROM THE MANUSCRIPT
OF THE REVEREND STAN MCINTYRE,
PAGES 51–53

I am indebted to Mr. Edward Anderson for the copy of the letter below. Edward and his wife Thelma have been friends of mine since I arrived at Cameron Branch, and Edward served as deacon for many years. A few years ago he and his wife went vacationing abroad to England. Maybe it was luck, perhaps it was divine intervention, but on a lark they dropped in at the West Suffolk Military Museum and found this letter in one of the many display cases. Thelma wrote it down on the back of a postcard, a couple of receipts, and their itinerary. The letter was written by one Lieutenant Jason Blackburn of the 63rd infantry while he was stationed in South Carolina during the Revolution. I think it relays much information about the state of the British Army at that time, and the last paragraph does offer some insight into Augustin Drummond. Here is the letter:

Camden District, South Carolina
18 December, 17 and 80

    My Darling Susan:
    I have been placed on temporary assignment and must turn these Scottish colonists into a trained army that can conquer this Swamp Fox. Earlier I worked closely with a dashing, fearless man from Liverpool, Lieutenant Col.

Banastre Tarleton, who loves horses, ladies, and games of chance. He is perhaps two or three years younger than I, and at first I enjoyed my brief tour with him. But, alas, he revealed himself as big of a scoundrel as Captain Jernegan and Major Wemyss.

You probably would not recognize me now. My uniform is in tatters. I have been forced to tear away the long tails of my uniform coat to repair other parts of my clothing so that now I guess it looks as though I wear a jacket. Others have likewise been forced to modify uniforms.

I cannot write you all that has occurred here, but know that I am in fine health, although I could certainly use some of your delicious pudding, and Oh, for a noggin of good wine.

Our luck against the Swamp Fox has not been good. I did make the acquaintance of one of his officers, a Lt. Drummond, a short time ago. He is the same one Major Wemyss held prisoner a few months ago. All I can really tell you about the rebel is that he is an excellent judge of horseflesh.

I will write more later. Give the children a kiss on their foreheads from me, and tell them that I shall come home as soon as we end this rebellion.

Your loving husband,
Jason

This is the only mention of Drummond I have found written by one of his enemies, and it is the first to tell of his rank. Various accounts have called our subject a private, a sergeant, even a captain, but it is clear he was a lieutenant, at least in the winter of 1780. Regarding "horseflesh," most militia rode horses, but would fight engagements on foot.

One letter from Francis Marion takes note of the many fine horses in his regiment. Marion rated his own favorite mount high, and commended a stallion named Charger ridden by Captain Ebenezer Moore, "but the most spirited animal in our army is the one procured by Lt. Drummond," he writes.

Chapter Twelve

December, 1780

The winds picked up and sent the temperature plummeting shortly after they crossed the Big Peedee, and, a few hours before reaching Britton's Neck, it started sleeting. They rid themselves of the Tory prisoners at a dilapidated chicken coop, and rode a few miles until finding a barn at an abandoned farm where they could wait out the storm.

Drummond's patrol consisted of Catawba Tom and Dobie, the only two who seemed to trust him. The blacksmith, Miles Jensen, had volunteered because he wanted to keep an eye on the new lieutenant, and Timothy Stokes went along because he always followed the smithy like an unweaned pup. Like Jensen, McGee joined the outfit to make sure Drummond didn't lead Banastre Tarleton's Green Dragoons back to Snow's Island. Levi, the taciturn mulatto, and the half-breed, Marcel, also volunteered; Drummond didn't ask their reasons, and none had given him any.

With Stokes playing "The Tobacco Box" on a German oboe and the travelers huddled close to fight the chill, Drummond led the buckskin out of the barn, and rode into the freezing night, stopping under an oak tree to allow McGee to catch up. He didn't expect Jensen or McGee to let him out of their sight.

"And just where are you off to on such a blustery night?" the Irishman asked.

"Scout the roads," Drummond replied, and pulled up the collar of his coat.

"Why? No gruel-loving redcoat will be out in this weather." Grinning, he added: "And, by the saints, the way that doctor's harlot of a daughter has been casting glances at you, I would think you would rather be there with her, pinching her sweet. . . ."

Drummond's backhand caught McGee squarely on his lips. The sudden movement caused both horses to shy, and, once they had calmed their mounts, McGee wiped his lips, and said: "Aye, bub, so I have found something you *will* fight for."

"Just watch your mouth."

"You think you can take ol' Paddy McGee?" he prodded with a snort.

"You might whup me, Paddy, but I'll break you of the habit."

McGee's smile seemed genuine this time. "No offense, Drummond. 'Tis worth fighting for . . . a woman like that. Truth be, the only reason I am here with you and not courting her is because Jensen and me drew cards, and I lost."

"You can ride back, Paddy, but leave her alone."

McGee laughed, but the unfriendliness had returned to his eyes and voice. "You'd like that, wouldn't you? Me riding back, that is. Well, forget it. I'm sticking with you like flies in a privy."

"Then keep your powder dry," said Drummond, kicking the buckskin into a walk. "An' your trap shut."

Over the next three hours, they didn't find one British patrol. They saw *two:* six or seven mounted dragoons, and then about a dozen shivering Highlanders in plaid kilts and red coats. The Highlanders marched so close to them, Drummond feared the Scots would hear his sword rattling.

He held his breath until the last soldier rounded the bend.

"What you make of all this?" McGee asked.

The question took Drummond by surprise. He never would have bet a half pence that the untrusting Irishman would ask for his opinion on anything. He shrugged, still staring down the road. "Could be anything. Might be they got caught in the weather and are high-tailin' it for camp. Might be Tarleton's figured to make things a mite tough on Colonel Marion from here on out. Could be Capt'n Moore raised a ruckus an' got redcoats lookin' for him."

"Don't reckon them redcoats found our Tory prisoners yet?"

Drummond shook his head. "The Dragoons we spotted weren't comin' from that direction. If them Scots had found 'em, they would have brung 'em along. Best get back to the barn."

It had stopped sleeting, but the wind refused to die, and the temperature showed no signs of rising until the sun re-appeared. Drummond knew the Tories would be discovered in a matter of time. That's why he had told Catawba Tom and Dobie to mention ever so casually that they would lead the doctor and nurse home after they left the prisoners, and to make sure they mentioned the good doctor's name— *David Langston*. That would send the enemy to the late doctor's residence in Georgetown, while Drummond could escort Rosemary and Dr. Oliver safely home to Cameron Branch, providing the two had been wise enough not to give their names while treating the prisoners on Snow's Island.

The weather had cleared by dawn, but it took Drummond two more days to reach Cameron Branch. With the increased activity of the British army, he didn't want to take unnecessary risks. They waited just off the Salem Road, along the path to the Madison cabin, while Dobie walked past Oliver's estate and back. Drummond picked Dobie because a lone freedman on foot would be unlikely to arouse suspicion. When Dobie returned late that afternoon and reported that the house looked as peaceful as Christmas, Drummond sighed with relief.

"You and your men are welcome to feed and water your horses at our barn," Oliver said dryly before looking at Drummond. "Then I demand that you take your leave and not trouble us again." Drummond remembered he was no longer welcome here because he had joined Marion. Oliver's curt hospitality surprised him, but he reckoned Rosemary had talked her father into letting the men care for their mounts.

"My slave, Ezekiel, will help you," the doctor went on. "I ask you not to tarry. See to your horses and get off my property. Come, Rosemary."

She hesitated, shot a quick look at Drummond, and kicked her horse forward. Drummond followed them down the magnolias to the front steps. Oliver was already mounting the steps, saying he needed a drink, and asking his daughter to bring in his medicine bag. He opened the door and disappeared inside.

Seeing Rosemary struggle to untie the strap holding the bag, Drummond slid from his saddle, and handed the reins to Catawba Tom. He walked to Rosemary's horse and began working on the knot, waiting for her to say something, but she just looked toward the barn. They hadn't said much since leaving Marion's camp.

The knot refused to give. *Who tied this blasted thing?* Drummond wondered, and swore out loud. Levi, the last of his men, dropped off his horse, mumbled something, and opened his pocketknife. He sliced the leather strap easily, and Drummond hefted the bag. Both men followed Rosemary up the steps. Once she reached the portico, she glanced again at the barn, where the men had gathered. The doors were closed. The whole place looked deserted.

"Where is Zeke?" Rosemary asked. As she reached for the knob, the front door flew open.

Her question had made Drummond suspicious, caused the hair on the back of his neck to bristle, so he reacted almost immediately as kilt-clad redcoats stormed outside. With a shriek, Rosemary fell on her backside, and Levi grabbed for the pistol stuck inside his belt. Drummond pitched the apothecary bag in front of the soldiers, tripping the first soldiers, and causing a massive pile-up, while he dashed across the portico. He flinched at the gunshot, realized he had not been the target, and leaped over the banister, crashing through the rose bushes that lined the side of the house.

More shots sounded from the barn, and Drummond cursed himself. He should have left all of his men at the burned-out cabin or sent them on back to Snow's Island, not that Jensen or McGee would have let him out of their sight, but at least he wouldn't have subjected them all to ambush.

Horrid cries came from the front of the house, blending with Rosemary's screams, tearing at Drummond's soul. He could picture the bayonets ripping into poor Levi, Rosemary watching in shock.

Drummond stumbled out of the roses. Thorns had scratched his face and hands, ripped his left sleeve. He drew his pistol, fired at the first face that appeared on the portico, knowing immediately that he had missed. The face dropped, and, when a second redcoat appeared, he let the empty flintlock fly. The pistol caught that soldier full in his face, sent blood spurting from the lad's nose as Drummond sprinted for the woods.

Wrong way. Green-jacketed Dragoons poured out of the trees in front of him, and he changed direction, darted to the back of the house, past the pigpen and chicken coop. A bullet whined over his head. Another clipped the already ripped left sleeve. He pivoted, slid behind the coop, grabbed for his sword. The damned thing only slowed him down. Ahead of him, he spotted a dozen soldiers at the barn, recognized one of his men on the ground, clutching a bloody shoulder, and saw the others raising their hands. He knew it was over, and released his grip on the sword, unmoving in its scabbard. Another bullet clipped the roof of the coop, causing an eruption of feathers and squawking hens. Hopeless. He had no chance of escape. Drummond lifted his hands well over his head, fully expecting a bullet to end his misery.

"I say, you must be the leader of this . . . *army*." The cock-of-the-walk officer greeted Drummond in Dr. Oliver's office. He had a face shaped more like a woman's, with neat red hair, and wore a green jacket with white piping, tight tan breeches, high-topped russet boots with large spurs, and a white neckerchief. Most British uniforms were soiled, patched, well worn from months, even years, of campaigning, but this rooster looked as if he had just stepped out of a Charlestown tailor's. His hat, a shako of black swan feathers, rested on Dr. Oliver's desk just behind him. "I shall have your saber, sir."

Drummond tugged at the sword twice. It remained locked in the scabbard. He glanced down, tried again, and finally unfastened the strap and handed both sword and sheath to the amused Briton. The gent took the proffered

saber, pulled at it once, and broke out laughing as he
handed the weapon to the blond lieutenant at his side. It
took a moment, but Drummond finally placed the lieutenant's face. He had been with Wemyss and Jernegan at
Cusack's and the Madison cabin.

"Your saber," the green-jacketed officer said, trying to
suppress more laughter, "has rusted in its scabbard. You
should take better care of your weapons, er. . . ."

"Drummond," he answered. "Lieutenant Augustin
Drummond, South Carolina militia, Colonel Marion
commandin'."

"I see. I am Lieutenant Colonel Banastre Tarleton of the
British Legion, and this is Lieutenant Blackburn, commander of our Peedee Loyalists. We have been waiting an
eternity, Mister Drummond, for your return."

Pouring himself a drink, Tarleton explained that Lieutenant Blackburn had been leading a squad of Loyalists
down the road when they spotted a wagon leave the Oliver
home in a cloud of dust. Blackburn was not suspicious at
first. He had merely stopped at the home to ask about Rosemary's health. That's when the slave, Jezebel, had informed
him that the doctor and Rosemary had raced off to treat a
smallpox outbreak at McAllister's post at Sparrow Swamp.

"Imagine Lieutenant Blackburn's reaction when he rode
to lend his aid at McAllister's and found everyone there in
perfect health?" Tarleton said before downing his drink.
"He deduced something was amiss, reported to me, and we
have been waiting for your return for . . . what, two weeks,
maybe longer? I was beginning to wonder if you would ever
show your faces."

"I'd like to see to my men, Colonel."

"The prisoners are being held in the barn at this time,"
said Tarleton, shaking his head. "You will join them

shortly. I'm afraid one of your darkies is dead, and another lout, some uncouth lad of questionable parentage, is wounded. They will be taken to Camden and from there to some prison camp, unless they . . ."—Tarleton winked— "are shot attempting escape. You, Mister Drummond, could avoid those consequences by leading us to your colonel's lair. Perhaps even make a profit." He lifted a leather pouch off the desk. Coins jingled as he hefted it.

"No, sir."

"Think it over, lad."

"No."

"Then you are unlikely to see Camden, Lieutenant. Perhaps one of your men will be more co-operative. Lieutenant Blackburn, escort our prisoner to the barn and bring in another prisoner . . . the Irish rascal."

Storm clouds darkened the sky, and the air smelled of rain. Blackburn and two privates led Drummond out the front door. Halfway down the steps rested Levi's body, and the mulatto's blood had turned the steps into scarlet waterfalls.

"Halt!" the British lieutenant called, and Drummond obeyed. "Private Fletcher, see that this rebel is disposed of. I do not wish for the Madison widow or her daughter to see such carnage."

After a salute, the private headed back inside to get help with the corpse. Drummond figured his odds wouldn't get better than this, so he turned swiftly and pushed Blackburn against the remaining private, sending both men crashing down the steps. Drummond sprinted around the rose bushes.

A cold rain began falling—Blackburn screamed the alarm—and Drummond could hear the movement of soldiers. He leaned against the chicken coop, heart and lungs racing, trying to think of a plan. It wasn't dark enough for him to make the woods without being seen. He needed a place to hide, had to find it quickly.

The chickens began squawking, sure to give away his position, so he took a few quick steps. "I think I see him!" someone shouted, and Drummond jumped back against the rickety building.

"Mistah Drummond." He almost jumped at the whisper right behind him. The voice shot out urgently but softly. "It me, Zeke. I jus' feedin' the chickens."

He heard Tarleton next, barking out orders to bring in the prisoner or they would rue the day they entered His Majesty's service. Drummond could see now as the slave tossed aside the feed bucket. The slave took Drummond's hand, and guided him to the pigpen. "In here. Hide in here."

Drummond couldn't quite comprehend. "You hide. I run, and they follow me. Too dark to tell it ain't you. Hurry. Gets in there."

Someone fired a shot, probably at a shadow, and he had no time to argue or develop a better plan. Ezekiel was right. He hurdled the wooden fence, and fell in the slop just as the slave took off running toward the woods.

"I hear him!" came a cry, followed by another shot and feet pounding the wet earth, chasing Ezekiel.

He started to mouth a quick prayer for his friend, but a grunting sow reminded him of his own dilemma. The sow waddled away from the uninvited guest and made her way out of the rain and into a ramshackle shed. Manure, hay, and slop he didn't care to identify lay in a pile against the shed. The whole place reeked, but he crawled to the pile and dug his way into the filth, holding his breath, trying not to gag, and then covered himself with manure and mud.

CHAPTER THIRTEEN

Although soldiers had escorted her upstairs and locked her in the bedroom with Jezebel and Rachel, Rosemary didn't feel like a prisoner—not with her daughter on her lap, locked in a bear hug. She fretted over Drummond, closed her eyes, and prayed silently that no harm would befall him, not now. Her heart ached that she hadn't revealed her feelings to him, let him know that she loved him. Where was he? Had he escaped? Or was he somewhere in the woods, his body pierced by Brown Bess bayonets? Jezebel kept her informed on the whereabouts of everyone else and what they were saying.

By opening the damper in the bedroom fireplace, the portly servant could hear clearly conversations being conducted just below in Dr. Oliver's office. Yes, Master John was with the rebel prisoners. No redcoats had been injured. Ezekiel was allowed to feed the animals. A door opened, and someone was shoved in. Drummond! Rosemary thanked God he hadn't been killed. "They kilt one man," Jezebel reported, and Rosemary closed her eyes and pulled Rachel tighter. She had witnessed that horrible murder, watched the redcoats stab the poor soul wickedly even as he begged for mercy. Another man had been shot in the shoulder, said Jezebel, listening intently, pausing only to fill a brass cuspidor with spit from her snuff. They would be taken to Camden, possibly murdered on the road if they did not reveal Marion's hide-out.

Drummond, she knew, would never talk. They'd kill him. The English muck would murder him and his men.

"They be takin' Mistah Drummon' outside," Jezebel said. "Gonna bring in another rebel, see iffen he take that Judas money."

The cry came from the lower portico, followed by sounds of a struggle. Rosemary jumped from the bed, Rachel still in her arms, hurried across the room, jerked open the door, and stepped outside. Cold rain and wind slapped her face, but she didn't care. She crossed the upstairs portico just in time to see Drummond disappear, followed by Tories. Shouts. Commands. An errant gunshot. Fading light and a steadying rain made vision difficult.

"Get inside, lady!" The young lieutenant, his uniform stained with mud, or blood, stared up at her. "Inside, I say. Immediately!"

"Mommie," Rachel said sleepily. "It's raining."

Rosemary obeyed, closed the door, and placed Rachel on the bed, drying her face and hands with the hem of her skirt. Biting her lip, trying not to cry, Rosemary curled up beside her daughter, desperately wanting to believe Jezebel's words: "Don't you fret none, Miz Rosemary. That Mistah Drummond, he be all right. Good Lord looks after that man, He surely does."

Jason Blackburn nodded at the Loyalist corporal from Kingstree who stood at attention, or as close to attention as one of these Back Country cretins could muster, beside the bedroom door. The soldier handed his Brown Bess to the other guard, and turned the key. After removing his hat, Blackburn rapped lightly on the door before entering Rosemary Madison's bed chamber.

"Colonel Tarleton sends his compliments, madam," he said, "and requests your presence outside."

She glared at him, but rose from the bed, and pulled a blanket over the seven-year-old button who reminded him so much of his own daughters. He cleared his throat. "The girl is to come, too, madam."

"She is asleep," Rosemary fired back harshly.

Swallowing, Blackburn stared briefly at his spatter-dashes. He felt suddenly uncomfortable, and not because of the blood and mud that stained his canvas gaiters. There was no telling why Tarleton wanted the women and children outside, but his orders had been specific. "Everyone," Blackburn said softly, and looked up. "Colonel's orders."

"It is dark, Lieutenant, and cold."

"Everyone is to assemble outside, including your daughter. Please do not force me to order one of my men to carry your child."

His uniform wasn't the only thing in tatters. Every last nerve felt raw, as well as his spirit, perhaps even his humanity after all that he had taken part in since landing in the colonies a lifetime ago. The young widow lifted her daughter, let the girl rest those precious curls on her shoulder, and walked briskly past Blackburn, the fat slave right behind, none of them speaking, not even addressing the soldiers with as much as a malevolent stare. Blackburn closed the door, and told the two guards to follow him.

It had stopped raining. Tarleton had lined up everyone in the front yard. A detail of his own Dragoons kept the rebel prisoners in line with bayonets. Several of Blackburn's Loyalist recruits held lanterns and torches, while the rest stood in formation. A sad-eyed Dr. Oliver stood at the front of the steps, leaning against the nearest stone column for support. Maybe the doctor was in his cups; Lord knows he had put away enough rum. His daughter stopped beside him, and the old slave peered over her shoulder.

"I want down, Mommie," Rachel said, and her mother acquiesced, although she kept a firm grip on the girl's right hand.

"What is going on?" Rosemary Madison asked her father. "Is it Augustin?"

Shoulders sagging, the doctor shook his head and took in a sharp breath. Two torch-wielding volunteers stepped underneath the closest magnolia, and the slave gasped at the sight of the hangman's noose. Blackburn's stomach began to quiver. He wanted to look away, but he was a soldier, an officer.

A pair of green-jacketed Dragoons pushed a blindfolded figure around the corner of the house, prodding him with their sabers until he rested on his knees just below the noose.

Although it remained chilly, Blackburn felt hot. A few soldiers had recently tested their firelocks, and the rotten-egg smell of gunpowder permeated the air. *Brimstone,* he thought, *brimstone and heat.* Someone had opened the gates of hell. " *'Long is the way'*," he muttered to himself, " *'and hard, that out of hell leads up to light'.* " He wondered if he would ever be able to climb out of this purgatory.

The Madison widow must have heard, because she looked back at him, just briefly. Maybe her eyes held some understanding, perhaps forgiveness, but he couldn't really tell. Candles burned inside the house, as well as lanterns on the portico, but he still couldn't see that well, and by the time he stepped closer, the woman had turned back to the assembly.

"This man," Tarleton shouted, "assisted the rebel

Drummond in his escape!" The arrogant redhead stepped forward and whipped off the mask. Rosemary and Jezebel gasped, Rachel looked up at her mother curiously, and Oliver just dropped his head. "He knows where Drummond is, but refuses to tell me. His master ordered him to reveal Drummond's location, yet still he plays deaf and dumb."

Tarleton leaned forward, cupped the slave's trembling chin, and lifted his head. "I give you another chance, Ezekiel," Tarleton said. "Slavery I do not condone, but I damn all seditionists, black or white. Tell me. Save yourself."

Rosemary Madison whispered the slave's name.

The slave shook his head, and Tarleton stepped back with a sigh. A slight nod of the colonel's head sent one of the men to refasten the blindfold over Ezekiel's head, while another lowered the rope. Two other men, carrying lanterns, stepped closer. Tarleton wanted to make sure everyone got a good view of this. One soldier fitted the noose over the black man's head while another tied the other end of the rope to the saddle before mounting the horse.

"Father," Rosemary pleaded.

"Ezekiel will not listen," the doctor said in a hoarse whisper. "There is nothing I can do. He will not obey. . . ."

Tarleton's head bobbed again, and the mounted Dragoon kicked the horse forward, lifting the slave, kicking fiercely, off the ground. Blackburn couldn't watch. "Father!" he heard Rosemary scream, and he forced his eyes open. The woman released her hold on Rachel, and took a step down, only to be stopped by points of bayonets. Retreating, she yelled: "Stop this, you butcher!"

On Tarleton's command, the hangman's horse backed up, lowered the slave to the ground, and Tarleton stepped over the man's supine body. He asked another question, shook his head at the unheard answer, faced the mounted Dragoon, and ordered: "Again. Longer this time."

When they lowered the slave, what seemed a millennium later, Tarleton had to empty a nearby Loyalist's canteen on Ezekiel's face to revive him. Another inquiry begat another negative response, and the colonel stepped back. "Let him rot from that limb," he snapped, and the horse bolted forward, jerking the slave higher. He kicked savagely for several seconds, and Rachel began sobbing. Rosemary alternated her screams at her father and Tarleton. Finally, when the slave stopped kicking, the fat black woman on the portico shoved her way past the first sentries, crying out fiercely: "You let'm down. Let'm down, I says."

It happened quickly, yet the scene would replay in Jason Blackburn's mind for the rest of his life, and possibly all of eternity. Jezebel charged halfway down the steps before one of Blackburn's own men, a stupid Cheraw recruit named William Colquhoun, stepped out of line, shouldered his firelock, and fired. The fat Negro spun around, gripped the banister as blood sprayed from her throat like some unholy artesian well, and collapsed on the steps near the very spot where that rebel had been bayoneted to death just this afternoon. Screams, sobs, chatter, and curses blended together. Before he knew it, Blackburn was cradling Jezebel's head in his arms, trying to stanch the pulsating blood with both hands. Rosemary Madison knelt down beside him, squeezing the slave's hand, begging her father to come quick.

Dr. John Oliver didn't move, just stood against his post as if in a trance. It didn't matter, though, for Blackburn knew even the greatest surgeon in London would be unable to save this life. Already the blood began to lessen. Rachel ran down the steps, weeping uncontrollably, begging

Jezebel to get up. Blackburn stared where the slave's blood had sprayed the poor girl's face.

Jezebel tried to say something. Maybe it was—"Don't worry."—maybe something else. Mostly, she just choked on the blood pooling in her mouth and throat. Her eyes rolled back into her head, and the streaming of blood stopped with the old woman's heart.

When Blackburn looked up, a frowning Banastre Tarleton studied the dead slave, crying woman and child, and dazed lieutenant. The colonel swore and pivoted. "Arrest the man who shot. I gave no order to fire." Removing his shako, he addressed Dr. Oliver: "Sir, you have my word that the idiot who shot your slave will face a firing squad himself, and I shall see that you are recompensed, even if it comes out of my salary. My apologies, Doctor. I did not mean for anything like this to happen."

Rosemary was at him in a second, cursing him, clawing at his face. The doctor still didn't move. Rachel just stared at the dead slave. A few soldiers came to the retreating colonel's defense, and shoved Rosemary away. She fell on her knees at the bottom of the steps, looked up, and spotted Rachel's bloody face. Screaming her daughter's name, she scooped the seven-year-old in her arms, and dashed inside the house, slamming the door behind them.

As it grew quiet, Blackburn took in everything: Tarleton's ashen face, the stunned look of William Colquhoun, the unmoving body of Ezekiel underneath the magnolia, the lifeless face of the black woman he held close. Then, from behind the house, came the cries of sentries, two shots, and a thundering of hoofs. A lone figure on a black stallion rounded the corner of the house, and for a moment no one else in the front yard moved.

"Drummond," Tarleton whispered. His eyes widened in

recognition, and he screamed: "It's Drummond! Stop him! Shoot him!"

The rider never slowed. He plowed over two Dragoons, spooking the hangman's horse that reared and sent its rider crashing against a magnolia. Two men fired, but their bullets thudded into trees, while another tried his firelock, but the weapon misfired. Horse and rider disappeared into the darkness, and, as the hoofs pounded the road, Drummond cried: "Thank Colonel Tarleton for the fine stallion. He can hang Augustin Drummond . . . when he catches him!"

"Colonel," one of the Dragoons said. "He stole your stallion, sir!"

As the rebel prisoners cheered, Jason Blackburn smiled.

"A bloody mess this affair has turned out to be," Tarleton told Blackburn the following morning, sweetening his green tea with Dr. Oliver's brandy. "Make your report, Lieutenant."

"Pursuant to your orders, Private Colquhoun is under arrest. I detailed a party of Loyalists to bury the slave, Jezebel. The man you had hanged recovered, sir, but his speech is impaired."

"He was a darky, Lieutenant. His speech was always impaired."

"No, sir. He slurs his words, sir. Doctor Oliver fears his mind has been damaged."

Tarleton sighed. "I suppose that will cost part of my bloody salary as well."

Ignoring the comment, the lieutenant went on with his report: "The Dragoons returned shortly after dawn, sir. They lost Drummond's trail. They plan to continue their search after breakfast."

The colonel shook his head. "No, they will accompany me."

"Sir?"

"Lord Cornwallis fears the rebels might attack Ninety Six. I am to proceed to the garrison immediately." He sipped his liquor, and smiled. "Perhaps I shall get to face a real soldier, like Greene or Morgan, and not this rabble. No, Lieutenant, Drummond and Marion will be your problem now, but I am sending you some help. Captain Jernegan should arrive in Camden by the end of the week. You will accompany me as far as Camden to await his arrival. Divide your force before we leave. I desire your best soldiers to pursue this Drummond, others should set up a base camp and guard our rebel prisoners. Wait one day, in case Drummond is captured. If not, have a squad take the prisoners we have to Camden." He winked. "The prisoners will not make it there, however. They will be shot while attempting escape."

"Sir?"

"Those are your orders, Lieutenant Blackburn."

"Sir, I protest. That is amoral. . . ."

"You have your orders, mister. If they are not carried out to my specifications and satisfaction, you will be facing a court-martial, alongside Private Colquhoun."

"Yes, sir."

"Anything else to report, Lieutenant?"

"Well, sir, Doctor Oliver's daughter and granddaughter are missing."

Drummond's eyes snapped open, and he reached for one of the horse pistols the Tories and Green Dragoons had so conveniently supplied him. He had not meant to sleep, just wanted to rest his eyes a mite before finding a place to hide until dawn. He could only think of the Madison place, which he knew he could find in the dark.

"Be still," Rosemary told him, and he lowered the pistol.

He took in the surroundings. It was well past dawn on a cloudy, cool morning. The blackened trees stood like quiet silhouettes behind the remains of the Madison cabin—a scorched chimney base, a few charred timbers, mounds of ash and trash. Drummond had tethered the black stallion to the sturdiest seared trunk, although he had dared not remove the saddle in case he needed to make a hasty departure. A few yards from the horse rested Rachel, sound asleep, wrapped in her mother's black cape.

"You reek," Rosemary said, reaching for some humor in the situation.

Drummond remembered hiding in the manure pile until well past sunset. He had heard some commotion in the front of the Oliver house, and thus decided to take advantage of the goings-on to steal away into the barn. There he had found the horses, and he quickly chose what he thought would be the fastest, already saddled, complete with a brace of horse pistols. A Tory had picked that moment to come into the barn, and, mistaking him for some waggoner or striker, stupidly asked him what he was doing with Colonel Tarleton's horse. Drummond had knocked him out with the butt of one of the pistols, relieved the bloke of his Brown Bess and hatchet, and rode away.

He explained all this to Rosemary, who, in turn, told him about the hanging of Ezekiel and death of Jezebel. He ground his teeth as she continued her story, feeling his rancor climb. His right forearm started trembling, and he realized he was clenching the pistol butt till his knuckles had turned white. Drummond relaxed his muscles and assured Rosemary: "Tarleton will pay."

177

She looked at him coldly, then jutted her jaw toward Cameron Branch. "Go to the bank," she said, "and take off these filthy clothes. I will wash them, and tend to your cuts."

"No time," he said. "Them redcoats be sure to search here. That lieutenant, Blackburn, he'll remember this place sure as Christmas."

"You shall do as I tell you, Augustin. If you ride around with pig. . . ." Her face reddened. "Those cuts will get infected. Now quit stalling. I will be down directly."

She scrubbed his hunting frock, leggings, socks, and breeches as best she could without soap, and used a handkerchief to scour his arms and face. Drummond bristled at the frigid water, and cursed when she daubed his cuts with rum from a jug she had taken from her father's house.

When Rosemary laughed, Drummond told her: "I don't rightly find it so almighty amusin'." He sat beside her like some pouting ten-year-old, embarrassed, cranky, in his dingy long-handle underwear, which he refused to take off. "I can wash myself."

"If I thought you would do a good job, I would let you. You keep forgetting that I am a nurse."

"I ain't forgettin' you're a woman, and I ain't."

Still smiling, she said: "Here, this will sting some."

"Least you could do is give me a swallow."

She relented, and Drummond tilted the brown jug. He coughed, lowered the rum, and Rosemary continued her treatment, checking his scarred back, and cleaning the cuts with her father's liquor. She leaned close to him and brushed her liquor-soaked handkerchief against the remaining lacerations on his stubbled cheek. He flinched as the rum burned, and their eyes locked.

Rosemary smeared the final cut. "There." She didn't move, and lost her smile. "You really made me mad," she told him.

"How's that?"

"When you said . . . 'Tarleton will pay'. That is just what Ebenezer would say. This revolution is not about the Tarletons and Jernegans. It is about justice. It is about liberty. It does not matter what those men do. They will pay. God will punish them, but you are a soldier."

"You're a dreamer, Rosemary."

Her jaw dropped, but she couldn't find a response before Drummond continued: "You an' your father, both. This be a war, and it ain't about justice an' liberty. That comes later, iffen we win. This is about killin' as many of the enemy as you can. It's butchery. It's beatin' the other soldier so far in the ground he don't want to get up no more. Hell, there ain't one damned bit of difference betwixt Tarleton an' me, 'ceptin' his uniform. It taken me a while, but I figured that out. Used to believe that I wasn't no real soldier, not cut out to be one, an' maybe I ain't. But I don't have much choice now, do I? I can be a dreamer, an' get myself kilt. Or I can be a fighter, like Colonel Marion, Colonel Pickens, or all them Cherokees I knowed. An' be just as low an' ornery as Wemyss, Jernegan, an' all them. That's war, Rosemary. That's what it does to a body."

He inhaled deeply and stared at the sky, letting his breath out slowly before continuing. "I tell you this, Rosemary, 'cause I be quite fond of you. Don't know how that happened. Sure didn't expect it to happen. But . . . well . . ." Their eyes met again. "I think your father's right. I think you should get on a ship with Rachel yonder an' set sail for Jamaica an' your ma. You'd likely find a good fellow down there, someone who can take care of the both of you."

"I'd like that someone to be you, Augustin." She hadn't meant to say it, certainly didn't expect to say it, but the words just came out.

He reached out and pulled her closer, slowly shaking his head. "Rosemary. . . ."

"Do not tell me that it is too soon, Augustin."

Drummond started to say something but stopped himself. "Never owned no clock," he whispered, and met her lips.

"Mommie!" Rachel's cry echoed from above.

Flushing, Rosemary stifled a groan. Her daughter called out again, and Rosemary glanced at Drummond, told him to get dressed, and she headed up the embankment, telling Rachel she was coming, that everything would be all right.

"I dare not take Rachel back to Father's house," Rosemary said as Drummond tightened the cinch on the stallion. "Not after all that has happened there. . . ." She shook her head.

"Got anywhere you can go till you can get to Jamaica?"

She shook her head sadly. "I was hoping you would take me back to Colonel Marion's camp. As a nurse."

"It's no fit place for a woman an' child."

"What is in the Back Country these days, Augustin?" she demanded, feeling her face flush.

Drummond swung into the saddle. "Try McAllister's tradin' post," he suggested. "He seems a good man for a Tory. Long walk, though. You up to it?"

"Where are you going?"

"Not to McAllister's," he replied. "An' not to Marion, neither."

Her eyes widened. "Augustin," she said softly. "You

can't. . . ." She reached for him, and he leaned forward to squeeze her hand before winking at Rachel. "Take care of your mother, you hear?" he said before kicking the stallion into a lope.

Chapter Fourteen

Irritated at the intruder, a turkey gobbled, took brief flight, landed a few yards from two dogwood trees, and glanced backward once more before scurrying away toward Little Lynches Creek. After Drummond and the stallion settled into the shadows, he pulled the Brown Bess to half cock, emptied the pan, and replaced the powder before closing the frizzen and making sure the flint had been screwed in securely. He did the same with the twin .65-caliber pistols thrust in holsters at the front of the saddle. They were handsome weapons with nine-inch barrels, shield escutcheons, and arrowhead frizzen finials. He hoped they shot as true as they looked.

The weapons gave him three shots, barring any misfire. He wouldn't have time to reload, would have to rely on his hatchet, and hope surprise worked in his favor. The redcoats guarding the prisoners were Blackburn's Tory recruits, not seasoned regulars like Tarleton's Dragoons, and Blackburn wasn't with them—but they numbered eight.

No one would blame him if he didn't try to free the militiamen, not against those odds, but, by God, if he would let Dobie, Catawba Tom, Stokes, Marcel, even untrusting Paddy McGee and hardcase Miles Jensen rot in some prison camp or be shot in the back.

Having trailed them since the wagon and men pulled out

of the makeshift Tory camp at the Oliver house, he figured they were, indeed, bound for Camden, and, following game trails, he dashed ahead through the forest to pick a spot for an ambush. Just across the Little Lynches seemed the best place. Too far from Cameron Branch and Camden to run into any likely redcoat reinforcements but deep enough in British territory that the Tories would feel a tad more relaxed. Any redcoats chasing Drummond would, he prayed, be searching the thickets, swamps, and barns far to the southeast, closer to Marion's den. This close to the creek's ford, the road grew wider, and he would have more room for movement. Then again, so would the Tories.

Just as wagon and riders pulled into view, they stopped, and the driver set the wagon's brake. Frowning, Drummond stood in his stirrups for a better view. Most of the Tories wore plaid kilts, red jackets with blue and white facing, and bluebonnets, but one donned leggings and a brown, single-breasted coat, and another wore a black flapped hat with a turkey feather and green and white striped breeches. Brown Coat ordered the injured Marcel out of the wagon, and he and Striped Breeches dismounted, tied their horses to the right rear wheel, then prodded and pushed the half-breed, shirtless with a dirty bandage over his shoulder, hands tied in front of him, toward an oak tree across the road. The shade tree rose out of a small clearing, several rods from the crossing, where travelers often waited for the creek's water level to fall. The ground was highest underneath the oak, so Brown Coat must have deemed it a likely stumping spot.

Drummond sat back in the saddle, balanced the Brown Bess across his lap, and retrieved Tarleton's spyglass from the saddlebags. He studied every detail, not missing a thing. He couldn't afford one mistake. Brown Coat handed

Striped Breeches his firelock to help Marcel climb in and out of a deep ditch. Both men struggled, for the water was knee deep, the banks slippery. Upon reaching the opposite side, the Tory pulled up Marcel, who moaned and held his wounded shoulder. Without pity, Brown Coat kicked the half-breed to his feet, pushed him against the massive oak, turned, and yelled: "I entreat you to tell us where to find Marion! Tell us, and I spare your life!" He addressed the other prisoners, although the words were meant for Marcel. Or were they?

What did Brown Coat plan to do? Hang him? He hadn't brought a rope. Drummond chewed on his lip and swept the telescope back to the prison wagon, a rickety farm vehicle pulled by four draft horses. Beside the wagon driver sat a guard armed with a blunderbuss, and both men gave Brown Coat and Marcel rapt attention. Each carried a sheathed knife, and the driver also had a belted pistol. Another soldier dismounted, wrapped the reins around the right front wheel, and lifted his kilt to empty his bladder. In the wagon, Catawba Tom and Dobie sat closest to the front, followed by McGee, Jensen, and Stokes, their hands tied in front of them, but their legs apparently neither bound nor shackled. Two other guards, one with a freckled face and the other sporting an unfashionable thick, gray beard, stood in the back, French-style firelocks butted against the wagon bed, equally captivated by the goings-on across the ditch. Trailing the wagon, rode the final soldier, fowling piece strapped over his back and without any other weapon. Drummond first scanned down the road toward Camden, saw only emptiness, then shifted his attention across the creek. Nothing. His heart quickened, his mouth turned to cured tobacco. He shoved the spyglass back in the saddlebag, hefted the firelock, prayed.

"Very well," the Tory across the ditch said, unsheathed his knife, and sliced Marcel's throat, pushing the wheezing, white-eyed militiaman into the ditch.

At first, the murder failed to register. If the Tories planned on killing the prisoners, he had figured they would have shot them, not cut their throats. Drummond caught his breath, comprehending the violence as Timothy Stokes cried out in horror and vomited over the side of the wagon, causing a ripple of laughter among the guards.

Dobie started to rise, but Blunderbuss turned on his haunches, trained the pitiless weapon on the prisoners. Muttering a curse, Dobie sat down. The driver joked at the pissing redcoat, who must have filled his kidneys with gallons of tea or rum earlier that morning. The cold-blooded killing had fazed nary a Tory.

"Alec," Brown Coat said as he wiped the bloody blade on dry leaves. "Bring the boy next. Let us learn if all he can sing is 'Johnny Has Gone For a Soldier'."

Striped Breeches or Alec, the guard nearest the ditch, carefully placed his weapon and Brown Coat's firelock on the ground, sprinted the short distance to the wagon, and practically dragged Stokes, still heaving, over the side.

"Up," Striped Breeches said, kicking Stokes in the stomach. "Up you damned rebel. Be a man."

Jensen stood and railed, but the bearded Tory, in the back of the wagon, lifted his firelock, and jammed the butt into the smithy's midsection. "You'll bring about your deaths quicker this way, laddies," the grinning guard said, and turned to watch Striped Breeches pull Stokes toward the ditch.

Drummond didn't remember cocking his firelock, kicking the stallion, or letting loose with a cry that would have chilled the most hardened Cherokee brave's blood. He had no time to think, just react, as the horse bounded out of the woods. Striped Breeches and Brown Coat were unarmed, and Pissing Tory had finished his chore and was trying to climb into the bay's saddle. The guard at the rear was on horseback, his weapon out of immediate reach, and too tough a target anyway, while the redcoats in the back of the wagon had butted their Charlevilles. The men in the driver's box spun around. Drummond shoved the reins in his mouth, shouldered the Brown Bess, pulled the trigger.

The guard with the blunderbuss somersaulted over the seat, crashing into Dobie. Drummond lost sight of the man's weapon. The horses pulling the wagon squealed, and the bay began kicking violently, rearing, giving Pissing Tory a handful as he held onto the reins with both hands, hurling curses at the terrified animal. Likewise, the two mounts tethered to the rear wheel tugged, pawed the road, whinnied, all of which made the farm wagon unsteady for Bearded Tory and Freckles, as well as the driver. Brown Coat leaped into the wide ditch, out of Drummond's sight, probably trying to climb out and grab his Brown Bess. Striped Breeches released Stokes, cried out, started for the weapons, only to fall face down. Stokes must have tripped him.

"Smart lad," Drummond muttered, then grabbed the reins and pulled the black to a halt. In the wagon, he saw Catawba Tom bent over the dead guard, Dobie working frantically at something, while McGee and Jensen leaped over the sides—the Irishman bolting for the woods and escape, the blacksmith charging Striped Breeches and Stokes. Drummond swore. That's not what he had wanted to happen. In his roughshod plan, once he had killed Blunderbuss, he envisioned Catawba Tom or Dobie jumping the driver, and McGee and Jensen attacking the two guards in the rear of the wagon, belaying any redcoats' defensive actions, giving Drummond just enough time to send the Scots to hell. Instead, the driver was standing, jerking his pistol, and Freckles and Graybeard were shouldering their firelocks. So was Mounted Tory with the fowling piece.

I'm dead, Drummond thought.

He had foreseen using the empty Brown Bess as a club, but the driver was too far away, so he threw it as hard as he could, leaned forward, reached for the twin pistols. That saved his life, for Mounted Tory picked that moment to fire, and the lead shot sailed over Drummond's back. Meanwhile, Drummond's sailing firelock caught the driver awkwardly with a *thud,* sent him toppling off the wagon where he disappeared under the kicking bay's hoofs, the crunching of iron shoe against bone rising above the chaos of battle.

Gripping the butts of both pistols, Drummond swung off the horse, ducked underneath the stallion's belly, dropped to his knees, and raised the weapon in his right hand. The nearest guard, Freckles, fired. The fleet stallion behind Drummond squealed, reared—its iron shoes barely missing Drummond—and bolted toward Camden.

Hoofs also clapped down the road and splashed across the Little Lynches. Drummond stupidly chanced a glance, saw Mounted Tory had dropped his empty weapon and was fleeing. Drummond stood, ignored Freckles, who was panicking, trying to reload his Charleville, tearing a paper cartridge with his teeth but spilling most of the powder. Graybeard, however, had Drummond dead to rights. He pulled the trigger, cursed as the pan flashed but failed to ignite the charge in the barrel. Drummond shot him in the chest—didn't bother to see him drop out of sight—let the smoking pistol fall, tossed the weapon in his left hand to his right, thumbed back the hammer, pulled the trigger as Freckles rammed ball and charge down the barrel. The Tory grunted, leaned against the Charleville for support, and pitched over the side.

"Drummond!"

Hearing Dobie's cry, he spun, tossing away his last firearm, reaching for his hatchet. Too late. Pissing Tory had wised up, let his spooked bay lope off after Drummond's stallion. The redcoat had circled the team, had his firelock sighted on Drummond. Little chance for two misfires in a row, Drummond figured, and braced for a bullet's impact.

The redcoat's face exploded in blood, bits of brain, bone, and bluebonnet while Drummond's ears rang from the blunderbuss' report. In the corner of his eye, he glimpsed Catawba Tom holding the smoking weapon, Dobie at his side. The scout had cut his bonds using the dead guard's knife. Catawba Tom dropped the empty blunderbuss, grabbed the knife, sliced through Dobie's bonds, and both men leaped off the wagon, and began searching for the weapons of dead Tories. Drummond tugged his hatchet free, crawled underneath the wagon, cleared it, spotted the driver, right arm hanging awkwardly, blood pouring from nose and mouth—wounds from the frightened, kicking bay—clawing for the pistol in front of him. Drummond buried the blade into the Tory's back. The Scot soiled his kilt and flattened, groaning. Drummond jerked the blade out, drove it deeper into the driver's back. The groaning ceased, and Drummond looked up.

Ahead of him, Jensen stood kicking Striped Breeches senseless, Timothy Stokes joining in, delivering blow after blow to the redcoat's head and chest. Brown Coat, however, was out of the ditch, had reached the firelocks, shouldered one, trained it on Jensen—a fatal mistake. Jensen wasn't armed, wasn't even considering Brown Coat, just focused on kicking Striped Breeches to death. The Tory should have concentrated on killing Drummond, or running into the woods to hide.

Drummond dived forward, grabbed the dead driver's pistol, fired without aiming, knew immediately that he had missed. The shot, however, startled Brown Coat. He pivoted, snapped off a round that slammed into right wheeler's head, killing the horse instantly. Other horses screamed, although Drummond couldn't hear much other than an intense ringing and dull buzzing.

Another shot rang out—Dobie or Catawba Tom, Drummond wasn't certain—but the ball only clipped bark off a distant tree.

Cursing, the Tory dropped the firelock, reached for the other. By then, Drummond had pulled the hatchet out of the driver's back, and ran, screaming, raising the bloody weapon over his head.

Brown Coat had both hands wrapped around the second Brown Bess, but he froze, took a few steps backward, tripped into the ditch, dropping the firelock. The Tory screamed something, trying to claw his way out of the ditch, managing only to finger mounds of mud and dead grass. Drummond leaped after the killer, sent water splashing. Brown Coat fell on his back, eyes wide, face white as Drummond straddled him. *"Noooooooooo!"* the redcoat thundered. "Mer. . . ." Drummond silenced his plea with the hatchet.

"Tarleton's quarter!" Drummond screamed, freed the blade from Brown Coat's breastbone, brought it down again. Over and over. Ignoring the blood, chopping until he grew too tired, until the ringing and faraway buzzing faded, until he recognized Dobie's voice.

"Drummond! Lieutenant Drummond, sir! Augustin!"

Less than three minutes, perhaps as few as two, had passed since Drummond had charged out of the woods.

He blinked, beheld the mangled body underneath him, realized he gripped a hatchet, its blade dripping, covering his right hand with blood. He looked up. Dobie reached out with both hands, and Drummond tossed away the grisly weapon, let the freedman pull him out of the ditch. He turned again, spotted poor Marcel, eyes closed, dark hair matted by blood and mud. The last thing Drummond could remember was the redcoat cutting the prisoner's throat.

A horse lay dead in its harness, a redcoat, face down, in the mud nearby, his coat ripped, stained with blood. Jensen still kicked one corpse, a Tory in striped breeches. The smithy swore and kicked, kicked and swore, had to be pulled away by Stokes. Catawba Tom had gathered the saddle horses, and began freeing the draft animals from harness. The scout kept calling out McGee's name. Leaving Jensen fuming over the man he had kicked to death, Timothy Stokes sat down, pulled his legs close, buried his head between his knees.

Closing his eyes, Drummond tried to remember the fight. Parts began fitting together, disjointed, far away, hidden in a fog. He could piece together the ambush he had led. Seven Tories lay dead, and he had slain six of them.

"One of the guards got away," Dobie was saying. "Not likely to run into any redcoats soon, but we best ride. Try to catch your horse and that Tory's, then get to Snow's Island. What you think, Lieutenant?"

The words barely registered. Catawba Tom put the reins of a Tory mount in Drummond's left hand, turned, and headed to the woods, crying: "McGee! McGee! Get your arse here or we leave you to redcoats!"

Miles Jensen was beside him then, pumping his blood-stained right hand, saying he would never doubt Augustin Drummond again, not hardly, no sir, bragging that the lieutenant had surely proved himself on this day, damn those Tory souls. Had murdered poor old Marcel, and would have sent the rest to Glory had Drummond not happened along.

"*Huzza! Huzza,* boys," Jensen went on. "We got us a real fightin' man here!"

McGee popped out of the woods, trying to ignore the taunts from Jensen, as the big man met him in the road and used a dead guard's pocket knife to cut the bindings around his wrists.

"Big fighter you turned out to be, Irish," Jensen said. "Figure to find any Tories in them woods?"

Glaring, the Irishman defended his actions. "Thought that's where the rest of Colonel Marion's men was, bub."

"Rest of 'em?" the smithy said with a chuckle. "Hell's bells, Irish, there wasn't no rest of 'em. Just Lieutenant Drummond here. That's all we needed."

Vivid memories of the battle suddenly stung Drummond like icy water, and, coupled with the grotesque scene, made his stomach quiver, almost overpowered him. He walked around the wagon, pulling the horse, also squeamish from the smell of blood and gunpowder, the gore. Freckles lay spread-eagled on the road, staring sightlessly at the winter sky. Graybeard was on the other side of the wagon, clutching his chest in death. Another redcoat, face blown away, lay in the center of the road in a vermilion lake peppered with bits of bluebonnet and gray brain matter.

He took a deep breath, held it briefly, exhaled slowly. His men, all but the sobbing Stokes, stared at him, silent now, worried. Drummond knelt beside the wagon, picked up the matched set of pistols, shoved them in his belt. He put his foot in a stirrup, mounted, choked down the bitterness. He had done what he had to do. *This is about killin' as many of the enemy as you can. It's butchery. It's beatin' the other soldier so far in the ground he don't want to get up no more. Well,* he thought, eying the ambush site a final time, *these lads wouldn't be gettin' up ever again.*

"Grab as many weapons as you can carry," he ordered, voice firm. "Ride double or walk. Tom, see if you can catch my stallion and the bay, then catch up with us. Let's get out of here."

FROM THE MANUSCRIPT
OF THE REVEREND STAN MCINTYRE,
PAGE 65

The turning point of the American Revolution was the Battle of Cowpens, if you ask me, which was fought on the seventeenth of January in 1781. There, General Danile Morgan defeated an overconfident Banastre Tarleton and crippled the British army. Meanwhile, General Nathanael Greene had replaced Horatio Gates as commander of the Continental army in the south, and he began preparing to drive the British out of the Carolinas. Like Morgan, Green knew he had to count on the militia. By the end of December, 1780, Governor Rutledge had promoted ~~Francis~~ Marion and ~~Thomas~~ Sumter to Brigadier Generals. Drummond, likewise, also became better known during this time.

A line in one of many letters on file in the Nathanael Greene Collection at Rhode Island Military Institute notes that a "militiaman under Gen Marian [sic], named Drummon[d], served well as a courier & travel'd many miles for Liberty's caus[e]."

CHAPTER FIFTEEN

January – March, 1781

"Quite the dandies," quipped Dobie, handing back Drummond's spyglass. "Ain't seen such perty uniforms in a 'coon's age." He chuckled, shaking his head, and added: "Reckon they can fight as good as they dress?"

Drummond shoved the telescope into the saddlebags without answering, and began tying the frayed sleeves of a shirt—a dirty piece of muslin that might pass for white—to the barrel of his long rifle. He had taken the .57-caliber weapon off a dead redcoat after a little set-to at Waccamaw Neck, and given the Brown Bess he had been carrying to a new recruit, a captured Tory who needed little persuasion to pitch his green coat and join General Marion. Not that Drummond needed a long rifle at this moment; a long branch would have sufficed.

"Why we need them Continentals to join us?" Miles Jensen argued. "We start winnin' the war, and them regulars decide to float their sticks alongside ourn, after we ain't seen hide nor hair of them boys since Camden. Hell, their hides would be in the loft weren't for us."

"Militia can't win a war," Drummond said. "Gen'ral Marion says that hisself. All we can do is mess up redcoat plans a mite, hit-an'-run. But by joinin' forces, we can stomp 'em like a cockroach, send 'em sailin' for Liverpool. Like Morgan done at the Cowpens."

"Maybe." Jensen snorted and spit. "But iffen that smilin' colonel tries givin' me an order, I'll be stompin' him. Or have Howard sic his dogs on'm."

Kicking the stallion, Drummond rode out of the woods, and stopped in the center of the road, waving the shirt over his head, followed by his two friends. The legion of Continental soldiers halted and considered him before four riders kicked their mounts, and rode ahead. Dobie had been right. In their buff, double-breasted waistcoats with green lapels and cuffs, tan leather breeches, high black boots, and leather caps complete with bearskin roaches, and green turbans, they appeared dressed for a parade, not a war. A dapper man, wearing the epaulets of a lieutenant colonel, smiled after reining in his buckskin mare.

"I am Lieutenant Colonel Henry Lee," he said, waiting for a salute that never came. Militiamen often dispensed with many military formalities.

"Lieutenant Augustin Drummond. General. . . ."

"Drummond?" Lee's eyebrows raised in suspicion. "I was informed a Captain Moore would rendezvous with us. Moore served in the Second South Carolina, you see. . . ."

Light Horse Harry Lee did not bother trying to hide his contempt. Ebenezer Moore had served in a regular Continental Army regiment. He was an officer and a gentleman, not some swamp-runner in gamy hunting frock, breeches, and moccasins.

"Yes, sir, but the capt'n's horse died of colic, so me an' the boys here come in his stead. Anyhow, Gen'ral Marion sends his compliments, Colonel. We're to escort you to camp."

That wasn't the entire truth, but enough for Lee's ears.

Shortly after receiving word of Morgan's victory at the

Cowpens, Drummond had been reporting to Marion when Moore, sobbing over Charger's death, entered Goddard's cabin. When Drummond tried excusing himself, Marion had held up his hand, then ripped into the gaunt captain.

"What has become of you, mister? You were once my most promising young officer and an excellent horseman. Now you act as if the devil has your soul. Charger is dead at your own hand, Captain. Mister Drummond tended to his fine black stallion after it was grazed by a bullet, but you inexcusably let yours die of colic." His head shook sadly. "I find your behavior these past few months unseemly."

When Moore reached for his sword—a cutlass he had taken after one of his attacks—Marion pounded his fist against the cabin wall. "Belay that, Captain! You shall know when I ask for your resignation."

Mouth trembling, Moore absently fingered his button necklace. "I have done my duty, sir," he said hollowly. "I protect my men and have killed. . . ."

"Yes, and I fear that has rendered you useless to our cause." Marion sighed. "See to your horse's burial, mister. Now, if you will excuse us, I have matters to discuss with Lieutenant Drummond."

The look the captain shot at Drummond as he left the cabin was unmistakable. That night, Drummond's straw bed had caught fire while he was sound asleep. Were it not for Catawba Tom, Drummond's legs might have been badly burned. Dobie had reasoned that an ember from one of the campfires started the blaze, but Drummond held another thought. Of course, he would never be able to prove Moore's hand in the matter.

Lee cleared his throat, snapping Drummond's focus to the present. The officer pored over Drummond, Dobie, and Jensen before bowing slightly and forcing another one of his thin smiles. "How pleasant, Lieutenant," the young Virginian said. "Very well, Mister Drummond, lead us on."

For a Loyalist, Reginald McAllister had turned out to be a delightful, generous man. He let Rosemary and Rachel stay in a little room behind his trading post. Of course, Rosemary had to earn her keep, but she found herself enjoying the work. It reminded her of the good years, none of Father's slaves to do the chores, just Richard and her. At Sparrow Swamp, she had relearned how to make johnnycake, forcemeat, and dumplings, how to use pear ash as leavening, pour applejack, and empty cuspidors, even barter with the best of them when McAllister was busy.

The trader had a son about a year older than Rachel, and the two of them hit it off immediately. McAllister's wife, Peninnah, made sure Rachel and Todd got their schooling, and read them a Bible chapter before supper.

There wasn't much to the settlement, just the post, the McAllisters' home, barn, and sheds, plus a Methodist meeting house across the road, cemetery, sawmill, and two other houses—one where sawmill owner Jacob Sanders lived, and farmer Mal Carter's cabin—not to mention a few necessary houses. It seemed two hundred miles from the Oliver mansion on the Salem Road.

Rosemary had written her father after news of the Patriot victory at the Cowpens. He had replied almost immediately, saying that a knife had been pulled from his heart to learn of his daughter's and granddaughter's well-being and whereabouts, that he had been sick with worry, that he cursed himself for being such a fool, and promising that he and Ezekiel would come to them as soon as he could shake loose of Jernegan and his wicked highwaymen.

She had not heard from him since.

Days dragged forever most of the time, and she had Sundays off to accompany the McAllisters to the meeting house, where the Methodist preacher, or whoever felt the call if the preacher couldn't make it, praised King George and those good Loyalists in the Peedee, and prayed for an end to the hostilities. She picked up a few tidbits of gossip and news after church, but most of her information came while working in the post on Saturdays.

Between totaling purchases, packing supplies, or serving liquor, she managed to hear the latest news of the rebellion, albeit with a Loyalist slant. Banastre Tarleton had left Ninety Six and was pursuing Daniel Morgan's Whigs somewhere around Charlotte. . . . Captain Jernegan had set up headquarters at her father's house, and had lost many a horseshoe chasing Marion's renegades. . . . Horrid news for the King! Tarleton's men had been practically slaughtered at the Cowpens just below the North Carolina border. Those unseemly Whigs targeted officers during the first attacks, creating confusion among the gallant English ranks! . . . Light Horse Harry Lee and Marion had joined forces in late January in a surprise attack on British forces at Georgetown, but Colonel George Campbell's men had driven off the Whig *banditti*. . . . The supply depots at Menial's Ferry and Wadboo had been destroyed. . . . Lee's Legion left South Carolina after Georgetown to rejoin General Greene, and routed a Loyalist force on the Haw River in North Carolina. . . . A Loyalist party was ambushed on the Santee Road. One survivor said he saw some fiend cutting a button off brave Major Harker's coat. . . . Captain Jernegan has struck back, destroying Whig Ben Coker's grist mill and slaughtering Will Draper's flock of sheep. . . . Thomas Sumter was dead. God save the King. No, the damned Gamecock was still breathing, tormenting decent Loyalists along the High Hills of the Santee. . . . Colonel Wellborn Ellis Doyle and his New York Volunteers had joined up with Jernegan, and Marion was soon to be caught and hanged. . . . Cornwallis, with the remnants of Tarleton's once-mighty British Legion, was bound to catch up with Greene's Continental Army and thrash him somewhere in North Carolina.

Often she fretted over Squire Marion and especially Drummond, and fought back a tear when Rachel asked her if it would be all right if she remembered Drummond in her prayers, even though he had forgotten her birthday back in November.

> *Forgetting the mercies of Great Britain's King,*
> *Who saved their forefathers' necks from the string,*
> *With hunting shirts and rifle guns,*
> *They renounce all allegiance and take up their arms,*
> *Assemble together like hornets in swarms.*
> *So dirty their backs and so wretched their show,*
> *The carrion-crow follows wherever they go. . . .*

The singing outside stopped, and Rosemary sighed with relief. She sat in the meeting house with Todd and Rachel, reading a verse from First Corinthians, trying to hold the interest of the children. The sermon had ended ten minutes ago, and the men had gathered outside to sing loyal songs like "The Rebel" while the women prepared a feast in front of McAllister's post.

Rosemary found her place and continued: " 'That your faith should not stand in the wisdom of men, but in the power of God. Howbeit we speak wisdom among them . . .'."

Peninnah entered, her face pale, eyes red. Something was wrong, and Rosemary closed the Bible, stood, waited.

Mrs. McAllister wet her lips, and whispered: "Rosemary, dear, you had better go outside. I will look after Todd and Rachel."

She handed the Bible to the post trader's wife, and took a hesitant step forward.

"Be strong," Peninnah said.

"I want to go with Mommie," Rachel began, but Peninnah shot out: "No, you have to stay!" Her voice softened. "Just for a few minutes, child. Let Miz Peninnah read to you from the Good Book."

Rosemary stepped outside into the March afternoon. Churchgoers had gathered around a mounted party, and she immediately recognized Francis Marion. Behind him rode Colonel Horry, followed by five or six partisans she didn't recognize. The last man was Drummond, and her heart pounded. She had feared him dead, had thought Squire Marion was bringing word of his death. Next she saw the pack animals trailing Drummond, two bodies wrapped in canvas, draped over the horses' backs. She knew.

"Oh, no," she said, gripping a wooden column for support.

Marion dismounted, hurried to her. The rest of his men looked down. "I am terribly sorry," he told her, taking her hands. "We found him and Ezekiel on the Salem Road. I warrant he was on his way to see you."

Tears cascaded down her cheeks. She made herself nod. "Father said he would . . . ," she began. "What happened?"

The general shook his head. "I. . . ."

"May I see him?"

"No, child. Remember him alive. Not like . . . this."

Someone, she thought it was Jacob Sanders, cursed, kicked dust at the partisans, and shouted: "A fine row have you hoed, Marion! You kill this poor lady's father and have the gumption to bring his body here!"

"A lie!" Peter Horry said. " 'Twas l-likely the . . . hand of . . . J-Jer-Jernegan's . . . D-D-De-Despoil-ers!"

"Despoilers," Mal Carter shot back. "A word you rebels use on His Majesty's soldiers, yet 'tis you who are the despoilers!"

"Be gone!" another churchman shouted, then hefted a rock, and hurled it at Drummond. It sailed over his head, but spooked a few horses. "You have delivered your bloody cargo. Be gone! We shall bury John Oliver with his own kind, men true to King George. Be gone, I say, damn your Whig souls."

Marion leaned closer, kissed Rosemary's forehead, and whispered: "Lieutenant Drummond and I will stay if it is your desire, no matter what these men say. Please believe that I had no hand in. . . ."

"I know," she said, sniffling. Salty tears landed on her tongue. "I know," she repeated, softer this time. "Still, you should ride away now, before this turns ugly. Tell Augustin. . . ." She choked out something unintelligible, and a woman grabbed her shoulder and pulled her close. Rosemary Madison buried her face and cried. She did not hear Marion walk away, mount his horse, and lead his men toward the swamp.

FROM THE MANUSCRIPT
OF THE REVEREND STAN MCINTYRE, PAGE 71

One of the oldest graves in neighboring Florence County can be found in the cemetery behind Sparrow Swamp Methodist Church. It reads simply "John Oliver, Murdered by Tories, 1781." The tombstone isn't original but one erected in 1813. A few yards away lay another weathered peace of marble, and this one appears original from the Revolution. The name on the gravestone had disappeared with age, but one can make out the epitaph: "A Loyal English Soldier." Strange, isn't it, that the words "Murdered by Tories" and "Loyal English Soldier" can appear so close together. But that was the Peedee in the early 1780s.

Who was this forgotten soldier? No one knows. Some claim it is the final resting place of James Jernegan, but historians discredit that. The legend of Jernegan had certainly grew about this time. It is said that as he burned one Whig's house, the wife of the estate cried out, "You bloody fiend. You and your men are nothing but despoilers." Like "Swamp Fox" and "Gamecock," the names "Bloody Jim Jernegan" and "Jernegan's Despoilers" took root.

CHAPTER SIXTEEN

March – April, 1781

Once they had forded Sparrow Swamp, Drummond galloped to the front of the column. "I'd like to go back there," he told the general.

"So would I, Lieutenant," Marion said. "Alas, we sha'n't. I asked Rosemary, but she knew our staying would have fueled a most ticklish affair. Mayhap we remained, blood would have spilled, and I loathe the day I wage war on civilians, especially on the Sabbath. No, Rosemary and Rachel will pull through this tragedy. Reginald McAllister is a God-fearing soul, a Tory perhaps, but an honorable man." Shaking his head, Marion sighed. "Like Doctor Oliver was. I shall miss him."

Peter Horry, riding on the other side of Marion, said tightly: "It . . . it . . . was . . . J-Jerne-gan. Only B-Bl-Bloody . . . Jim would do . . . that."

The corndodgers and rum in Drummond's stomach began boiling. He swallowed down the venom, and, staring straight ahead, spoke: "Wasn't Jernegan done it."

He felt the stares of Marion and Horry bore into him, but he still looked ahead, though he would have been hard pressed to tell anyone what he saw, and he had traveled this path many a time. "The killer taken a button off the doc's waistcoat," Drummond said at last, "an' one offen Zeke's shirt."

* * * * *

Ebenezer Moore slipped the necklace over his head, put on his sword harness, and finally his leather helmet. The buttons numbered twenty-three now, but he had lost the one he had pulled off Ezekiel's smelly shirt. The wooden button had broken shortly after Moore had pocketed it. No matter.

Funny, he had once liked John Oliver, yet felt not even a farthing of remorse. The man was a Tory, even had the gall to let a killer like Jernegan camp on his property, the same lout who had flogged Rosemary. A man who harbored such a cut-throat was no better than those despoilers and deserved to die. As for Ezekiel, well, the slave was just another casualty of war.

He adjusted the hat, spun around, marched to Goddard's cabin, entered without knocking, and stood in front of Brigadier General Francis Marion. The partisan leader did not wait for Moore to pull the door closed.

"How dare you, Captain! How dare you butcher a good man like John Oliver. Why?"

"He was a Tory, General."

Marion shook his head. "A pet Tory, yes, practically neutral. Not some fire-breather. Have you forgotten what Oliver did for our cause? Have you forgotten that last autumn he saved many of our men's lives? Do you not remember what he and his daughter did?"

"I have not forgotten a thing about Rosemary," he heard himself saying, turning her name into a hiss.

"Who rode with you in this affair?"

"McGee. Howard. Turner, Pierce, and Strickland." He quickly added: " 'Twas I, however, who killed John Oliver, General, and the slave."

"So I gather. This time I shall have your saber, Captain Moore."

He had expected this—why else would Marion demand that he report at once?—so he simply pulled the cutlass from its scabbard, and dropped it in front of Marion. Besides, he was sick of Francis Marion and Augustin Drummond, wanted to be rid of the whole damned militia, yet he still felt the need to safeguard his men. "Will you run off McGee, Howard, and the others?"

"No, but I will meet with them. I will inform them of the way we must conduct ourselves. We fight men waging war on us. We do not kill the innocent and plunder, no matter where their loyalty lies."

That made Moore laugh. "You'll lose a lot of your boys, General. They'll join up with Sumter. I hear the Gamecock wants to let his boys share any loot they can get from Tories and the like, anyone who is not a Patriot."

"Brigands," Marion said. "I'll not go down in history being compared to Jernegan's Despoilers. I am putting your name in my book, Moore, of disgraced officers no longer under my command. I am also writing a letter to General Greene and Governor Rutledge. You are no longer associated with my militia."

"Washing your hands of me, sir?"

"Get out!" Marion spat. "Make haste, Moore, and leave Snow's Island. If ever I see you again, I swear we shall meet on a field of honor, and I will avenge John Oliver's death."

"You'll see me, General," Moore said as he turned to leave. "In hell."

Drummond swung from the saddle, and handed the stallion's reins to Dobie. He had ridden hard the past two days, dodging redcoats, greencoats, and two or three armed parties that might have been partisans but could also easily have been Tories. He found Marion's camp on the Sampit River, northwest of Georgetown, and, before Dobie led away his lathered mount, he pulled from the saddlebags the message General Greene had given him in North Carolina.

"Where's the general?" he asked while stretching. His legs felt cramped, and his back ached like blazes.

Dobie jutted his chin toward a campfire, and Drummond hurried to hand the sealed papers to the commander. Marion looked a fright, pale, unshaven, his Second South Carolina uniform in tatters now, barely distinguishable from the other outfits worn by his militia. Horry, Captain Hunter, and a few other officers surrounded the general. No one said a word.

Marion took the paper, glanced back at Drummond, and offered him his tin cup. Drummond thanked him, and drank greedily before remembering Marion always added vinegar to his water. He forced down the liquid, set the cup on a table, and tried not to gag.

"Colonel Lee is on his way back," Marion told the officers. "General Greene wants a joint attack on the redcoat fortresses along the Santee."

He expected that to cause a few huzzas, but the officers stared at their feet. Studying the camp, Drummond noticed nothing but long faces. No music. No laughter.

"Too late for us," one of the officers muttered.

Drummond glanced at Marion, but the general was lost in thought, so he turned to Hunter for an explanation. "Redcoats and Tories under Doyle, Jernegan, and Blackburn captured Snow's Island," the captain said heavily. Feeling suddenly weak, Drummond squatted.

"Got our stores, horses, several men," Hunter continued. "We are considering disbanding. Not much we can do."

Cursing underneath his breath, Major James snapped a branch, and tossed it into the fire. Drummond looked to Marion, but the general had not moved. Drummond's head shook as he thought of those left on Snow's Island: Miles Jensen, Paddy McGee, Clarence Howard and his dogs. He hoped they had escaped but realized, if they had, they would likely be in camp by now. Drummond muttered an oath.

The men began gathering around the officers' fire now, their weary faces reflecting the firelight. Maybe one hundred, probably not that many. Four months ago, four hundred had camped on Snow's Island. These weren't the part-time fighters who joined Marion between plantings and harvests. These were true Patriots, men who had weathered disease at Snow's Island, bullets, canister, bayonets. Some had been with Marion since 1775.

"Sir?" Dobie spoke softly. "What news, General?"

Marion turned, swallowed, straightened. "Men, sighing and croaking will do us no good," he said. "We have lost many men. News comes that General Greene's army was badly bloodied at Guilford Courthouse in North Carolina. Bloody Jim Jernegan has burned many of your homes. I know your hearts are weary. So is mine. I know you have tired of this war, as have I, but, friends, if we have been ruined by resisting these tyrants, what will become of us if we lie down tamely and give them our firelocks?"

Gripping the hilt of his sword, one fashioned from a saw-mill blade by Miles Jensen, Marion continued: "Disband, many of you say." His voice grew louder, his eyes harsher. "I say no." Softer again, thoughtfully: "Yet any of you who wish to retire to his home, so be it. I bid you no ill will.

Nevertheless, if my eyes do not deceive me and I read your faces truly, then those of you who stay, know we will fight." Now his voice rose to a crescendo. "Colonel Lee comes with his legion. Liberty is not lost, but, even if it were, I would rather die fighting than live in wretchedness under a tyrant King." He practically shouted his final sentence: "Look sharp, Captain Jernegan, for you shall soon feel the bite of Patriot buck and ball."

The men answered with a resounding—*Huzza!*—and Drummond joined their cheers.

He sat underneath a mulberry tree near the Tory sawmill at Sparrow Swamp, spyglass in hand, peering across the road and fields at McAllister's post. Ebenezer Moore had decided against joining Thomas Sumter's militia. He had met the Gamecock once, and found him too haughty, too political. Briefly he had considered riding to North Carolina, finding General Greene, offering his services to the Continental Army, but that was no good. That cocksure Marion had sent a letter to Greene, denouncing Captain Moore, and Marion had much influence among the Patriots. So he sat here, spying on Rosemary Madison, working up courage to ride over there, to face her. He wasn't sure if Marion or Drummond had told her who had killed her father. He didn't really care if they had.

Word came a day earlier of Colonel Doyle's raid on Snow's Island. The partisans had been caught with their breeches down, and the Swamp Fox had lost his impregnable fortress, leaving him nowhere to hide. Jernegan would now be able to run down the ruffians. The Tories at McAllister's celebrated well into the night. Moore felt like joining them, but he just stayed hidden in the woods, laughing at the foolish Francis Marion.

He downed a stirrup dram of rum, which heightened his courage, and swung into the saddle, adjusted the button necklace, and started to spur the dun into a lope but stopped when another figure rode out of the swamp. Moore adjusted the spyglass for a better look. A redcoat, leaning forward, about to fall off a worn-out bay. Another time, another place, and the British soldier would have soon joined the dead, and Moore would have collected another button.

The horse faltered in front of the store, and the redcoat fell into the dust. The door opened, and Rosemary Madison hurried to the man, turned him over, and started shouting orders. McAllister and his rotund wife came to her aid, helped her lift the wounded redcoat, and they all disappeared inside the post.

Frowning, Moore shoved the telescope into its case. He thought of the auburn-haired beauty who had spurned him, of Marion, of all he, Ebenezer Moore, had done, and, cursing himself, pulled his helmet down tighter, turned the dun around, and rode into the forest.

His eyes fluttered open, then closed tightly, blinded by the light. Voices spoke to him, soothing, feminine, an angel's. Jason Blackburn forced his eyelids open again, and slowly the faces came into focus. A striking young woman was telling him something, her face intense. Behind her stood a bald man and plump woman. He knew these people, just couldn't place them. The younger woman's lips kept moving, but he heard only some thick drone. He could smell something, too, something awful. Had he soiled himself in the fight at Snow's Island?

Snow's Island. His eyes darted as he tried to remember. He had been there, could recall the screams of battle, deafening musketry, calls of the swamp. Dogs. Barking dogs.

They had attacked him, ripping his right arm, biting, scratching. Intense pain. He knew he had shot one with his pistol, and his recruits had come to his aid, killing the beasts from Hades. Then some rebel had charged them, screaming at them for murdering his dogs. A sergeant had shot the man in the chest, and he dropped atop his animals. Other kilt-clad Loyalists fell upon the wounded man with bayonets. Blackburn remembered pulling himself in the saddle, kicking the animal, telling his troop to follow him, to keep the attack going, and he let the horse carry him on, through briars and moors. Tears blinded his vision, and finally he saw only the blazing light.

The woman felt his forehead, bit her lip. He recalled her, Rosemary Madison, who had been flogged, the daughter of the good doctor. He knew the other two as well, Reginald and Peninnah McAllister, loyal subjects of His Majesty, set-,tlers at Sparrow Swamp. What were they doing?

Rosemary Madison spoke again, stood. The trader, his face ashen, climbed on top of Blackburn, leaned forward, gripped his shoulders, pinned him down. His wife took hold of Blackburn's right arm, stretched it, squeezing her eyelids tightly as she did so.

Blackburn bit his lips in pain, mouthed a prayer, called out for Susan and his children, stopped, watched in horror. . . .

Rosemary Madison, her face a mask, brought an axe over her shoulder, took a step forward, exhaled, said something again, and swung. Blackburn screamed as the blade came down.

FROM THE MANUSCRIPT
OF THE REVEREND STAN MCINTYRE,
PAGES 82–83

In his petition for pension, filed in 1819, a copy of which can be viewed at the University of South Carolina Archives, Augustin Drummond notes that he returned to his company in the spring of 1781, and engaged in battles at Fort Watson, Fort Motte, and other militia affairs, surviving the bloody charge at Quinby, as General Greene returned to South Carolina. Greene's Continental forces had been battered at Guilford Court House, but while technically a British victory, Cornwallis army was itself bloodied and the English lord took his forces north to Virginia, where destiny awaited him and George Washington at Yorktown.

Greene fought Rawdon in an indecisive battle at Hobkirk's Hill that April and staged an unsuccessful siege at 96 in May-June. At length, however, his Army hooked up with Marion, Lee, Sumter & Pickens. Greene's arrival meant that Marion's militiamen were now part of the Continental Army, and the combined forces was bound to meet Col. Alexander ~~Stuart's~~ Stewart's forces, Lord Rawdon having returned to England in ill health, near the Santee River. The Battle of Eutaw Springs for some reason has been overlooked by historians, lost in the shadows of engagements like Cowpens, Kings Mountain and Fort Moultrie. It was also Drummond's last official action in the Revolution.

CHAPTER SEVENTEEN

September, 1781

Croaking bullfrogs echoed through the dense pines that trapped in suffocating heat and steam. A brief afternoon shower had brought some relief, but now the sun had reappeared, turning the forest into a furnace. It had to cool off soon, although the summer had been one of the hottest Back Country settlers could remember. Drummond remained crouched, long rifle cradled over his thighs, tense, not moving, hardly breathing, peering through sweat at the deer trail.

A dark figure moved easily toward him, running without making a sound, stopped suddenly, and ducked behind a pine. Drummond smiled and whistled the piercing *bob-bob-bob-white* of a quail. A crow's *kaw* answered the signal, and Drummond stood with a groan. His back ached again, probably always would. Catawba Tom stepped around the tree.

"You get better," the Indian said. "Almost no see you."

Drummond enjoyed the compliment but got down to business. "Spot Stewart's camp?"

The scout nodded with a grunt. "At big plantation at Eutaw Springs. Got Nelson's Ferry guarded. Heap redcoats. Foot soldiers, horse soldiers, big guns."

"More'n we got?"

" 'Bout same. Come big fight. Be many dead. Bluecoats. Redcoats. Maybe me. Maybe you."

"Maybe." There had been enough deaths this summer. Captain Roche had fallen during the slaughter at Quinby, and Sergeant Pierce had also been wounded there, dying three days later on the banks of Lynches Creek. Caleb Turner fell to dysentery, and camp fever had claimed the lives of Ben Strickland and sweet-singing Timothy Stokes, who had not sung much at all since Miles Jensen's capture during Doyle's raid on Snow's Island. Paddy McGee had escaped capture, though. Captain Hunter had found the Irishman near Sparrow Swamp, hiding in the brambles, and brought the fighter back to camp in time for the assault at Quinby, where he was shot in the thigh but recovered. Two former Tories, Robert Embleton and Sean Devlin, had fallen beside McGee there. Drummond had gotten to know the two men, even liked them. A pity. A waste. Too many had already died, and Catawba Tom was right—more would fall tomorrow.

Drummond wiped his forehead, sighed, and studied the Indian in amazement. "Has anyone ever seen you sweat, Tom?" he asked.

"No." The Indian grinned. "And nobody will."

Francis Marion drained the last of his vinegar and water before rising from the table to face his officers. Andrew Pickens, back at arms against the British after redcoats had torched his home, stood beside him, eyes trained on a map. Drummond had not spoken to Pickens since Kettle Creek. His stomach bubbled as he wondered what his old boss thought of him, but soon his attention turned to his immediate commander.

"General Greene," Marion said, "has given us a great honor. We lead the assault." No one spoke, likely too exhausted from the heat and campaigning all summer. "We will face hardened warriors, the Sixty-Third and Sixty-Fourth regiments of Foot, as well as the Irish Buffs, but Colonel Stewart has been waiting for the weather to cool, and he expects us to do the same, so we shall take him by surprise, drive him into the Santee." Marion offered a rare smile. "I know I ask a lot of you men, but we must not fail, not with victory within our grasp. Do your best, and remember . . . it has been an honor and privilege to serve with you gallant Christians. Report to your troops. Dismissed."

Drummond turned with the other officers to leave, but Marion called his name and beckoned him over. He approached tentatively. Marion's face remained unreadable, and Pickens, no longer focused on the map, stared like a preacher about to deliver fire and brimstone. Of course, that was his nature. "Lieutenant," Marion said softly, placing an arm around his shoulder, "I desire you to take over Captain Roche's company. Sergeant McGee has been leading them, but I want an officer in command tomorrow."

Almost all former Tories comprised Roche's company. They would be facing old comrades, and Drummond knew that would entail some of the bitterest fighting. What was it he had heard General Greene say, only partly in jest? *The way this war is going, we shall soon be fighting the enemy with British soldiers, and they will be fighting us with ours.*

"I'll do my best, sir," Drummond said.

"I know you will, son," Marion said kindly.

"So do I," Andrew Pickens said, extending his hand. "You always have."

He marched at the head of his company, mentally checking his accouterments for battle. Long rifle primed and charged, patch box and powder horn full, spare flints, lead balls in hunting bag, hatchet and knife in his belt. He had also bored five holes into a small board and covered the holes with a patched ball for quicker reloading. Most officers carried only saber and pistol into battle, maybe a spontoon, but Drummond preferred a rifle. He would be fighting alongside his company.

Beside him marched Paddy McGee, his firelock loaded with a .69-caliber ball and three .30-caliber projectiles. Buck and ball, it was called, and quite deadly. A lot of the militiamen had charged their Brown Bess and Charleville weapons that way. Some had even rammed old nails and bits of scrap iron down the barrels, anything they could think of to perfect this art of killing.

They broke camp at Burdall's Plantation at four o'clock, began covering the seven miles to Eutaw Springs, following the River Road. The predawn gray sky began lightening, and the coastal moss, dripping from the blackjack limbs, hung still. Not a breath of air, and an hour later, the rising heat and humidity could be felt. It would be another scorcher. Drummond reached into his leather pouch, grabbed three balls, and stuck them in his mouth. A Delaware major had given him the tip. They would slake his thirst and provide easier access for reloading, as long as he didn't swallow them.

The command came to halt, and Drummond found the sun. Eight o'clock maybe. They had covered three, four miles. Pot shots sounded to his left, toward the Santee. Thundering horses. A skirmish. The word passed down the line that Major John Armstrong's North Carolina cavalry and John Henderson's South Carolina militia had ambushed a redcoat cavalry patrol, managing to capture about a hundred unarmed regulars who had been sent out to gather yams.

"Yams," one of the old Tories in Drummond's company said. "I could use some yams myself."

"Don't care much for yams," another said.

"Hush," a third voice called out. "You makin' me hungry."

The fourth voice was General Marion's. "Quiet, men. Companies, form for battle."

Drummers and fifers put down their instruments, picked up the jugs being distributed, and walked down the lines, letting each soldier take a swallow of rum. A blue-eyed boy held the jug up for Drummond, but he shook his head. Drinking finished, the soldiers fell in line, Marion's militia on the right, Malmedy's North Carolinians in the center, Pickens's men on the left. Behind them came the Continentals from Maryland, Virginia, and North Carolina, with Kirkwood's Delaware troops and William Washington's cavalry in the rear, Lee's Legion on the right flank, and Henderson's infantry and Hampton's cavalry guarding along the Santee.

"Forward," Marion said. "March."

Suddenly Drummond wished he had taken a slug of spirits. He could see skirmishers lining the clearing just ahead. He thought of the black stallion stabled back at Burdall's with most of the militia horses, and wondered what Rosemary was doing back at McAllister's. Drummond ground his teeth. *Block those thoughts. Stay focused. Think of nothing but killing.*

The British line fired first. A few slugs dug up the ground thirty rods in front of the partisans, out of range. "Hold your fire," Drummond said. "Hold your fire." Other officers echoed similar orders down the militia line.

Gunfire erupted on both flanks. "Eyes front!" someone barked. Another order was lost as cannons opened fire. The foot soldiers ahead had reloaded, fired again. A bullet whistled over Drummond's head. A second later came the sickening *thunk* of a British ball tearing into flesh and bone.

Marching on. Sweating. Stopping. The din of commands: Poise firelock! Cock firelock! Take aim. Fire!

The stock of Drummond's rifle slammed against his shoulder. He heard himself yelling—"Prime and reload!"—found himself doing just that, pulling the hammer to half cock, grabbing his horn, priming the pan, closing the frizzen, filling the tip charger, pouring the powder down the barrel, grabbing his loading board, positioning a patched ball over the barrel, ramming it home.

"Forward, march. Halt. Poise firelock. Cock firelock. Take aim. Fire!" Repeating the process. His eyes burned from smoke. The pan flashed, the rifle boomed, echoed by hundreds of other rifles and firelocks. The painful ringing and dull buzzing in his ears returned, but not enough to drown out the wretched screams of men torn apart by buck and ball, rifle shots, and the mutilating fire of nail and iron. "Reload. Fire at will!"

On a knee now, out of the smoke, he located a redcoat holding a spontoon. Aiming. Pulling the trigger. Flash. Explosion. Kick in the shoulder. Cloud of smoke lifting. The British officer on the ground. Priming again. Realizing his bullet board was empty. He had already fired six rounds. Grabbing a bullet from the bag, patch from the box carved into the rifle stock. Feeling his men move past him, their firelocks, quicker to reload than long rifles, ready. Standing, falling in line. The redcoats vanishing in acrid smoke. His own men screaming. Tripping over bodies. Standing, firing, reloading, and Colonel Peter Horry stammering: "C-c-ch-ch-cha. . . . Oh, d-d-damn it. You k-know what I mean!"

"Charge!"

Howling like a Cherokee, sailing into the redcoat line, he had no idea what was happening around him—whether the British had turned back Malmedy's and Pickens's troops—

if Marion's militiamen were the only ones here—even if Marion himself had retreated. Drummond planted the barrel of the long rifle against a stunned redcoat's chest. "Please," the Englishman began, releasing his spontoon, but Drummond pulled the trigger. In the corner of his eye, he glimpsed one of his men killing another Briton at point-blank range before falling with a bayonet in his back. The infantryman withdrew the bayonet, started to thrust it again, but fell, tackled by one of Drummond's men. The Carolinian raised his hatchet, brought it down violently, stood, surged forward.

The balls in his mouth were gone. He wasn't sure if he had fired them, spit them out, or swallowed them. He started to reload, thought better of it, grabbed the barrel, and swung his weapon like a club, hearing it connect against the back of a redcoat's neck. Suddenly Drummond was down, pinned by a white-faced soldier, who slashed with a knife. Hot pain and blood shot out of Drummond's left forearm. The redcoat withdrew the blade, and his face changed expression. Blood seeped from both corners of his mouth, his eyes rolled back in his head, and he dropped the knife, pitched over. Drummond looked at the knife in his own hand, had not remembered pulling it from his belt, but understood he had jammed it to the hilt in the soldier's belly, twisting the blade relentlessly. He checked his left arm, glanced at the blood streaming down his torn shirt sleeve, dripping from his fingers. It hadn't struck an artery, would have to wait.

He sheathed the knife, replaced it with his tomahawk, just in time to parry a bayonet thrust. He became only vaguely aware of his own actions. Kicking the man in his groin, seeing him gasp and crumple, bringing the hatchet blade down into the man's back. Pulling the blade free, slashing another soldier's neck, throwing the hatchet, losing it in the smoke but hearing it strike flesh. Screaming, slashing a coatless soldier with the knife, practically disemboweling the fellow.

He bent over, grabbed the barrel of his long rifle again, picked it up, swung. Blood poured from a British officer's nose and mouth. The redcoat spit out teeth, staggered, groaned as a bayonet ripped into his back. Moving forward again, driving the redcoats back. Realizing he had broken the rifle's stock, Drummond dropped the useless weapon, bent over, pulled a pistol from a dead officer's belt. Cocked. Fired. Tried to reload.

Air exploded from his lungs, and he was down, struggling, clawing at some giant redcoat on top of him. He couldn't breathe. The man's weight was crushing. He fended off a bayonet thrust aimed for his throat, felt the blade bite into his shoulder, nicking the skin like a razor. An iron fist slammed into his left temple, stunning him. Shaking his head, vision returning, he spotted the soldier raising the broken bayonet—his firelock gone—over his head with both hands.

Drummond was free to move his arms, but he had no weapon, and the giant assailant's weight had knocked the wind out of him. Thinking of Rosemary, he braced for the blade to shred him, kill him. Waiting. Nothing. The redcoat had frozen, but still had Drummond pinned. Drummond looked up, saw the man's face, the agony, and recognized Miles Jensen.

The big blacksmith whispered Drummond's name, closed his eyes, brought the bayonet down swiftly. Drummond held his breath, stunned to see the blade curve upward and pierce Jensen's own chest. The man sank, toppled, and Drummond scrambled to his knees, looked down at Jensen, still clutching the bayonet as blood soaked his chest.

"I'm sorry," the smithy said, barely audible, before death shut his eyes.

Drummond breathed deeply, making his lungs work, staring at the dead man who had been captured at Snow's Island, forced into the British service rather than face summary execution, only to take his own life rather than kill a friend.

He scrambled away, picked up a rifle, ran forward, ignoring the pain in his arm, back, shoulders, and neck. Whoops. Cheers. Musketry. Groans for water, for mothers, for mercy. The cannon had fallen silent. Stewart's troops kept falling back, retreating, and suddenly Patriot militiamen were sweeping through rows of tents. Shrieks for mercy were answered with "Bloody Tarleton" or "Tarleton's quarter." He barely recognized his own voice taking up the cry of vengeance.

Drummond staggered on, fired the weapon, pulled a bullet from his bag, realized his .57-caliber balls were too big for the rifle he had grabbed, cursed, primed and charged the rifle anyway, left the ramrod in the barrel, aimed, pulled the trigger. The ramrod whistled as it spun after the fleeing soldiers.

The wave of attackers slowed, stopped. Redcoats ran without order, hurdling a fence, hiding in a garden beside the red brick house. The Patriots could turn this into a rout if only they kept at it, but his men were quitting, gobbling down hot rice gruel, sipping tea over British campfires. Others plundered the abandoned enemy tents. Stopping! Overpowered by their own hunger and weariness. One man dropped on his knees in front of a fire, began sobbing.

"Come on!" Drummond shouted. "Don't stop. Get up. Up. Keep on fightin'!"

One soldier answered him with a curse, stuffed his mouth with a peach, washed it down with scalding coffee. A bullet slammed into the back of the man's head, and he spit out blood, peaches, teeth, coffee, and fell face down in the fire.

The redcoats were storming back in a counterattack. Stewart's Buffs had seen the attack falter, realized they could save the day. Drummond grabbed a sobbing soldier, shoved the boy back toward Greene's line, shouting: "On your feet! Here they come!"

A bullet cut a furrow across his ribs. Other soldiers dropped. Some shot. Another officer yelled: "Fall back! Fall back! Keep order!"

Moving again, carefully, taking a few steps, trying to prevent his men from running. Something gripped his left ankle, pulled him to the ground, and he landed with a *thud*. A bloodied hand gripped tighter. "Please," the redcoat whispered. "Help me." A wave of panic swept through Drummond. He would be captured, executed, all because of this badly injured man. With his free leg, Drummond kicked the soldier in his powder-stained face, kicked him again and again until he let go and slipped into unconsciousness, or death. Drummond pulled a hatchet and loaded pistol from a nearby corpse, tried to stand. Another redcoat charged him, and Drummond fired. The man fell into a tent.

Standing, wielding the hatchet, falling back in a steady withdrawal. They might make it back to the Continental line alive. His head seemed to explode, and he welcomed a dark void that knew no pain.

"How you feel?" Dobie asked him.

"Dead," Drummond answered. He started to sit up, but

dizziness dropped him onto a bed of straw. When the spinning faded, he sucked in fresh air, and asked: "What happened?"

"To you? No telling. Your thick head deflected a ball, someone poked a knife all the way through your left arm, looks like a bullet tickled your ribs, and something cut your shoulder. To us? We took a big hurt, but the redcoats took a bigger one. They pulled out last night, running to Moncks Corner. General Greene sent General Marion and Colonel Lee after them. Want some tea?"

Drummond nodded, and the freedman handed him a steaming tin cup. It burned his lips, so he set it aside to cool. "How's Catawba Tom?"

"Lost an earlobe is all. Damned redcoat bit it off. He's scouting for our Swamp Fox. General Greene says we fought gallantly. He was a little irritated that a bunch stopped at the redcoat camp and started looting, filling their bellies, but that passed." Dobie shook his head. "Lost a lot of good boys, though."

"McGee?"

"Naw, he's one lucky Irishman. Nary a scratch. Hell, no one seen him once the battle commenced till Captain Witherspoon pulled him off some prisoners he was hacking apart."

Drummond shook his head. "Miles Jensen."

"Huh? What you talking about, Lieutenant? Jensen got captured at Snow's Island."

"He was there, Dobie. Fightin' with the redcoats. You know how things's been. Was 'bout to gut me with a bayonet. Then turned it on hisself. Died right 'side me. Last words was 'I'm sorry'."

"I'll be damned."

"Yeah."

FROM THE MANUSCRIPT
OF THE REVEREND STAN MCINTYRE,
PAGES 90–91

Having suffered by some estimates 47 percent casualties, the battle of Eutaw Springs made the British army no longer a threat. South Carolina was held by the Patriots, with the exception of a stretch from Charleston to Savannah, GA and so, shortly after the battle, General Francis Marion disbanded his militia. In a letter to his good friend Peter Horry, the great general mentioned his parting words to Augustin Drummond. The letter reads: *"I reminded Drummon[d] that in war, we all do things would to God we could forget. We are soldiers, and, as such, are all despoilers. This is what I told him. But when this war is over, we must return to being just men, and leave our bloody past behind us."*

So Augustin Drummond, it can be assumed, returned to Cameron Branch. Of course, there remained a few skirmishs between Tories and Patriots in the Back Country, including the bloody retaliation raid of James Jernegan. At the Luke Jones Memorial Library in Cheraw, South Carolina, is the only discovered copy of The South Carolina Patriot, published in Charleston on 17 Oct. 1781. One paragraph in a editorial reads: *"King George's protectors are doing a grand job making sure the wares of our city's Taverns shall not fall into the hands of Gen Greene, but lest you think the war is over, this editor reminds loyal Patriots that peace will not come to the Back Country as long as men like Bloody Jim Jernegan draw a breath. "*

That is the only edition the editor managed to print. Royal forces destroyed his press and office the following day.

CHAPTER EIGHTEEN

November, 1781

The dogwood leaves were beginning to lose their red blaze, smoke hung thick in the woods, and the morning wind carried the hint of frost. Summer had finally ended, and now autumn prepared to give way to an early winter, which made Drummond think he had better quit loafing and get back to work.

He emptied the dregs of his coffee, tossed the tin cup to the ground, grabbed the axe, and walked to a pine log. He braced his right foot against the log, and swung the axe. The loud *thump* echoed throughout Cameron Branch as he began the notching progress. An ox snorted in the distance, telling him Catawba Tom was hauling in another load.

They had cleared the burned ruins of the old Madison cabin and started anew, working six days a week, taking Sundays off to ride over to Sparrow Swamp and visit Rosemary. The British army remained bottled up around Charlestown; Francis Marion was tending to his affairs at Pond Bluff; and Bloody Jim Jernegan, after burning the Oliver mansion upon learning of the redcoat evacuation of Ninety Six, had led his Despoilers to the safe haven of Savannah. Up in Virginia, word came that Cornwallis had surrendered to George Washington in October. War continued—Peter Horry still led a few partisan firebreathers against warring Tories—but not for many, including Drummond and Catawba Tom.

"Whoa!" The Indian pulled the team to a stop, and moved with a purpose toward the tent the two men shared, not bothering to unload the three new logs he had felled this morning. Drummond lowered the axe to follow, recognizing that something was wrong. The Indian picked up a long rifle, tossed it to Drummond, and grabbed his own, muttering: "Riders."

Drummond cocked his head, didn't hear a thing, but, after serving a year with the scout, he had learned not to doubt Catawba Tom's instincts. A few minutes later came the unmistakable sound of hoofs sloshing down the trail that led off the Salem Road. Drummond cocked the rifle, and his friend disappeared into the brush.

He waited, licking his lips. The riders were likely friendly; there hadn't been any Indian trouble this far south or east in years, and revenge-seeking Tories would have left their horses behind to sneak in afoot. Still, it was best to be prepared. Once the three riders rounded the bend, Drummond eased down the hammer, and leaned the long rifle against a tree.

"Hello, Dobie," he said as the men reined in their horses. "Capt'n Hunter, Paddy."

Catawba Tom reappeared, put his rifle aside, and squatted.

"Building a cottage?" McGee said, swinging from the saddle without waiting for an invitation. "Where's that heavenly figured woman of yours?"

Ignoring the Irishman, Drummond asked Andrew Hunter: "What brings you out this way, Capt'n?"

"After a turncoat," the partisan answered. "We aim to hang him."

For a second, Drummond wished he still held the rifle

until Dobie read his eyes, and reassured him. "Not you, Lieutenant. Nobody thinks you'd do anything like that any more. Mind if we sit a spell? My arse is raw."

"Gladly. Don't get much company. Help yourself to coffee, too."

When they had stretched their muscles and drained the coffee pot, Andrew Hunter began talking. "The three of us agree that somebody led those redcoats to Snow's Island. Whoever did that bargained with Lucifer, and such treachery I do not abide."

Drummond considered this for a moment before asking: "You don't think they just found the hide-out? They was lookin' an awful long time."

The reply came from Dobie: "You recall when we were captured by Tarleton? You told us later how the colonel had offered you money."

With a nod, Drummond said: "He offered all of us money." Finding McGee, remembering Tarleton planned to bring in the Irishman after Drummond had refused the bribe, he added: "Right, Paddy?"

"Aye. The smiling bloke offered us all some coin, by the saints. Except Dobie."

" 'Cause I'm a Negro," the freedman explained. "Warrant he did not feel like interrogating a man of color, free or not."

"The money makes sense," Hunter chimed in. "Someone had to bring those redcoats to Snow's Island. Traded us in for thirty pieces of silver."

"So what do you want of me?" Drummond asked.

"Ride with us," Hunter said. "Help us find that scoundrel."

He shook his head before replying: "War's practically over, Capt'n. We won."

"Hayes Station, Stevens Creek," McGee argued, referring to recent skirmishes in the Back Country. "And the English dogs still control Charlestown."

"Not for long," Drummond answered. "We all know that. Cornwallis surrendered his whole army. France is on our side. It's a matter of time."

Dobie cleared his throat, and asked: "And what of Bloody Jim Jernegan? He rode out of Savannah with a hundred men. They've left a lot of dead 'twixt Georgia and Camden. May be heading here."

Drummond had not heard about Jernegan. His back began to throb, and he pictured the murderer flogging Rosemary, laughing as the cat-o'-nine-tails struck again and again. He would love to cut Bloody Jim Jernegan's throat, and, if General Marion asked him to rejoin the militia, he would. Yet for all he knew, Miles Jensen had been the informer, if, indeed, there had been a traitor. That would explain why the giant smithy was fighting with the redcoats at Eutaw Springs, why he had killed himself with the broken bayonet.

"What say you, Drummond?" Hunter said. "Ride with us. The man who betrayed us should be killed."

"There's lots of things I done in the war that I ain't proud of," he said, staring at the pine cones at his feet. He omitted the recurring dreams, the nightmares in which he saw the faces of the men he had killed, usually the two or three who had begged for mercy before he slew them. "Lots of things I'd like to forget. I was once a peaceable man, Capt'n. I need to see if I can be that man again." He looked up. "You understand, sir?"

"I do," answered Hunter, his head bobbing slightly. "There are things I have done of which I am ashamed, but I will not lose any sleep by hanging our betrayer." He stood, gesturing at McGee and Dobie that it was time to ride. "Watch for Jernegan," he told Drummond and Catawba Tom. "He rides for revenge, knows the war is lost, simply wants to kill as many Patriots as he can."

Drummond thanked the visitors, but thought that an officer like Andrew Hunter should be chasing Bloody Jim Jernegan, not some phantom traitor.

He and Catawba Tom walked alongside the three militiamen as they led their horses down the path to the main road. He told Hunter about Jensen, how the blacksmith might have been the traitor, but the captain dismissed the theory. "Jensen was on the island during the attack. Captain McCottry remembers seeing him there. No, it was someone else."

They shook hands at the road, and, after the three riders had mounted, Drummond said: "Capt'n, it probably won't do you no good. Well, I doubt iffen he'll tell you nothin', but that redcoat lieutenant might know the informer's name. I mean, Blackburn was with Doyle and Jernegan."

Hunter looked down in bewilderment. "What are you talking about?"

"Lieutenant Blackburn, sir, the redcoat commandin' them Peedee Tories. He's been at McAllister's for I don't know how long. Rosemary's been tendin' him after amputatin' his arm."

The three riders exchanged glances. McGee started to say something, but Catawba Tom suddenly pointed to the northwest, muttering: "Big smoke."

They saw the thick black cloud stretching into the cloudless sky, rising from what had to be Weaver's Settlement, where John Oliver had done most of his doctoring and drinking.

"Jernegan," Dobie whispered, although he had no way of knowing.

"Mayhap it is," Hunter said, and shot Drummond an intense stare. "Will you ride with us now?"

"Yes, sir," he answered. "Ride on. We'll catch up."

Catawba Tom was already running down the path to saddle their mounts. McGee was saying that he would gallop to McAllister's, question the redcoat lieutenant, in case Jernegan was on his way there next, or at least warn Drummond's lady-fair. *McAllister's?* Drummond thought. *Would the Tory murderer raid his own? Perhaps.* Loyalists barely outnumbered Whigs at Weaver's Settlement, and Jernegan really didn't care who won the war. Drummond had always guessed that. He and his men were nothing more than thieves and killers. The name they had been branded with fit: Despoilers.

He ran faster.

Sparrow Swamp again. Well, Ebenezer Moore always knew he would be back. The coins in his waistcoat pocket jingled as he dismounted. He slipped in the mud, and landed with a *splat*, his helmet falling beside him. He let out a drunken laugh, checked the priming powder in the Jägerbusche's pan, closed the frizzen, and stared across the barren fields at McAllister's post.

It would be simple—ride down to the store, call out her name, and, when Rosemary Madison appeared, shoot her dead. Let Drummond sort that out. Ebenezer Moore would be out of his misery. Reginald McAllister or one of the damned Tories below would kill him for murdering the lovely woman. If they lacked the nerve, a pistol holstered on his saddle would do the trick. He would kill himself— silence his tormented soul.

He fingered the button necklace, a habit he had only recently noticed. The pewter, bone, wood, and brass pieces numbered thirty-seven now, although for the past few months he had been picking off lone travelers on the Back Country pikes, caring not a whit whether they were Whig or Loyalist. Once a devout Patriot, he had become nothing more than a bandit, no better than one of Jernegan's lot.

A rider loped down the road, and Moore mumbled— "Thirty-eight."—laughed, and braced the stock against his shoulder. Out of range, likely, and riding too fast, so he lowered the Jägerbusche, and tried to shake off his drunkenness. The man knocked on the door of the trading post, disappeared inside. A few minutes later, Rosemary Madison and the stranger stepped out the rear entrance, and hurried to the McAllister house. He wet his lips, watching them until they went inside.

"Whore," he said, spitting out the detestable taste in his mouth.

He sat in the mud some thirty minutes, not moving, waiting for her and that "friend" to come outside—till echoing hoofs drew his attention. His mouth fell open at the horde of men. They shouted curses as they reined their lathered mounts in front of the post. Others raced to the house, while some struck flints to fire torches. "Bloody Jim Jernegan," he whispered. A moment later, he heard himself say, almost in a panic: "Rosemary!"

Suddenly sobered, Moore realized the raiders would certainly come to the sawmill, see him, kill him before he could. . . . No matter. He staggered to his feet, grabbed his horse's reins, led the animal hurriedly into the woods. "Quiet," he said, slipping beside a tree, watching. His eyes flamed as the Despoilers plundered the store. A shot rang out from the house, followed by more rifle fire behind the store, and, later, laughter. Moore became aware of his own rum-scented, sour sweat.

There had to be almost a hundred men. What could he do? He couldn't help anyone. They'd cut him down before he got halfway to the house. Suddenly Ebenezer Moore did not want to die. Confusion wracked him. Help Rosemary Madison? Hadn't he wanted to kill her? Well, Jernegan would do the job for him.

He sat there, trembling. When Bloody Jim Jernegan himself rounded the store, waving two bloody scalps, Moore looked away and trained his eyes on the battered leather helmet he had left in the mud. For six years he had been wearing that headgear, now scarred, filthy, barely recognizable, except the polished silver crescent that reflected the sun, staring back at him like the eyes of a serpent.

Chapter Nineteen

A light tapping on the door stirred Jason Blackburn from his slumber. He swung his legs over the cot, and reached up to push the hair out of his eyes, only to remember he no longer had a right hand. Rosemary Madison had severed the arm just above the elbow with an axe. He stared at the stub a moment, used his left hand with a sigh, and called out: "Enter. I am awake."

Rosemary Madison opened the door, smiled weakly, and asked: "Are you up for a visitor today, Mister Blackburn?"

Who would come to see him? Before he could answer, a man moved in front of the young woman, and for a moment Blackburn found himself looking into a mirror. A one-armed man wearing the uniform of the Sixty-Third Regiment of Foot stared back at him. Not a perfect reflection, though, not as gaunt, haggard, and pale as Blackburn knew he looked. The figure blinking before him needed a bath and shave, but did not resemble a cadaver. The fog lifted over his brain, and he heard Sergeant James Talley say: "Good day, Lieutenant. My, but it is good to see you again, sir."

"I will leave you alone," said his nurse, closing the door.

After removing his cap, Talley settled on a stool by the bed, the same stool where the Madison widow and Mrs. McAllister had spoon-fed him, bathed him, did just about

237

everything because he was too weak. Blackburn awkwardly filled two glasses with water. From the children's bedroom, he heard Rosemary Madison reading from the Bible to her daughter and the McAllister boy. He handed Talley one glass, gripped the other tentatively—he wasn't used to living with one hand—and took long pulls, surprised at his thirst. After draining the water, he put his empty glass on the stand, and faced Talley. The sergeant stared at Blackburn's empty right sleeve.

"Begging the lieutenant's pardon, sir, but how did that happen?"

"Snow's Island," he answered stiffly. "I was attacked by some rebel's dogs. Badly injured . . . somehow I mounted my horse, and the next thing I remember, here I was. The Madison woman saved my life, I do believe. Infection had set in. She performed the amputation, sealed it with hot tar. She and McAllister's wife have been nursing me for months now. I came down with the ague, chills, and fevers. They have been angels of mercy, Sergeant." He shook his head, eying the empty sleeve. "Although there are many hours when I wish they had let me die a whole man."

"Nonsense," Talley fired back. "You are alive, sir. That is all that matters. Trust me, Lieutenant, living with one arm is better than dying with both. You will grow accustomed to this, sir, as did I."

He didn't care for this topic. "How did you find me?"

"I was in a tavern in Charlestown, sir, when an angry settler entered. He was a Loyalist who had been tortured by the rebels. Anyway, he operated the sawmill here and just happened to mention how the McAllisters and their house guest were caring for an English officer. The pieces fit. I guessed mayhap it was you and rode to bring you, or whoever, back to Charlestown. Can you ride?"

Blackburn's spirits lifted. He pictured himself sailing the Atlantic, back in England, kissing Susan and his daughters. Yes, he told James Talley, he could ride like the devil. They talked more of news, of Cornwallis's surrender, of Jernegan's latest raid, of all that had happened since Blackburn had been wounded during Doyle's raid.

They were still talking when the first gunshot echoed.

As he reined in the stallion at Weaver's Settlement, Drummond cursed. Flames engulfed six cabins; shoats, ewes, and cows lay slaughtered in their pens; women and children knelt sobbing over the bodies of husbands and fathers; and other blood- and soot-covered settlers staggered about in a daze or waged fruitless attacks against burning homes. Dobie, Abe Weaver, and two teen-agers formed a brigade inside the tavern, tossing out kegs, cornmeal, anything they could save before the inferno forced them out.

A woman pointed on the ground at two blanket-covered bodies, screaming at Andrew Hunter: "They strung up my Luke and Matthew by their hands to that oak yonder! And Matthew, I hear him say . . . 'What will we tell Mother?' Then the big man with the red beard, he says . . . 'You shall tell them nothing, you rebel nits.' He cut their throats! They were not rebels. My husband was loyal to King George, served with. . . ." She broke down, sobbing uncontrollably in front of the blood-soaked blankets.

The fire grew too hot, chased Dobie, Weaver, and the boys outside, and they walked toward Captain Hunter. A few other settlers gave up on their cabins to join the circle.

"Jernegan?" Hunter asked.

"Aye," Weaver replied. "He had an army with him, too many for us to fight, and most of our men were out hunting, anyway. We told him we were Loyalists, and most of us are, but he said he has less use for pet Tories than he has for outright rebels. Said if we had gotten off our haunches and served with the King's army, the war would not be lost."

A collapsing roof showered the area with sparks, but few paid any attention. Drummond kept watching Catawba Tom circle the settlement on horseback while half listening to the conversation around him, wondering what the Indian would discover. The scout finally loped back to the gathering.

"Many horses," Catawba Tom told the captain. "More than I count. Follow cut-off trail."

The cut-off trail wound through the forests and creeks before intersecting the Salem Road just before the Sparrow Swamp-Lynches Creek turnoff.

A fisted ball of mud splattered Hunter's hunting frock, and the captain twisted in the saddle to draw a pistol holstered in the front of the saddle.

" 'Tis your fault!" a white-faced woman shrieked. " 'Tis all you rebels' fault!" She gathered up another ball of mud and hurled it, this time at Drummond. The stallion shied a little as the projectile sailed between the rider and big black's neck.

"Sally speaks the truth," cried a balding man whose hands and arms were badly burned. "You should have solved your differences with His Majesty in peace, not by bloodshed. Look around us. Look at what you've done!"

"This was wrought by Bloody Jim Jernegan," Hunter said, "not by Whigs."

Dobie reached for his horse pistol, but, spotting the movement, the captain shouted: "Belay that! No more blood shall be spilled here." He holstered his own pistol.

Hunter straightened in the saddle, swept one quick look

240

across the crowd, and began: "I have four men with me. One is already riding to McAllister's to give warning. Four men against one hundred, perhaps more. I ask you to put aside our differences, ride with us, help us send this scourge of the Peedee to Hades."

"Differences!" the bald man shouted. "You rebels refuse to put aside those differences. Jacob Sanders of Sparrow Swamp was tarred and feathered on the stagecoach road two weeks ago, forced to abandon his sawmill and run to Charlestown. You rebels. . . ."

"Silence, Aaron Hall!" Abe Weaver said. Wiping soot from his face, staring at the militia captain, the tavern owner spoke urgently: "I would ride with you, Capt'n, but Jernegan stole or killed most of our horses. Even if we all rode double. . . ."

"Billy Rudd!" a woman called out. "Billy raises horses by Lake Swamp. If Bloody Jim has not raided his place. . . ."

"That be some miles out of the way," Drummond told Hunter.

"Quite so," agreed the captain, facing Drummond. "I shall lead these men to Rudd's. You, Dobie, and Tom follow Jernegan's trail. We will catch up as soon as we can and endeavor to enlist any man we meet along the way."

Drummond did not wait for Hunter's call for volunteers. He kicked the stallion into a gallop, digging up mud and grass as he raced for the cut-off trail, Dobie and Catawba Tom lagging behind.

One minute Rosemary Madison had been reading the Bible to Rachel and Todd, and the next she was hurrying the children out the back door, practically pushing them, screaming: "Hide! Hide in the swamp, and don't come back no matter what you hear!"

Blackburn stood beside her suddenly, and she pushed him after the boy and girl. "Stay with them! Go! Hide. There are too many to fight!"

"But. . . ."

"For God's sake, do it!" She turned, disappeared inside the house, pulled the rifle from above the front door, and jerked back the hammer. A bullet shattered a pot outside. Another shadow rounded the house, fired once at the *banditti*. They answered with a dozen or more shots, and the shadow disappeared.

The front door flew open with a *bang*, and Rosemary turned the barrel and pulled the trigger. The man's face disappeared in a cloud of putrid smoke, and she dropped the empty gun. Her eyes stung, but she could see the soles of the intruder's feet, knew she had killed him. She could also make out Peninnah and Reginald running from the store, pursued, shot, staggering, falling.

Others made their way for the house, and she abandoned her fight, screaming Rachel's name, knocking over a dining room chair, making it out the back door, running between the house and the summer kitchen, trying to make the woods. She caught the blur of movement on her right, attempted to dodge her attacker, knew she was too late. A man's shoulder rammed her side, knocked her breath away, and she landed, stunned, rolled over, tried to crawl, but a weight crushed her legs. A giant hand grabbed her hair, jerked her head up, slammed her into the ground. She smelled mud and blood, felt herself being rolled onto her back, forced her eyes open, saw the man atop her, grinning.

She knew him. . . .

Pillars of smoke told Drummond they were too late. He rounded the bend, prodding the big black relentlessly with the stock of his long rifle, Catawba Tom and Dobie trailing a good half mile by now. McAllister's trading post and sheds were still burning, along with Mal Carter's farm house, but the Despoilers had left alone the sawmill, McAllister home, and Methodist meeting house. Too busy maybe. Too religious? He swung from the horse in front of the store, ran toward the McAllister home, realized Jernegan's cut-throats had tried to set the house on fire, but it had failed to catch. Maybe that's why the sawmill and church remained untouched as well.

He called out Rosemary's name as he ran, spotted the scalped bodies of McAllister and his wife on the ground just behind the store. Tears began to sting his eyes. *Not Rosemary. Please, God, not Rosemary.* Drummond hurdled a corpse blocking the open front door, ran through the house, searching each room. Nothing. Outside then, through the back entrance, and he saw her, her long hair, Paddy McGee kneeling over her body. The anger, the animal inside him, returned.

Tossing away the cocked rifle, he charged. The Irishman looked up just as Drummond hit, knocking McGee aside. "Get away from her!" Drummond shouted, and jerked the handle of his hatchet.

McGee was backing away on hands and feet, pleading, saying he had everything wrong. He was repeating a name over and over. Drummond raised the hatchet over his head, heard the hoofs of Catawba Tom's and Dobie's mounts, and this time recognized what the sobbing Irishman was saying.

"Captain Moore. Captain Moore. He done it. He was the traitor. Ebenezer Moore. Jesus, Mary, and Joseph, it was the captain I tell you. He done it all. Captain Moore."

Drummond lowered the hatchet, turned, ran to Rosemary, found Dobie already beside her. The freedman looked up, said solemnly: "She's alive. Need to get her inside."

Her eyes fluttered, and Drummond dropped the tomahawk, fell to his knees, leaned closer. Her nose and lips were busted, caked with dried blood, her face stained with mud, grass, blood. She saw him, must have recognized him, said out loud—"Rachel."—and slipped back into unconsciousness.

He spun around, found McGee, still shivering on the ground, snapped: "The children! Where be the children?"

"Don't know. Didn't see them. Jernegan might have taken them. They killed that redcoat, too, the one-armed man." He pointed to the body.

Drummond didn't care how many soldiers Jernegan had murdered. He didn't think for a second that the savage would kidnap a young boy and girl unless he wanted hostages, and Jernegan had never relied on hostages.

"Small tracks," Catawba Tom said from the edge of the woods. "And one man's. Maybe chase them. I follow."

"To the swamp," Dobie whispered. "Sweet Mary, there are 'gators bigger than pines back yonder."

Drummond was moving now, picking up hatchet and rifle, telling Dobie to look after Rosemary. He swung into the saddle, kicked the black into a run, Ebenezer Moore's face chiseled into his mind. Moore had put his filthy hands on Rosemary Madison. He had betrayed General Marion and the partisan cause, sold out the militia for Judas money. Drummond followed the trail, crossed the swamp, picked up the road. All of his life, he had been denied his revenge. Zack Gibbs and the settlers of Long Canes had tracked down and killed Salâli's murderers while he was traipsing around with Pickens. Thomas Sumter's men had wounded and captured Major James Wemyss. Tarleton had been defeated, humiliated by Morgan. Even if he had wanted to track down his father's killers he couldn't, for those Cherokee renegades were dead as well. Drummond might not be able to get close enough to kill Jernegan, but Ebenezer Moore would pay. This, he swore.

The horse was played out, but Moore kicked harder, ground his teeth, pounded the trail from Sparrow Swamp to the Georgetown-Cheraw stagecoach road. The horse wheezed, and Moore knew it was finished. He kicked free of the stirrups, and leaped from the saddle as the dun twisted in the road before collapsing.

Moore ignored the dying beast, ran. He had to run. Faster. Find another horse maybe, keep riding. For twenty minutes, he kept at it, ignoring his blistered feet.

He had waited until after Jernegan's Despoilers left the burning settlement, then crept around the side of the house and almost laughed. Rosemary was dead, or soon would be. Of this he felt certain. The sound of horses had startled him, and, in a panic, he had galloped for the swamp. He should have felt vindicated, relieved, but every time he closed his eyes, he saw that crescent moon on his old helmet, staring at him, haunting him, cursing him as a traitor and a fiend. *Run,* he told himself, *faster. Escape.*

Thunder rattle sounded behind him. Not thunder, but a galloping horse. He spun quickly, dropped to a knee, saw the flash of smoke, heard the boom. The bullet kicked up dirt behind him, and the rider pitched the empty rifle, whipped out a hatchet.

"Drummond!" Moore said hoarsely. Mouth open, he just stared, frozen, uncomprehending. Survival instincts ultimately took over, almost too late. The horse was practically on top of him. The tomahawk swung. Moore parried the blow with the Jägerbusche, which was knocked from his hand but also spilled Drummond from the saddle. Moore reached for the Jägerbusche, lifted it, spun, pulled the trigger. Nothing. Just a spark from the flint. He tried to change grip, use the weapon as a club, but knew he was too late. Drummond lowered his shoulder, tackled him. The German firearm fell in the dirt.

Moore just managed to draw up his knees, rocked, sent Drummond somersaulting. He landed in the center of the road, and Moore found his feet, cursing himself. He had forgotten the pistols holstered in the saddle on the dun; he could have used them now. Drummond recovered quickly, charged again, not human. No man could act this way. Moore ducked his wild swing, dodged another, planted a solid fist in Drummond's stomach. The man grunted, and Moore gripped the greasy hunting frock, shoved his attacker into the road.

Damn it all! Drummond landed beside the tomahawk he had dropped. Moore ran, kicked him in the chest as he tried to rise, but Drummond grabbed Moore's boot, twisting it, sending him to the ground.

He collapsed, sucked in air, tried to move, felt Drummond's moccasin slam into his gut, turn him on his back. Drummond fell on top of him, left hand clamped against Moore's windpipe. With both hands, Moore tried desperately to free the grip, but exhaustion overtook him. The hard ride from Sparrow Swamp, the running. It was over. Drummond raised the tomahawk with his right hand.

Moore froze, mouthed *Rosemary* as the blade slammed forward.

Chapter Twenty

Emotionally drained, he forced himself into the McAllister house, entering with Captain Hunter at his side. Paddy McGee asked if they wanted something to drink, but both men shook their heads. Standing in the parlor, the three men kept their eyes locked on the closed bedroom door. Inside, Dobie looked after Rosemary.

Several members of Hunter's posse had stopped at the settlement to bury the dead in the little cemetery behind the meeting house. Drummond had met Hunter and the others on the far side of the swamp, and the militia captain had put Abe Weaver in charge and returned to McAllister's with the backwoodsman.

"Did you kill Captain Moore?" McGee asked.

Drummond didn't answer, just stared at the door, but Hunter replied: "Ebenezer Moore is dead."

No one spoke again until Dobie came out of the bedroom, shut the door, and sighed.

"She'll live," the freedman said. "Some broken ribs. Cuts and bruises. Busted nose. Was choked, but . . . I'd like to kill the man that done this."

"Drummond done it for you, bub. Is she awake?" McGee asked.

"Sleeping. She needs rest." The freedman found Drummond. "So, you caught Captain Moore?"

He nodded, cleared his throat, and asked: "Catawba Tom back with the children?"

"Not yet. Think we should go ourselves?"

"Aye," McGee answered. "You do that, bub. I'll look after wee Miz Madison. . . ."

"When we served with Pickens," Drummond said sharply, now staring at the Irishman, "you was always hankerin' for a fight, Paddy. But that ain't been the case lately. No one saw you at Eutaw Springs 'ceptin' when Capt'n Witherspoon, here, pulled you off them prisoners you was butcherin'. An' when the capt'n an' us rode off to Weaver's, you didn't need no arm-twistin' to volunteer to ride here an' warn the settlers."

The Irishman's eyes flamed. "If you are calling me a coward, Drummond. . . ."

Drummond cut him off. "Where were you during the Snow's Island raid, Paddy?"

"Fighting redcoats. Barely got out with me life." McGee looked first to Hunter, then Dobie for help, but saw only suspicion. "Don't listen to this bub," he began. "I came here as fast as I could. He's just riled that I didn't get here in time to save his precious Rosemary."

"Why did you murder those prisoners, McGee?" Andrew Hunter asked.

"Tarleton's quarter!" he snapped. "I have not forgotten that, even if you have."

"And Snow's Island?" Dobie said suspiciously. "We all thought you had been captured till Capt'n Hunter found you here. You knew where to look for us, Paddy. You. . . ."

"You listening to his rubbish? I was here hiding from redcoats. They practically. . . ."

"Why would you hide near a settlement filled with Tories?" Dobie asked.

"Listen to me, you swine. Fighting the English for years have I been."

"Here's what I think, Paddy," Drummond said. He found himself surprisingly calm, unlike the rage he had felt when he had killed Ebenezer Moore. "I think you sold out our brothers on Snow's Island. You, an Irishman. I think you rode here to kill Blackburn, feared he'd point to you as the turncoat. An' if it was you that hurt Rosemary, not Moore, by God, I'll kill you."

"By the saints," McGee screamed, "you got everything wrong!"

Hunter and Dobie looked doubtful.

"Blackburn's dead," McGee shot back. "The Despoilers killed him. Not me."

"Jernegan would not kill a redcoat officer." This came from Captain Hunter. "Tories, yes, but he would not dare murder a Royal soldier. Then he would have no safe lair."

Drummond added: "Besides, Paddy, that ain't Lieutenant Blackburn lying dead. That be some redcoat sergeant. Same one that had whipped me at Cameron Branch." He glanced out the window. "No, Paddy, you killed the wrong man."

"You have no proof. You. . . ."

"The proof be walkin' here, now," Drummond said, nodding out the window. "Catawba Tom found Rachel. The McAllister boy . . . an' Lieutenant Blackburn."

Jason Blackburn's face turned white at the sight of the smoking ruins and dead bodies being moved toward the cemetery. He found his voice, although he barely recognized it, called out to two unrefined rebels to halt, and staggered forward. They were carrying a British soldier, and Blackburn knew it was Sergeant Talley. Unashamed, he wept, staring at the dead man's face. Talley had given his life to protect Rosemary Madison, the children, even Jason Blackburn.

I should be dead, too, he thought, *were I a decent soldier. I should have sent Talley with the children. I should have done more. I. . . .*

What did it matter? His shame, his feelings of cowardice, were soon replaced by something stronger, and he lifted his head toward the sky, cursed Jernegan and Tarleton, cursed this war. He roared like some injured lion. Jernegan! Blackburn had fought alongside that murderer, that devil. Blackburn suddenly felt fear, and he bolted inside the house. "Miss Madison!" he yelled. "Rosemary Madison!" The sight of other rebels shocked him, yet he couldn't quite place the faces, not yet, not still blinded by tears, pain, hate, and regret, but he did recognize one.

"You son-of-a-bitch!" he yelled, and tackled that Judas, Paddy McGee, clamping one powerful hand on the Irishman's throat.

Drummond watched as Dobie pulled Blackburn off McGee. The freedman wrapped his arms around the enraged officer, surprisingly strong considering all he had gone through, and mumbled something about proof and no need for a court-martial.

Gasping for breath, rubbing his red throat, McGee quickly pulled himself to his feet and began pleading. "You got it all wrong." He wet his lips, turned quickly toward Hunter. "I swear to you, this is a mistake. By the saints, I am Irish. You think I would do a thing like this? I hate the English. These blokes is trying to trick you. Rosemary, she can set the truth straight. Here. . . ." He spun, ran, jerked open the bedroom door, took a step inside.

The pistol shot was deafening.

McGee staggered back into the parlor, clutching his chest with both hands, choking, spitting out blood, sinking to his knees. Drummond ran past him, into the bedroom, took Dobie's horse pistol from Rosemary's trembling hand.

Clad in a chemise, she sat on the bed. "I heard him." Her voice was hushed. "I heard. . . ."

"It's all right," he said, eased her back into the bed, pulled the covers over her. "Everything's all right." He squeezed her hand.

Her eyes widened. "Rachel?"

"Rachel's fine. So is Todd and Blackburn. You get some sleep."

"Augustin!"

"I'll be here," he told her. "I'll be here."

Drummond found Jason Blackburn standing beside the coach. He approached the officer tentatively, not knowing what he would say.

Captain Hunter had ridden off to join Abe Weaver, but Bloody Jim Jernegan's men had split up, and the settlers returned empty-handed. Dobie and Catawba Tom had dumped McGee's body in the swamp, where it would feed alligators and crows. Abe Weaver's wife was looking after Rachel and Todd at the settlement being rebuilt a few miles from Cameron Branch.

"Bound for Charlestown?" Drummond asked. It was a start at conversation.

"Yes," Blackburn replied. "While we still hold it."

A cloud of silence hovered over them a minute, maybe two, before Blackburn spoke again. "I will send a headstone for Sergeant Talley's grave, Mister Drummond. Will you see that it is properly placed?"

"Aye."

More silence.

"I am sorry for . . . ," Blackburn began.

"No need to apologize," Drummond said. " 'Tis war."

"Yes." Blackburn sighed. "War. But I fear I am no better than Jernegan, no better than McGee, Moore, Tarleton. . . . War changes men. Well, it changed me. I feel I have permeated into some despoiler."

Drummond understood this too well. He had killed men trying to surrender, had been unable to control his rage in battle. One push, and he easily could have descended into the hell that eventually consumed Ebenezer Moore. Maybe his actions would not be deemed as unspeakable as Moore's, or Paddy McGee's, but they would always haunt Augustin Drummond. Blackburn had done nothing so horrible, had simply followed orders. "No diff'rent than me, neither," Drummond said at last. "But I'll tell you somethin' Gen'ral Marion told me. After we disbanded, he said . . . 'We're soldiers, so we all be despoilers. But after the war, we need to be just men again, an' forget our bloody past'."

"Just men," Blackburn said softly. When he looked at the house, tears began rolling down his face, but he found strength deep inside him, wiped his eyes, and said forcefully: "Rosemary Madison is a strong woman, but she shall need a strong man to help her recover. Be that man. The war is all but over, Drummond. You have Rosemary and Rachel. Take them back to Cameron Branch. Maybe rebuild Doctor Oliver's mansion."

Shaking his head, Drummond corrected the officer. "The cabin on the branch."

"Yes," Blackburn agreed. "That suits her better. She

talked of it often while nursing me back to health."

"What of you?"

Blackburn turned from the house, glanced at Drummond, and stared down the road. "England, I imagine. Not much use for one-armed lieutenants in the colonies. Perhaps back home, with my wife and family, I can find the old Jason Blackburn again." Awkwardly he climbed into the coach.

"Ready, sir?" the driver asked.

"God be with you, Augustin Drummond," Blackburn said softly. "God be with us all." He turned away. "Drive on!"

After the coach disappeared, Drummond walked around the house, and found Dobie coming out of the kitchen, balancing a steaming kettle, cups, and sugar cubes on a tray.

"She awake?" Drummond asked.

Nodding, the freedman asked: "You want to bring her this tea?"

Maybe I can find the old Augustin Drummond again, he thought, and took the tray.

FROM THE MANUSCRIPT
OF THE REVEREND STAN MCINTYRE,
PAGES 103–105

The final Tory surrender happened on 8 June, 1782, and the British army evacuated Charlestown on Dec. 14. Men like our subject and Francis Marion lived out his days in peace. The Tories, however, defeated and chastised, were forced to flee our new United States. Many settled in Canada, others in Jamaica.

Francis Marion became commodant of Ft Johnson after the war and served in the state senate and state constitutional convention. He remained the gentleman planter at Pond Bluff, too, and died on Feb. 27, 1795. Andrew Pickens served in the state legislature and went to Congress in 1793–95. He became a major general in the state, dealt with Indians, & died in 1817.

Among Drummond's enemies, Banastre Tarleton returned to England, wrote his memoirs of the Southern campaign, served a few stints in Parliament, was knighted in 1820 and died on Jan. 25, 1833. James Wemyss recovered from his wounds inflicted by Sumter's men, was promoted to lt. col. in 1787 but had faded from history by 1790. Lt. Jason Blackburn retired from the army, became a solicitor and died in 1829. Thelma Anderson took a photo of his headstone in a cemetery in West Suffolk. I have it in my possession. James Jernegan somehow escaped the gallows and Patriots, most historians agree, to die penniless and drunk in Nova Scotia in 1785.

After his marriage to Rosemary Oliver Madison in 1783, Augustin Drummond seems to have disappeared from the face of written history. He and Rosemary, accorrding to records, had at least four children. One, sex unrecorded, died shortly after birth. Other children were a son, Oliver, born in 1786, death unknown; and two daughters, Virginia, 1788–1839, and Rebecca, 1790–1863. An adopted son, called Todd McAllister Drummond, died of yellow fever while fighting against the British during the War of 1812. Rosemary died on January 3, 1808, and was buried, tradition has it, at the Drummond homestead.

As I finish this manuscript, I am struck by General Marion's words to his scout and friend: "We are soldiers, and, as such, are all despoilers."

For fifty years, I have been troubled by something I did in World War II. Not, personally. As far as I know, I never took a human life but I was on board the U.S.S. Indianapolis. We delivered the uranium used in the first atomic bomb dropped on Japan, after which our ship was torpedoed. Many men died, as we spend spent four days and 5 nights in a brutal Pacific Ocean before those of us who had not drowned, fell victims to sharks or perished in some other un-Holy method, were rescued. Often have I dreamt that the Jap sub sank us before we delivered our precious cargo. I have awaked happy—until realizing this was only a dream.

More than ten years ago, I met a roving reporter in the church cemetery. Though we only spoke briefly, I gathered that he too has been haunted. He told me he served in Vietnam. He told me nothing more, but I senced he wanted to talk. Perhaps he shall come by my church someday and we will talk. I'll tell him what General Marion told

Augustin Drummond: "We are soldiers, and, as such, are all despoilers. . . . But when this war is over, we must return to being just men and leave our bloody past behind us."

Amen.

EPILOGUE

I finished the manuscript shortly before the 737 began its descent into Kansas City. After landing and grabbing my bags, I picked up my Jeep Cherokee, and drove to my apartment, where I decided my expense report could wait. Stan McIntyre's manuscript wasn't publishable. Way too sloppy and unprofessional, too short, inconsistent, too many typos, dangling participles, not enough documentation. I might be able to fix it up some, but I didn't think it would ever find much of an audience. No, I decided, the best course of action would be to donate it to a library, perhaps Darlington or Florence. Maybe some other historian could use it to expand on McIntyre's thesis and write that history. I showered, shaved, drove to chow down on a Gates barbecue turkey sandwich, returned home, read the *Star*, drank two Negra Modelos, and went to bed. I didn't sleep.

I could hear Francis Marion, or maybe it was the Reverend Stan McIntyre, telling me: *We are soldiers, and, as such, are all despoilers.*

I could picture everything so clearly. Smell it, too.

The stink of decaying mud, of putrid rice patties, human sweat and piss, the god-awful humidity. Night ambush patrol at Binh Long. A nineteen-year-old grunt in 1971 with cottonmouth and an M-16, waiting to kill somebody.

259

Everyone was asleep, but me, watching the road but not seeing anything—or wanting to. Then spotting the movement. Black pajamas in the moonlight. AK-47. One gook. Wait. Two. No, at least six. Six. A Charlie patrol. I glanced at Kemosabe, my best friend, wanting to kick him but too afraid. He might wake up shouting. Kemosabe was known to do that. I couldn't move. The VC came closer down the road, cautious, but not expecting anything. I closed my eyes. If only I could move. . . .

Yet I did. Don't remember it, but, when my eyes opened, I held the grenade, pin already pulled. Waiting. Sweating. Waiting. Not sure if my heart still beat. The closest VC spotted me, and I hurled the grenade. Moving. Popping. Screaming.

"Charlie! Damn it, Charlie on the road!" Squeezing the trigger like a madman. Not hearing my buddies joining in, not hearing the grenade explode, not hearing the screams.

Then it was over.

"Christ, Price," Kemosabe was telling me. "You's a regular friggin' John Wayne."

Kemosabe had been the one who stopped me. As the patrol joined in on my ambush, I charged out of the jungle, chasing a wounded soldier as he crawled for safety. He wasn't getting far because the grenade had blown off his right foot. Yet I was relentless, like Kemosabe would say in his New Jersey snarl, "a regular friggin' John Wayne." I caught up with the soldier as Sergeant Potato Head and Lieutenant Tibbles finished off each dying VC with a coup de grâce.

The VC I was after stopped and rolled over. I braced the M-16's stock against my shoulder. . . .

And saw it was a woman.

Black pajamas, blood-caked hair, treacherous eyes. Praying to Buddha or something. Maybe simply cursing me.

I felt sick. Outraged. Yet crazy. I blamed this woman, so I emptied a clip into her body and face. Until Kemosabe stood by me, forced me to lower my weapon, and said: "Christ, Price. You's a regular friggin' John Wayne."

"It was a woman," I told Lieutenant Tibbles later that morning as we walked back.

"She would have wasted you, Price. She was nothin' more than a VC bitch."

That's what I tried to accept. She was Viet Cong, and would have killed me if given the chance. What I couldn't understand was me, son of a Mobile, Alabama, plumber and housewife, emptying an M-16 into a young woman, watching her body jump, blood spurt, as the slugs tore through her, ripping her face and chest apart. A wounded soldier, and I had murdered her.

Maybe that's why, after the war, I moved from job to job and never told anyone about Binh Long. I wanted to, yet never could. Not my parents, not my friends, not Stan McIntyre, not two girlfriends-turned-ex-wives.

So now I wondered: How did Augustin Drummond feel after the Revolution, after all the horrors he had witnessed, after all he had been forced to do? Somehow, he had lived with his demons, had been happily married, had fathered several children. Stan McIntyre had been haunted, but he became a minister, and died a respected man. I imagine he was happy. He came to terms with what he had done in World War II, and he had not done anything. His ship delivered uranium used in the Hiroshima bomb. Well, if the *Indianapolis* hadn't done this, another ship would have. Me? I had committed murder. Killed a woman. Mutilated her body.

But when this war is over, we must return to being just men, and leave our bloody past behind us.

Maybe I can do this now. The war's some thirty years

behind me. I'm a sportswriter at a major metropolitan daily, have been here for five years. There's a divorcee I meet for coffee every Saturday morning at Starbucks, and we've had a few dates. Yeah, what I did at Binh Long was horrible, but I don't think that was me. That was a nineteen-year-old boy given an M-16 and lousy orders. I'm different.

I'm no longer a despoiler.

Author's Note

If you turn off U.S. Highway 76 at the stoplight in Timmonsville, South Carolina, my hometown, and head toward Darlington, you won't find Cameron Branch Baptist Church or Augustin Drummond's final resting place. However, not far past the Darlington County line, although certainly not as close as in this novel's prologue, a historical marker at the Lake Swamp Baptist Church cemetery commemorates Augustin Wilson, whose grave was once marked by a cannon barrel.

Augustin Drummond is a composite of my own imagination and several Revolutionary War historical figures, including Wilson, Andrew Hunter, Andrew Pickens, William Clay Snipes, Daniel Morgan, and many forgotten Patriots. "The Swamp Fox," Francis Marion, and "Wizard Owl," Andrew Pickens, existed, of course, and along with "The Gamecock," Thomas Sumter, did as much to defeat the British as George Washington—at least in the biased opinion of a Sandlapper who once hunted and fished around Marion's old stamping grounds. Likewise, Lord Charles Cornwallis, Major James Wemyss, and Colonel Banastre Tarleton really lived and fought against the rebels during the Revolutionary War, while Ebenezer Moore and "Bloody Jim" Jernegan are fictional composites, the latter being loosely based on Loyalist butcher William "Bloody

Bill" Cunningham, sometimes spelled Cuningham.

I have used period spellings throughout this novel. Charlestown became Charleston in 1786, the Peedee is now the Pee Dee, and Lynches Creek has been promoted to Lynches River.

South Carolina's Back Country of the Revolution has been compared to the Kansas-Missouri border of the Civil War era, even Vietnam. It was chaos and anarchy, neighbor against neighbor, not just British against Patriot, with crimes being committed on both sides. That's what I have tried to describe here.

Much material for this novel came from *Rise Up So Early: A History of Florence County, South Carolina* by G. Wayne Hill. *Parson Weems' Life of Francis Marion* by General Peter Horry, one of the earliest Marion biographies, was consorted, although it's more hyperbole than history. On the other hand, W. Gilmore Simms's *The Life of Francis Marion*, originally published in 1844, is an excellent account. The best biography of Marion, however, is Robert D. Bass's *Swamp Fox: The Life and Campaigns of General Francis Marion*. Indeed, Bass's other Revolutionary War titles—*Ninety Six: The Struggle for the South Carolina Back Country*, *The Green Dragoon: The Lives of Banastre Tarleton and Mary Robinson*, and *Gamecock: The Life and Campaigns of General Thomas Sumter*—are excellent material for readers interested in learning more about the American Revolution in the South. Other sources included *Rambles in the Pee Dee Basin, South Carolina* by Harvey Toliver Cook; *South Carolina: A History* by Walter Edgar; *Southern Campaigns of the American Revolution* by Dan L. Morrill; and far too many more to list here.

I'd also like to thank the staffs at the Florence County Library; Darlington County Historical Society; Hampton

Plantation State Park; Historic Camden Revolutionary War Site; Cowpens National Battlefield; and Kings Mountain National Military Park. Patricia Fountain of Litchfield Beach helped refresh my memory about Georgetown and the Pee Dee basin, and my father often pointed out historic places, including Snow's Island, while taking me fishing as a boy.

Leigh Jones Handal, an old drinking buddy during my University of South Carolina days who now works for the Historic Charleston Foundation, was a wonderful resource and tour guide around the city. This novel is warmly dedicated to Leigh and her husband, Chris, another long-time friend from college. Chris and Leigh, I couldn't have done it without y'all. *Huzza!* The next pitcher of beer and order of shrimp and grits are on me. Thanks.

Johnny D. Boggs
Santa Fe, New Mexico

About the Author

In addition to writing Western novels, Johnny D. Boggs has covered all aspects of the American West for newspapers and magazines on topics ranging from travel to book and movie reviews, to celebrity and historical profiles, to the apparel industry and environmental issues. Born in South Carolina in 1962, he published his first Western short story in 1983 in the University of South Carolina student literary magazine. Since then, he has had more than twenty short stories published in magazines and anthologies, including *Louis L'Amour Western Magazine*. After graduating from the University of South Carolina College of Journalism in 1984, Boggs moved to Texas to begin a newspaper career. He started as a sportswriter for the *Dallas Time Herald* in 1984 and was assistant sports editor when the newspaper folded in 1991. From 1992 to 1998, he worked for the *Fort Worth Star-Telegram*, leaving the newspaper as assistant sports editor to become a full-time writer and photographer. Boggs's first novel was *Hannah and the Horseman* (1997). His first non-fiction book was *That Terrible Texas Weather* (2000), a history of some of the worst natural disasters in the state from the 1800s to the present. He is a frequent contributor to *Boys' Life*, *Wild West*, *True West*, and other publications. His photos have often accompanied his newspaper and magazine articles, as well as appearing on the covers of many Five Star, Thorndike, and G.K. Hall titles. He won a Spur Award from Western Writers of America for his short story, "A Piano at Dead Man's Crossing," in 2002. Subsequent novels have included *The Lonesome Chisholm Trail* (Five Star Westerns, 2000), a trail drive story, and *Lonely Trumpet* (Five Star Westerns, 2002), an historical novel about Lieutenant Henry O. Flipper, the first black graduate of West Point. Boggs lives in Santa Fe, New Mexico, with his wife, Lisa Smith, and son, Jack. His next **Five Star Western** will be *The Big Fifty*.

The employees of Five Star hope you have enjoyed this book. All our books are made to last. Other Five Star books are available at your library, through selected bookstores, or directly from us.

For information about titles, please call:

(800) 223-1244

or visit our Web site at:

www.gale.com/fivestar

To share your comments, please write:

Publisher
Five Star
295 Kennedy Memorial Drive
Waterville, ME 04901